MADDOX

Maddox—Vested Interest #3 by Melanie Moreland
Copyright © 2018 Moreland Books Inc.
Registration # 1148534
All rights reserved
ISBN: 978-1-988610-07-8

Edited by
D. Beck
Lisa Hollett, Silently Correcting Your Grammar

Cover design by
Melissa Ringuette, Monark Design Services

Interior Design & Formatting by
Christine Borgford, Type A Formatting

NEW YORK TIMES AND USA TODAY BESTSELLING AUTHOR

MELANIE MORELAND

DEDICATION

Love is an all-encompassing,
passionate emotion found in all my books.
But there are other forms of love,
and I am blessed to have them in my life.
Friendship and family
To my friends, thank you for being part of my life-
You brighten my days and make my world sparkle.
To my sisters, Sandy and Kerry, you are my heart. I love you.
To my Matthew who is my world.
There aren't enough words-there never will be.

PROLOGUE

MADDOX

I RAN INTO the house, skidded to a stop in the kitchen, and stared in horror at the boxes.

My father turned, glaring at me. "Pack your stuff. We're leaving."

"No!" The word was out before I could stop it.

Pain exploded in my cheek from his backhand. He knew how to hit to cause the most agony. After all these years, he was an expert at it.

"You have half an hour. Anything that isn't packed, we're leaving behind."

My eyes smarted from holding in the tears. I grabbed two boxes, trying not to flinch at the sight of them. Stained, partially torn boxes that, no doubt, my father had grabbed from a dumpster or behind a store.

In my room, I glanced around, knowing he was serious. Anything I didn't have ready I had to leave behind. Every time we moved, it was the same. Once again, he would pull me from the routine I had fought to establish. The thing I needed to cope. Now I would have to face a new place, new school, new people.

None of which I would stay at long enough to become attached to. He made sure of that.

I hurried to pack my things, being careful. I didn't have much in the way of clothes or possessions, so I tried desperately to take care of the few things I had. My father found it amusing to destroy anything that might mean something to me, so I had learned never to let him see what I liked. I acted nonchalant even when I found him rifling through my things. I knew he was looking for money or anything of value to sell. However, I'd learned to hide anything I really loved. Loose floorboards, wall vents with covers he would never think to check in, became my friends.

I listened at my door, but he was down the hall in his room, so I hurried and pushed aside my mattress to get to the loose floorboards hidden underneath. Briefly, I wondered if the next place would even have the luxury of a mattress on the floor to sleep on at night. I grabbed the small, hidden shoebox and shoved the bed back into place. Using some frayed jeans and T-shirts, I wrapped the box and placed it into the old cardboard box, rushing to add the rest of my meager wardrobe on top. I added my few books and folded the torn lid into place. Into the second box, I put my worn shoes and the one item that went from place to place with me.

An old lamp, chipped and worthless. It meant nothing to anyone except me. But what it represented was everything. My mother used to read to me with the lamp sitting on the table by her elbow. Her voice was always soft as she spoke the words on the page and her touch gentle as she stroked my head.

I shut my eyes and stuffed my thin pillow around the lamp to keep it safe.

It was one of the few things I had left of hers. He had no idea of its existence or the memories it held for me.

Her gentle, loving voice, sweet words, and a time when I had been happy. Dim recollections of a long dead childhood.

That was all I had of my mother. Reminders of being loved.

I fought to keep them alive in my head.

No matter how he tried to beat them out of me.

He appeared in my doorway.

"There's room for one box. Move your ass."

"But—"

He shoved me aside, my shoulder burning with pain when it met the edge of the doorframe.

I didn't make a sound.

He reached into the box, tossing my shoes carelessly. "Carry these." Pushing the pillow aside, he lifted the lamp, a frown creasing his face. All that remained was the decorated base, the lampshade long ago broken, bent, and discarded. The truck with the loader lifted high was dull, the streetlight it sat beside pieced together with glue. The edges of the truck were worn from where my fingers had rubbed, wanting to play with it when I was a child. I could hear my mother's patient voice talking to me.

"No, Maddy, just to look at, baby boy. One day, you can have a real one."

A glimmer of recognition flitted over my father's angry face. "What the fuck? Where did you get this?"

I shrugged and tried to bluff. "It's a stupid lamp. I need something to use when I read. It was in one of the houses, and I took it."

He wavered, his saturated memory unclear. "Oh yeah? Well, leave it behind. We ain't got room."

"No! Please!" I couldn't help but beg.

Satisfaction glimmered in his dark eyes, confirming his thoughts. "Well then, let's make it fit."

Frozen, I watched as he lifted the lamp, cracking it against the window frame. It broke, the truck separating from the stand, the streetlamp shattering as it all fell to the mattress on the floor.

"There," he sneered. "Fit it in or leave it. You have five minutes."

With shaky hands, I lifted the truck and tucked it into the corner of the one box he allowed me to bring. The rest of the lamp was garbage, damaged beyond repair, so I left it behind. I would have to safeguard the last piece and keep it well hidden.

Tears dripped on the box as I flipped closed the lid.

I lifted my box, and placed my shoes on top, leaving the pillow.

I wiped my face roughly. I would never allow him to see my tears. I would never give him that satisfaction again.

I didn't look back as I left another piece of my life behind.

There was no point.

CHAPTER 1

MADDOX

WITH THE LIGHTS of the city spread out below me, I stared out the window, sipping my whiskey, enjoying the way the rich flavor rolled around my tongue. The low lights reflected my condo in the large pane windows. Tidy, organized, everything in its place. Exactly the way I liked it. Needed it.

Behind me, I heard a light tap. I hit the button on the remote, unlocking the door, knowing who was waiting. Soft footfalls headed in my direction, and Dee's reflection appeared in the glass. Turning, I offered her a smile and a tumbler of whiskey. I knew she'd like this one.

"Hey, neighbor."

She shook her head, taking the glass from my hand and settling into the club chair. "You are such a dork. I live ten floors below you. I'm not your neighbor."

I shrugged. "Close enough." I sat across from her on the sofa. "Seriously, are you settling in?"

She held up her whiskey, studied its dark golden color, then took a sip. Her eyes drifted shut as she swallowed. Her hand swept through her hair, the strawberry color catching the light. She was artless, sexy.

I liked it.

She opened her eyes. "Nice choice."

"I knew you'd enjoy it."

She smiled and reclined her head. "I'm settling in. I wasn't expecting to be on my own, but it will be nice to have a home office to work from on occasion."

"Still in shock?"

She chuckled. "I shouldn't be, given it was Cami, but I am."

"I think this was all on Aiden, which makes it the biggest shock of them all."

We went to Vegas for a quick trip away. Everyone needed a break, and rather than the girls going on their own, we joined them. The first day was fun with sightseeing and dinner. We went to a show and even did a little gambling. The next night, we ended up pairing off the way we usually did: Emmy and Bent, Cami and Aiden, Dee and me.

Bent and Emmy went to another show. Dee and I checked out a whiskey bar we'd heard about, Cami and Aiden spent the night doing the usual touristy things. They visited the Eiffel Tower, took a gondola ride, and watched the fountains dance. Then, Aiden being Aiden, he had gone for broke, and since we were in Vegas, married Cami.

They showed up at breakfast the next morning, and neither of them said a word. But they looked guilty, yet so happy; I knew something was going on. They simply ordered their meals, talked about the day's plans and acted as if nothing was amiss. Until Emmy spotted the rings on their hands.

"What the hell? Cami . . . are you . . . oh my God, are you married?"

All of our heads snapped in their direction. Aiden lifted Cami's hand, pressing a kiss to her knuckles. The light glinted off the matching ring on his left hand.

"We are," he stated.

We gaped at them, shocked.

"Is it legal?" Dee asked, looking between Cami and Aiden. "Or did you

do this for fun?"

"It was fun, but it is very legal," Aiden confirmed.

Suddenly, the table exploded. Hugs, kisses, backslaps, and congratulations were exchanged all around. Aiden looked like the happiest man on earth, and beside him, Cami beamed. When Emmy asked if they were going to have a real wedding, Cami shook her head.

"It was exactly what we wanted. Only us." She smiled at Dee in apology. "We thought we'd renew our vows next year and bring everyone to join us."

Dee covered her hand. "That sounds perfect. I'm happy for you."

I had wondered then, the same way I wondered now, if Dee was as okay with the marriage as she seemed to be. In the weeks since we had returned, life had been busy with work, moving Cami in with Aiden and moving Dee in to her new place in the building where I lived. I helped move boxes at night. Movers handled the furniture, but it still took a lot of hours. We'd barely had time to see each other.

Or, in other words, fuck each other.

"You were very calm about the whole surprise wedding."

She sipped her whiskey, looking contemplative. "I was a bit hurt, but I realized it was Cami's decision and her life. She was much too happy for me to be upset." She huffed a long breath. "I hope it wasn't a rash decision they'll both regret."

I scowled, feeling the need to defend my friend. "Aiden loves Cami. He loves her so much it terrified him. When he accepted what he was feeling, it changed him. *She* changed him—for the better. For the first time in his life, he accepted something good for himself. I don't think you have to worry about any regrets from him."

She tilted her head, studying me. "That was spoken with conviction."

I shrugged. "The two of them work."

"They do." She grinned. "That was also spoken like a true romantic, by the way. Which you insist you are not."

I chuckled. "I have my moments. I'm okay with romance . . . for other people."

"Me too."

We stared at each other, not speaking. Slowly, the air shifted, growing more intense.

"So tell me, *Deirdre*, what are you wearing under that businesslike navy suit you have on?"

She loved it when I murmured her full name. No one used it but me, and I only uttered it when we were alone.

She traced the rim of her glass, eyeing me. "I'm sure you'd like to know."

I shifted, my erection lengthening as I thought about it. Wondering what secret I would discover tonight.

Dee was a walking contradiction. Classic, dark suits, neutral-colored blouses. No-fuss hair. Simple makeup. No jewelry.

However, underneath the linen and cotton was an entirely different story.

Lacy, push-up bras, tiny triangles that covered silky curls and a sweet little cleft I knew intimately.

Satin, lace, silk, and sin.

Black, pink, red, every color of the rainbow.

Cutouts and high tops. Thongs, boy shorts, strapless, bustiers, stripes, polka dots, pin-tucked, bedazzled, and sexy.

She had them all. She was sex on legs.

"Why don't you show me?" My eyes raked down her body.

She stood, her fingers drifting to the pearl buttons under her neck. I settled into the cushions, anticipation waking every nerve in my body.

"Slowly."

She tilted her head.

"I want it slow tonight, baby."

She shrugged out of her jacket, the fabric a dark pool on the floor.

"Is that so?"

"Yes." My cock grew harder as she moved. Slow. Sensuous. Exactly the way I instructed her.

"Do I get a reward?"

I palmed my erection. "You get me. Buried so deep inside you, you'll feel me for days."

Her blouse joined her jacket, showcasing the cream lace bustier encasing her torso that made me groan. Her breasts were high, ready to spill over the tight lace. I wanted to bite them. When her skirt fell, revealing the thigh highs attached with tiny straps of lace, I almost lost it. The scrap of material nestled between her thighs was so minute it was ridiculous. And sexy as hell.

I widened my legs. "Come here."

She stood between my knees. I trailed my fingers up and down her thighs, tracing the ribbons and lace, teasing the satin of her skin. I jerked her forward, burying my face in her pussy, breathing her in.

She whimpered as I pressed my mouth to her, hard.

"You want me. I can smell how much you want me."

She dug her fingers into my scalp, lifting my face.

"Yes. But the rules still apply, Maddox. Sex. That's all it is. Nothing has changed."

I smiled grimly. "I wouldn't expect it to."

"Then fuck me."

Never breaking eye contact with her, I shredded her panties. Tore them away from her skin with one firm yank of my fist.

I would fuck her. I would fuck her because that was what we did.

To the outside world, we were the same: cool, calm, and collected. Detached.

When we came together, alone, things changed. We were relentless. Explosive and insatiable.

She fucked with my control.

I fucked her to get it back.

That was our game. It always had been.

Until one of us changed the rules and fell in love.

CHAPTER 2

MADDOX

I WAS ALONE once again. Dee never stayed. It was one of our rules. There were many, but that one had never changed or been broken.

Pouring another shot of whiskey, I sat on the sofa, thinking of when we met.

Deirdre Anne Wilson slid into my life as easily as she slid into the back seat of the limo on the night out for Emmy's birthday that Bentley arranged. She sat beside me with her long, sexy legs crossed demurely and a smile playing on her full lips.

"You must be Maddox."

"Dee, I presume?"

"Right in one."

She looked around the interior of the car. "Nice limo."

I grinned and pulled a bottle of champagne from the bucket. "Thanks to Bentley."

She arched an eyebrow my way knowingly. "I think my sister insisted.

She has no boundaries." She glanced over at Cami. "I'm afraid Aiden has his hands full."

I poured her a glass of the bubbly with a chuckle. "I wouldn't worry about Aiden. He can handle himself."

I thumped the roof of the car and yelled at Bentley to move things along. I was hungry, and I wanted to get the evening started.

When Bentley and Emmy finally entered the limo, I handed them each a glass of champagne and toasted the birthday girl. I already had a soft spot for Emmy. She was bright, vivacious, and a good match for Bent. I had never known him to be so taken with someone.

Aiden seemed caught in Cami's spell, and she only had eyes for him. I had a sense she was going to keep him on his toes, and he might prove to be a good partner for her—if he allowed it.

That left Dee and me. I was prepared to endure the evening being friendly, for Bentley's sake. I didn't know what I anticipated Cami's older sister to be like, but the alluring woman sitting beside me wasn't part of my expectations. She was average height, with a willowy build. Unlike Cami's vivacious looks and personality, Dee was sedate and pretty in an understated way. Her clothes were simple and unfussy, her hair cut chin-length, and her face makeup-free. Yet, there was something intriguing and sexy about her. Her large green eyes were intelligent and her movements graceful. She had a low and husky voice, and she chose her words carefully. When she smiled, her face lit up, but in a different way from her sister. Cami beamed, while Dee's expression softened and warmed, like the diffused light of dawn.

It was highly attractive.

For the next weeks, I had gotten to know Dee as our little group formed. I enjoyed talking to her, and we conversed on a variety of subjects. She had a wicked sense of humor and did incredible imitations of people that made me laugh. She was strong and seemingly unflappable, and I suspected there were hidden depths under her no-nonsense façade. She was well read and we had a lot in common, but neither of us pursued anything outside of our group get-togethers. It was nice to have someone to chat with when we were all together. Given the way Bentley was falling for Emmy, I had a feeling I'd be seeing a lot of Dee. I liked her company and found myself thinking of her a great deal, but I never followed through with my distracting thoughts. As much as she intrigued me, I didn't pursue her.

Until one day, I was browsing my local bookstore for something new to read.

Studying a book jacket, I was distracted when a woman's silhouette caught my attention. She was lissome and pretty, the sunlight catching her light red hair. She was reading the back of a book, her finger running over the spine. Something about her beckoned to me yet seemed familiar. With a grin, I realized it was Dee, and I approached her. "Find something good?"

She glanced at me, startled. I was close enough to see the flecks of brown in her wide green eyes. She smiled and slid the book back onto the shelf. "Not really." She indicated the books I had in my hand. "I think you've had better luck."

"You can borrow one if you like. I tend to buy in batches."

She tilted her head, silently mouthing the titles. She looked up with a smile. "That would be lovely."

"I was gonna grab a cup of coffee. Can I interest you in joining me?"

"I'd love to."

Seated across from her, I realized it was the first time we'd ever been alone.

"You come here often?"

She shook her head with a wry grin. "Is that your best pick-up line, Maddox?"

I chuckled. "I don't think I've ever seen you in here until today."

"I was in the office for a short while, then dropped in here. Usually I browse on my lunch hour."

"That makes sense."

Silence fell as we sipped our coffee, but it wasn't uncomfortable. I noticed she nibbled at the end of her thumb, and it struck me as odd. Given her stoic persona, I found it rather endearing.

I found my thoughts strange. Endearing wasn't a word I used often—if ever.

She met my gaze. "So, is it?"

"Is it what?"

"Is that your best pick-up line?"

I studied her as I drank my coffee. "I don't typically do pick-up lines."

She smirked. "I'm not surprised."

"Sorry?"

"With that whole silver fox thing you've got going, I'm sure you don't have to."

I frowned. "Silver fox?"

"Maddox, the silver fox. Young, sexy, wealthy, plus that premature gray? I bet you beat them off with a stick."

I shook my head, amused at her thoughts. "I'm sorry to disappoint, but no."

"Really? I'm surprised."

I sat back, crossing my legs, swinging one foot. "What about you, Deirdre? All prim and pretty. You drive the lawyers crazy at your firm?"

She laughed. "Dee. No one calls me Deirdre. It's stuffy and formal."

"No. It's a lovely name for a lovely woman. It suits you. The lawyers you date don't call you by your full name?"

She ignored my comment about her name. "I don't date lawyers, or anyone else at my firm," she stated firmly. "In fact, I don't date."

"Ever?"

She hesitated, then shook her head. "No. Love, romantic love, isn't for me."

I took in a deep breath and spoke. "Why is that?"

"It's dangerous. It overwhelms and kills you."

At my raised eyebrow, she continued.

"I'm not saying I don't see people. I have . . . needs. But I don't do romantic relationships. I've seen the way love destroys people." She held up her hand before I could speak. "I know it works for some, but I'm not built that way."

I drained my coffee, then leaned forward. "Neither am I."

She widened her eyes. "Really?"

"Love equals power. The power to destroy. The ability to hurt and cause pain. The chaos it causes. That's what love means to me. It destroys trust and leaves you weak."

"You feel that way about everyone?"

"There are a few exceptions. And I will never break them for a woman."

Our eyes met, silent understanding passing between us. The air shifted, and I felt our mutual desire grow. It stretched out, pushing tentatively against the boundaries we had erected. She propped her elbow on the table, lifting her thumb to her mouth. Her small teeth gnawed at the flesh. It was an innocent gesture, yet I found it provocative.

"I have needs too," I murmured. Reaching over, I tugged her thumb from her mouth, inspecting it. From the roughness of the skin, and the fact that it was the second time she'd done it since we sat down, it was clearly a nervous habit for her. I slowly dragged my fingers across her palm, then laid her hand on the table.

Her breathing hitched. *"I'm older than you are."*

"Three years," I scoffed. *"It's nothing."*

"I'm serious. I don't do relationships."

"Nor do I." I bent forward, lowering my voice. *"May I be blunt with you?"*

"I prefer blunt."

"I find you incredibly attractive, Deirdre. Very sexy in your buttoned-up clothes and calm exterior. I'd like to see what happens when you're naked and aroused." I tilted my head, studying her. *"Like now—are you aware in the past few minutes, your breathing picked up and your eyes darkened? You have the loveliest color across your cheeks. Even the tips of your ears are pink. I wonder how far down I could make you flush that way."*

Her color deepened, but she didn't flinch. She shifted closer, our knees pressed together under the table. Her normally husky voice was even lower, turning me on. *"You want honest?"*

I nodded.

"I think you're one of the sexiest men I've ever met, Maddox. I see how your toned body moves when you walk, and I imagine you moving in me. You use your hands a lot when you talk, and I want to feel them on my skin. Your muscles flex under your expensive suits, and I want to feel them tighten under my touch." She ran her finger over her lips. *"I want to taste you and watch you fall apart."*

"Then maybe we should go and explore each other."

On the table between us, her phone pinged with an incoming message. She ignored it, never breaking our gaze. It rang out again. With a sigh, she picked it up, her brow furrowed, and she grimaced.

"Problem?"

"My boss needs me to return to work."

"Could you refuse?"

She sighed, her posture slumped. "Probably not." She met my gaze with a slight shrug of her shoulders. "I could postpone him for a short while."

I shook my head, disappointed yet resigned. The moment had been broken, and it was probably a good thing. Given the dynamic of the group we had, no matter what we said, sex might complicate things.

And I hated complications.

I stood, offering her a smile. "I'll walk you to your building."

"You don't have to do that."

"It's not a problem. It's on my way."

We were quiet as we walked. Strangely, my disappointment lingered, and the desire I felt hadn't ebbed at all. Before we got to her office building, I pulled her into an alley and yanked her close. Without a word, I crashed my mouth to hers. She flung her arms around my neck without hesitation. I traced her lips with my tongue, sliding into her sweetness as she parted her mouth. I explored her, tasting and teasing, our tongues dueling for control. With a low growl, I fisted her hair, angling her head and taking over. She melted into me; her body was supple and her quiet whimper a total turn-on. I licked at her mouth, nibbled her lips, sucked and pulled at her tongue. I tugged on her hair, holding her tight and controlling her movements. She tasted of coffee and sweets and all things Dee. She gripped my neck, sliding her fingers into my hair, twisting the strands. All too soon, we broke apart, both of us breathless, our mouths swollen and cheeks flushed.

I brushed her cheek with my fingers. "A taste of what should have been."

She captured my hand, pressing a kiss to my palm. She teased the skin with her tongue. "Damn cockblocking boss."

The words were out before I could stop them. "Make sure that's the only part of his cock you're ever near, Deirdre Wilson."

I spun on my heel and left her.

⌒

OUR TRYST REMAINED *a memory until Emmy was kidnapped. After she came home, we all sat in the living room waiting for Bentley to join us. Eventually, Emmy gave up, and wandered upstairs mumbling about studying. Cami followed her not long after, and Aiden watched her leave, his eyes following her until she was gone. Dee disappeared into the kitchen, and Aiden stood.*

"I don't think we're doing pizza."

"No."

"I'm heading upstairs."

I knew exactly where he was going, so I nodded. After he was gone, I was restless and edgy. It had been one hell of a few days, and my nerves were stretched tight. I paced the room a bit, then decided to get a drink.

In the kitchen, Dee was perched against the counter, nibbling on some grapes. She was casual, dressed in sweats and an old, plaid button-down shirt. She looked . . . edible.

"Hi," *she murmured.*

I grabbed a beer from the fridge and took a long swallow, leaning against the counter across from her. "Hey. How you holding up?"

"I'm fine. You?"

I shrugged.

"Is your head aching again?"

"No," *I assured her. The night before, she had made me lie down, and she stroked my head to ease the pain until I fell asleep. I had felt oddly comforted and cared for.* "I need something. I just don't know what I need."

"I could make you something."

I smiled and, without thinking, pushed off the counter. I moved a stray piece of hair from her cheek. It was soft against my fingers and I rubbed the silken texture. Suddenly, I knew what I wanted.

What I needed.

"Always looking after everyone, aren't you . . . Deirdre?"

Her eyes grew round, and her hand holding a grape froze partway to her mouth. With a low chuckle, I bent and sucked the grape into my mouth, chewing it slowly. "Mmm, sweet. Delicious," I murmured. I set down my beer bottle on the counter. "You know what else I remember being sweet?"

She shook her head, the motion slow and deliberate.

I lifted her to the counter, sliding my hands along her thighs, parting them wide and slipping between them. Her breathing picked up, the flush of color I remembered so vividly staining her chest.

I traced the streak of color with my index finger. "Ah, I like this. I recall wanting to know how far it went." Teasingly, I popped a button, then another, my fingers finding the warm skin and rosy color on her chest.

I leaned into her, almost groaning when her legs wrapped around me, pulling me in closer. "I remember how sweet you tasted on my tongue, Deirdre. How you felt pressed into me. How much I wanted to drag you to my place and fuck you. I didn't even care if you got in trouble with your cockblocking boss. I wanted you. Does that ring a bell with you?"

She curled her hands into my shirt, fisting it tight. "Yes."

"I know what I need from you right now. Are you willing to give it to me?"

"Oh God, yes."

"Are you sure?"

She slipped her fingers into a pocket of her flannel shirt and held out a condom. "I've been waiting for you to come find me all day."

I yanked her tight and kissed her. I fisted her hair in my hands, tugging and twisting the silk between my fingers. I devoured her mouth, licking and nipping at her as she whimpered and moaned. She grabbed at me, her need as strong as my own. I heard the kitchen door open, but I couldn't stop. I knew Bentley had seen us, but he left quickly, and I didn't care. In seconds, I had her sweats stripped away, revealing frilly pink underwear so minute they barely covered her. In one twist, I tore them from her body, sliding my fingers into her wet heat. She bucked against my hand, her groan loud in my ear.

"You like that, Deirdre? You like my fingers in that sweet pussy of yours?"

"Not as much as I want your cock."

"First, you're going to come on my hand, then you get my cock. Do you understand?" I hissed in her ear. "We do this my way. Always my way."

She tensed, her muscles fluttering.

"That's it, baby. Let go."

She arched, her mouth open in a silent scream as she came. I tore her shirt open, sucking her tight nipple into my mouth right through her pretty pink lace lingerie. I bit down as she arched again, her body straining for more.

I yanked down my sweats, my hard, aching cock springing free. I rolled on the condom, her eyes wild and watching, her breathing hard.

"Oh God, you're so big." She moaned.

"You want this, Deirdre? You need to tell me what you want. What you need."

"I need you to fuck me. Take away the ache with that huge cock of yours."

I stroked myself, pleased with her answer. "I'll take away the ache, baby. I promise you that."

I buried myself in her. The entire world narrowed down to mind-blowing pleasure. She was hot, slick, and tight. She met my thrusts, matched my rhythm, driving me crazy with her mouth as she licked and nipped at my neck. I pumped steadily, gripping her hips hard, lost in the vortex we had created. Sweat pebbled around my scalp, and my back grew damp. I wrapped my arm around her waist, holding her tight as I fucked her with everything I had.

"I'm going to come," I groaned into her ear. "Let me feel you, baby. Take me with you."

Minutes later, she cried softly into my neck, her body locking down. I stiffened, letting my orgasm wash over me. Ecstasy raced through me as I shuddered, enveloped in her arms until I was done.

I lifted my head, meeting her gaze, wondering what I would see. She grinned, sated and relaxed. "I don't think Bentley would approve of what we did in his kitchen."

I grinned back; relieved she was still simply Dee. "I don't think we should tell him."

"I don't think we should tell him how you fucked me in my room later either."

I quirked an eyebrow at her. "Is that a fact?"

"I think so."

I kissed her. "All right then."

My smile faltered as the memories grew dim. Whether I admitted it or not, my feelings for her had already started to grow even then.

I was fucked right from the start.

CHAPTER 3

MADDOX

AIDEN STROLLED INTO my office, a file tucked under his arm, a box in one hand and coffees in the other. With a grin, he sank down in a chair across from my desk.

"Hey, Mad Dog."

"Hey."

He opened the box with a flourish and handed me a cinnamon bun, one of my weaknesses. I took it with a shake of my head. "I think you keep the café downstairs in business."

He bit into his lemon Danish, chewing and swallowing. "They make amazing baked goods." He handed me a coffee. "Sandy is out with Bentley, so I had to get creative."

I laughed at his statement. "You know as well as I do there is always coffee in the thermal pot."

He shook his head. "Nope. Reid pulled another all-nighter. He has the pot on his desk with a straw." He rolled his eyes. "The kid is gonna be wired."

"In more ways than one. What's he working on now?"

"More Ridge Towers stuff. He's full of ideas."

"He's full of something." I sipped my coffee. "Where are Bent and Sandy?"

"Looking at some houses with Van and Olivia."

I chuckled. "More flips?"

"Yep."

Bentley still loved finding houses, fixing them up, and flipping them for a profit. We had a busy department dedicated to the endeavor. I had to admit, he knew what he was doing. He kept it small, hiring the best, and handpicked each project. Vince Morrison, or Van as we called him due to his incredible guitar-playing abilities, oversaw the construction, and Olivia Rourke handled all the design work. They each had their own team that worked well together. It was a profitable arm of the company.

"How many?"

"Two on the same street, both selling. Big places, in North York."

"Great. That'll keep Van busy."

"Yep." He leaned back with a yawn.

"Tired? Your new wife wearing you out?"

He smiled, glancing at his hand. His thick band caught the light, glinting brightly. It almost equaled the glint in his eyes and the brilliance of his smile. I realized it was the first time I had ever seen Aiden truly happy. It had taken him a long time to allow himself to feel that way.

"We were sort of celebrating last night. You know, she's all moved in, and yeah, I get to keep her."

I chuckled at his bashful remark. Something else new for Aiden.

"Good for you, man."

"At least I have an excuse. You look exhausted."

I waved my hand, dismissing his words. "Headache. Nothing to worry about."

He frowned but didn't respond. He finished his Danish, then relaxed into the chair.

"She got a tattoo."

"Cami did?"

"Yeah."

"Should I ask, or is it way more personal than I want to know?"

He chuckled, tapping his arm. "She traced one of these red flowers and put it over her heart with my name on it. She said that way I knew I lived in her heart all the time." He glanced at me with a shrug. "Cheesy, right?"

Normally, I would have agreed, but I saw how it made him feel. It was a different side of Aiden, softer and open, with the love he had for Cami. It made me feel odd, as if I were missing something.

"Actually, Aiden," I said quietly, "that's pretty deep. Astounding, in fact."

"Yeah, I guess it is." He leaned forward, excited. "I got her something too, but I haven't given it to her yet."

"Oh?"

"Darlene made me a ring for her. I picked it up this morning."

Darlene was a jewelry designer we knew who'd made Bentley an engagement ring for Emmy. Darlene specialized in high-end diamonds and custom work.

"You want to see it?"

I had to laugh at his eagerness.

I held out my hand. "Give it over." I flicked open the lid of the box and whistled. "Wow."

"Yeah. It's spectacular. Cami is going to flip."

I glanced at it again, the brilliance of the stone stunning. "You asked about this cut when we were looking at rings for Bent."

"Yeah. I liked it a lot."

"You knew even then, Aiden?" I asked, curious, handing him the box. "You were in love with her?"

He sighed and slid the box into his pocket. "I think I was, but I was too afraid to admit it. Too afraid to give someone else the chance to hurt me."

"I don't think you have to worry about that with your wife. She adores you."

He grinned. "Yeah, she does. I'm glad she stuck around until I got my head out of my ass."

I reached into my drawer and pushed an envelope across the desk. "You can share this with her tonight. It can be a double celebration. Spare me the details tomorrow."

He opened the envelope and studied the contents. "What is this for?"

"A wedding gift."

He frowned. "A trip to Hawaii?"

I nodded. "It's open. When school is done for Cami and you know the dates you want, I'll book it for you. It's all covered. Flights, villa, car."

"Maddox, this is more than generous. It's not necessary either."

"I disagree. You got married and deserve a celebration. You never take time off unless it's to rescue a damsel in distress, and you've earned it. Bent and I can handle this place for a couple of weeks. Take your wife and go away on a honeymoon."

"It has been a while. I remember you pointing out I took some time off four years ago. I don't remember what I did, though."

"I do."

"Oh? Remind me."

"You were off because you insisted on eating tacos from a sketchy street vendor after a Leafs game. Bent and I warned you not to do it, but you wouldn't listen. Your gas was far too much to handle in the office. Thank God."

His brow furrowed, then he began to laugh. "Oh, right. It wasn't pretty."

"You overshared, even then."

He reclined, chuckling. He tapped the envelope. "Thanks, Mad Dog."

"I think Bent has something for you too."

He lowered his head, fiddling with the envelope. "You guys . . ."

"We know."

Before he could say anything else, there was a knock at my door, and Jordan Hayes came in, holding a folder. He was the head of our team for Ridge Towers and oversaw every aspect of the project. An older man, he projected an air of calm and authority. He ran a tight crew, had great attention to detail, and didn't believe in cutting corners.

"Great news!"

"What's up?"

"We got a whole bunch of building permits pushed through. We're right on schedule—in fact, ahead at this point. We'll be breaking ground in a few months."

Aiden and I exchanged grins. "You're right, that is great news."

"I'll send you projected dates and you can start your marketing plans."

"Thanks, Jordan."

With a wave, he left.

"Bent will be happy to hear that news."

"Yeah, he will." Aiden reached for the file folder he had carried in. "He wants to go ahead with his idea of exploring other companies for marketing. He wasn't happy with the last firm."

"I know. Did you come up with some candidates?"

"Yeah. I got the research done, made some inquiries, spoke to them myself, and narrowed it down. A few candidates looked good. One in particular." He paused. "Are you sure you want to be involved with this aspect? You usually stick to the numbers side."

I pursed my lips in thought. He was correct, but lately, I'd wanted something different. Things in my department ran smoothly, and I found myself with extra time on my hands. Ridge Towers was going to be huge for us, and like Bentley, I wanted to make sure we had the best of everything for it. Including the marketing. The firm we'd used in the past had changed ownership, and we weren't impressed with their new strategies or marketing plans.

"Yeah, I need a new project. This is such an exciting event for us, and I want to be involved with you and Bent on it."

"Okay." He handed me the folder. "Here's our short list. We both have notes on the top three. You can speak to them and add your thoughts, and then we'll start the process of face-to-face interviews, listening to their ideas, and picking one."

"Great."

"One is local. The other two are out of town. One of the firms stands out."

"Which one?"

"The one based in BC—The Gavin Group. A family-run business. Great track record. I spoke with the owner and the guy who would be our rep. Straight shooter, no bullshit. Eager to hear about the project and create ideas."

"We've never gone outside the city before. Bent likes having someone close."

"That's the added bonus. This group agreed to have a local person on hand at our disposal. We'd provide office space, and they'd provide the body until the contract is done."

"Great. I'll read this through and make some calls."

"Okay. I'll leave you to it." Aiden stood, taking the envelope containing my wedding gift. "Thanks again, Maddox. Cami will love this." He held out his hand. "I appreciate you thinking of us."

I shook his hand and he left.

I spun in my chair, staring out the window.

Us.

I had never thought Aiden would be part of an us. Or Bentley.

I wasn't sure what I had thought. Given our various traumatic pasts, it seemed inevitable we would stay married to the business, none of us willing to put ourselves on the line on a personal level.

But they had and were now happy.

I turned back to my desk, my gaze sweeping around my well-appointed office. Its organized appearance calmed me. My days were busy and productive. I knew what to expect. I was always prepared and ready. I controlled my department tightly, the same way I controlled my emotions. I wouldn't allow anyone to take away that control.

That was what made *me* happy.

Or at least, it used to.

⌒

THAT EVENING, MY phone rang, and I hit the speaker button, the file I had been reviewing open on my desk.

"Maddox Riley," I announced.

"Richard VanRyan of The Gavin Group speaking." A deep voice resonated over the line. "I believe you were expecting my call."

"Yes, Mr. VanRyan. Thanks for returning my call this evening."

"It's Richard, please. You're working late tonight." He chuckled. "It's past six here, so it's going on past nine in Ontario, I believe."

"I'm working from home, yes. I wanted to get the initial call taken care of."

"Happy to be at your disposal. I've been reviewing your file. Quite the concept you have going with Ridge Towers."

"We're proud of it."

"As you should be," he stated. "I won't take much of your time, Maddox. May I call you Maddox?"

"Of course," I murmured.

"As I said, I've gone through your file and looked at your project. I've spoken to both Aiden and Bentley and got a feel for what they're looking for. Do you have anything else you want to add to the mix?"

"Aside from the fact that this is a long-term deal and we want something classic and catchy that will carry the brand to its completion, not that I can think of right now. You do know you're in the running with two other companies, yes?"

He didn't hide his laughter. "Trust me, I have every confidence we're the company you'll go with. I'll make sure of it."

I liked his directness.

"We want a face-to-face meeting."

"You name the time and date, and we'll be there."

"You'll come here?"

"Aiden said you preferred that, so we'll make it happen."

I glanced at my notes. The local company had insisted we come to them so they had the home-field advantage, and the other had agreed to come to us, though I had sensed some reticence.

"Do you have any concepts?"

"I have an entire campaign done."

Now, I was impressed.

"And if we don't like it?"

"I'll start again. However, I think you will. It ticks all your boxes. Classic, simple, but high impact. In addition, you'll have us at your disposal for any changes, adjustments that you want to make. Here at The Gavin Group, our clients get the best. Every time."

I smirked at his bluntness, even as I felt a grudging respect for it. I sensed he wasn't bragging—simply stating a fact. I had gone through all the notes Aiden and Bentley had made. I'd looked through the various examples of their campaigns, along with those from the other candidates. I had reviewed the stats Reid had pulled for us, which were impressive. The Gavin Group had ranked as the top pick for both Aiden and Bentley. I made a decision based on all the facts we had accumulated and my first instinct speaking to Richard.

"I think we need to arrange that meeting."

"Excellent," he responded. "I'll get my assistant in touch with Sandy. We'll figure out the best dates, and Graham and I will fly in." He paused. "I'm going to bring Rebecca with us. She's the woman who will be in Toronto as our liaison with you. I've been training her myself, and she's perfect for the job. You can meet her and us, and we'll go from there."

A chime sounded on my computer, and I glanced at the screen, smiling when I saw Dee's face peering into the camera at my door. I pressed the key to unlock it and returned my attention to the call. "Sounds like a plan."

"I'll be in touch. Have a good evening, Maddox."

"You as well, Richard." I ended the call.

I jotted a couple of notes on the file. We'd meet with the three candidates, but after speaking to all the reps, I liked what I had seen and heard from The Gavin Group.

Dee appeared at my door, looking confused.

"There you are!" She laughed. "I'm not used to the door unlocking and no one there."

"Sorry, I was on a call." I tapped the screen. "I love this feature, I have to say."

"Am I interrupting?"

"Not at all." I waved my hand. "I need to finish this thought. Grab us a whiskey if you want."

A tumbler appeared in front of me as I flipped the file closed and tossed my glasses on top. Dee and I clinked glasses, and I took a deep sip of the amber liquid with appreciation. I studied her over the rim, taking in her shining hair and casual attire.

She fidgeted under my scrutiny, lifting her thumb to her mouth. As I discovered that first day in the coffee shop, it was her biggest nervous trait. She worried at the skin of her thumb whenever she was upset or nervous. It hadn't taken me long to notice her habit and to realize she often did it unconsciously.

"What's going on?"

She scowled, dropping her hand. "Do I have to have a reason to drop by?"

I chuckled and shook my head, although deep inside I hoped there was a reason. "No, simply wondering."

"Well, to be honest, I got tired of online shopping, and I fancied some company. Plus, I wanted to see if you would like to come to dinner tomorrow?"

I was surprised. Dee never invited me to her place. "Dinner?"

"I'm having Cami and Aiden for supper. His favorite food is fried chicken. I thought you might like to join us."

A home-cooked meal, good friends, and the pleasure of her company?

"I would. Thank you."

She settled into her chair with a sigh. "Great."

"You don't strike me as the type to online shop."

"Oh?" She laughed lightly. "What type am I?"

"Tactile," I answered promptly. "You're the kind of person who would want to touch the fabric, feel the textures of something you purchase."

I knew that because I was the same way.

She smiled in acknowledgement. "Normally, I would agree with you. But when it comes to this sort of shopping, I'm simply looking for serviceability that is in my budget."

"What are you shopping for?"

"A desk, maybe a couple of shelves for the extra bedroom that was supposed to be Cami's. I found a nice sofa bed in case I ever need it for company, but I want to add the rest."

I tapped the edge of my glass. Dee was fiercely independent. I knew she lived frugally and would never accept a handout, but I wanted to help her in any way I could. If making her comfortable in her new space was something I could do, I would make sure it happened.

"We have an entire room of surplus desks and bookcases at the office. Chairs, file cabinets, you name it. I'll take a look and send you some pictures. If there is something you like, it's yours."

"Really?"

"We remodeled some offices last year—the stuff is taking up space, and it's all good quality. I remember one set in particular. I think you'd like it."

Her brow furrowed. "Are you sure?"

"Dee, something is constantly being remodeled. It's unlikely we'll ever use the pieces again. We let the staff go through it on occasion to thin it out. Liv uses a piece or two every once in a while, but often we donate it to a charity." I shrugged. "But it builds back up. The room is full, so I know it's time to get rid of some pieces again."

"Liv?"

"Olivia—Liv. Our designer. She works with the residential side for the most part—Bentley's house flips. But she's done work on some of our bigger projects too. She handles all the décor, both inside and out. If she's creating an office, she might dip into what we have, although she has her own warehouse of pieces."

"You guys have a lot of irons in the fire, don't you?"

"We do. Bentley has built quite the empire. Residential, commercial, real estate, holdings, investment properties. We have our own architects, builders, contractors . . . The list seems endless at times."

"And the three of you love it."

"We do." I took another sip. "So let me send you a couple of pictures. If you like something, I'll have it delivered." I lifted an eyebrow. "No charge."

"I—"

I shook my head. "No charge."

"Fine." She huffed. "You'll do it anyway."

Satisfied, I nodded, but I noticed she was still apprehensive.

"Are you nervous about dinner tomorrow? You seem . . . tense."

"Nervous? No." She laughed. "But it's odd, you know? Having my sister and her husband for dinner. She'll be a guest, and it struck me today, that's how it'll be from now on. She's not coming home, since her home is with him, not me. She'll be visiting. We'll have dinner, and they'll leave." Her voice sounded strangely thick. "I thought having you there might help me."

"Dee," I said quietly, waiting until she met my gaze. "I understand. I would love to join you. I like fried chicken too."

She blinked, and the sight of her misty eyes did something to me. I knew she was struggling with the situation and hiding it.

"What else can I do to help you?"

"Nothing," she assured me. "You coming for dinner and being able to come see you, helps. It really does." She dropped her gaze to the floor, hiding her expression from me.

I sipped my whiskey and set the glass to the side.

"Deirdre."

Her head snapped up, her eyes meeting mine. "I think I know what else you need." I pushed my chair back, widening my legs. "Come here."

She stood, and the action pulled her sweatshirt off her shoulder.

Her creamy skin glowed in the light. She didn't hesitate to come around the desk and stand in front of me, which pleased me.

I wrapped my arms around her and pulled her in tight. She clutched the back of my head to her stomach, restlessly combing her fingers through my hair. I absorbed the pleasure of her touch for a moment, then bunched up the material of her sweatshirt, kissing the smooth skin of her taut stomach with light touches of my mouth. I grinned as her muscles contracted under my lips. I stood, removing her sweatshirt and tossing it aside. Her breasts sprang free, and I cupped them in my hands, the fullness perfect in my palms. I teased her tight nipples, and her breathing picked up.

"No pretty lace for me tonight?"

"No," she whispered, breathless.

"I think you knew exactly what you needed when you came here."

She met my gaze, her wide green eyes brimming with desire.

"I needed you."

I hovered over her mouth. "What did you need from me, Deirdre?"

"I needed your cock. Inside me."

"Then that's what you get." I crashed my lips to hers, sweeping my tongue into her mouth. She clutched at my neck as I continued to tease her nipples, the buds erect and pushing against my fingers. I kissed her hard, needing her taste, wanting to feel her tongue wrapped around mine. I sucked and licked at her, biting her lips and teasing her breasts. She arched into my touch, whimpering low. I broke away, and before she could react, I spun her around. I ran my fingers down her arms, placing her hands on my desk and easing her torso down to the cold glass of the desktop.

"Like this, Deirdre. Tonight, I'm having you like this."

She shivered, spreading her arms wide and lifting her ass. Slowly, I peeled her leggings down, smirking at the lace stretched over her ass. Red. Sexy.

In the way.

Hooking my fingers around the sides, I tugged. "I hope these are disposable."

She groaned. "I just bought them."

"For me?" I tugged again, feeling the elastic begin to tear. I already knew the answer. She bought them, I ripped them, then she bought more. I had given her a credit card to use, with the silent agreement that was why I was giving it to her. I liked to rip lingerie off her body. It was like a gift on Christmas morning I couldn't wait to unwrap. And she was the best gift of them all.

"Yes," she whimpered. "For you."

The sound of the material surrendering made me smile, and my dick got harder. I ground my hips into her, hissing as she pushed back, her tight ass rubbing against me in the best possible way. I covered her with my torso, pressing her into the glass. Entwining our fingers, I stretched her arms over her head.

"Grab the edge of the desk, Deirdre. Don't let go. Don't move. Do you understand?"

Her response was a low moan and her fingers tightening around the edge.

I kissed my way down her neck, biting at the sweet juncture where it met her shoulder. I pulled the skin between my teeth, knowing it would leave a mark only she would see. I slid my hands under her, cupping her full breasts as I licked, kissed, and nipped across and down her back, tracing the delicate ridges of her spine with my tongue. I pinched her tight nipples, making her groan. I eased back, dragging my hands around to her ass, cupping the cheeks and biting them hard. She twitched, one hand smacking the desk.

"Oh, baby. You moved." I feigned disappointment. Leaning over her, I curled her hand around the glass. "Now I have to start all over."

And I did—taking my time, playing with her, knowing how ready she was for me.

I wasn't ready to give it to her, not yet. I wanted to play with her a little more. I loved her reactions, and I wanted her begging me.

Her legs were trembling when I finally returned to her ass, my teeth nipping at the smooth flesh. I paid extra attention to her breasts, knowing how much she loved it when I manipulated the nipples, making them sensitive and stiff. The cold glass added to the sensations I evoked. She whimpered, but her hands stayed locked on the desk.

"Good girl," I praised, sliding my hand between her legs. She was beyond ready for me.

Hot, wet silk met my touch. My fingers glided over her cleft, stroking her clit. She gasped, widening her stance, begging in silence for my touch.

"I need to hear you tonight, Deirdre. I need you to tell me what you want."

"Play with my clit, Maddox. Please."

"Do you want my fingers or my mouth?"

"Both."

I ran my finger up her slit, teasing her tight back entrance. "What if I want something else?"

"Whatever you want. Maddox, please, I need you."

"You need me?"

Her body shuddered as I touched her again. I strummed her clit with my thumb and slipped two fingers inside her, stroking, curling them to find the spot that made her cry out.

"Yes!" She gasped, pushing against my hand. "Take me. *Fuck me*, Maddox. Lose yourself inside me. *Please.*"

I reached into the drawer for a condom, my need for her at the forefront. Grabbing one of her knees, I bent it up to the desk, opening her wide for me. I gripped her hips and sank in deep, causing us both to shout. Bending over her, I began to move. Long, deep thrusts that pushed her into the desk. She gripped the edge to hold on, groaning my name. I wrapped my arm around her waist, lifting her as I kept driving into her heat. She moved with me, arching to meet my movements, gasping my name. I slid my hand to her neck, threading my fingers into the silk of her hair and twisting her head to meet my mouth as I hovered over her. She flung her arm around my neck, holding me tight. Our lips moved, teeth clashed, and tongues dueled in a heated dance. Her breathing was ragged, her moans low and pleading.

"More, Maddox. Make me forget everything but you."

I gripped her hard, lifted her from the desk, and sat on my chair. She cried out at the depth I had my cock buried into her, but I kept going.

Pounding.

Taking.

Driving into her.

She flung her head back on my shoulder, and my mouth covered hers, kissing her as fiercely as I fucked her. She used the arms of my chair to lift and bend with my thrusts. The sounds of our sweat-soaked skin sliding and thudding against each other filled the room. My chair creaked and shook, and I didn't care if it ended up in splinters on the floor. I couldn't stop. Her gasps and my groans echoed off the walls. Everything became magnified.

Everything narrowed down to her.

To us.

I glided my finger over her hard clit, strumming it as she pleaded for more. I pressed harder, moving it faster, giving her what she wanted, what she needed, because I needed it too. Her body tightened and she came, screaming my name in ecstasy. Her muscles contracted around my cock, tightening and setting off my own orgasm. I pulled her down hard, stilling and cursing as I spilled inside her, the pleasure greater than I had ever known.

Gradually, our movements ceased. She collapsed on my lap, becoming limp, her breathing ragged and her body bowed in exhaustion. Her head flopped onto my shoulder again, her hair a wild mess around her face. I pushed away the strands and buried my face into her neck, breathing her in deep. She smelled of the soft citrus perfume she wore, of sex, and of me.

I liked the combination.

Still buried inside her, I lifted my head and stroked her cheek.

"Open your eyes, Deirdre."

Blinking, exhausted, sated green met my light blue. "Okay, baby?"

"Wow," she breathed out.

"Was I too rough?" I raised her wrist to my mouth, kissing the soft skin. I forgot sometimes how fragile she was—I lost myself with her, with the moment.

"No, you were exactly what I needed."

"I think we both needed it."

"You always have condoms in your desk?"

I smirked, kissing the end of her nose. "I put them in there the other day. I must have known you'd be dropping by."

She sighed, the sound low. "I like how controlling you are."

I brushed her hair away, tucking it behind her ear. "I like how you let me control you."

She nestled closer, surprising me. Usually once we had sex, she was gone. I wrapped my arm around her waist, holding her close and enjoying the unusual after-sex time with her. Her breath was warm on my skin as I slipped from her. I reached between us and removed the condom.

"I think-I think I need it. I need that from you, Maddox."

"Tell me."

"I have to be in control all the time," she confessed. She shivered, and I grabbed her sweatshirt, draping it over her body. I was afraid if I moved, she would stop talking.

"When I'm with you, you take over. I don't have to think. Only feel." She sighed again. "I so rarely get to feel."

"I like making you feel." I flexed my hips, feeling myself begin to harden beneath her. "I like when you lose yourself with me." I slipped my hand under her chin, bringing her to my mouth. "I like being with you."

"Me too."

She tightened around me as I slid through her wetness, making me groan.

"Are you sore?"

"A bit."

I lifted my hips, making her whimper. "I can be gentle." I guided my hand between her legs, teasing her. "We can take it slow and easy." I kissed her mouth, dipping my tongue inside her sweetness, tapping her clit with my finger. "One more time, Deirdre, for me."

"Slow," she whispered.

"Yeah, baby," I promised, reaching into my desk for another condom. "Slow."

CHAPTER 4

MADDOX

SANDY ENTERED THE boardroom and placed a file on the table. "The Gavin Group sent this over. They arrive next week and will be here for three days. They refused the company suite. They prefer to stay at the Fairmont. Mr. Gavin explained they have a young woman with them and would prefer not to share an apartment, but thanked you for the offer. He was most appreciative of the gesture."

Bentley nodded. "I never thought of that. Good call on Graham's part. Make sure they have what they need, Sandy."

She pursed her lips, giving him the evil eye. "I'm ahead of you on that subject, young man. Frank will be at their disposal. I have arranged for flowers and fruit trays in their suites. The boardroom is booked exclusively for you while they are here. I've preordered catered lunches, and I've cleared your schedules to accommodate the visit."

Bent and Aiden grinned, and I chuckled. "As usual, Sandy, you have dispatched your duties admirably. Thank you."

With a smirk, she turned on her heel, leaving us alone.

Aiden pushed the file my way. "Bent and I think you should run lead on this."

"Me?"

He nodded. "We'll all be in on the decision, but we're going on your recommendation."

"All I said was I liked this Richard guy. He sounded like a straight shooter, and their track record is impressive."

"Our thoughts exactly."

"I had a call from both the other companies this morning. Advance wants to do a video presentation instead of coming here, and Zip is open to whatever we want for an initial meeting." I paused for a sip of coffee. "Both feel a body here isn't necessary with today's technology."

Bentley shrugged. "They're right. It's not, but I want it anyway. If I'm willing to pay for it, they should be willing to give it."

"We should listen to the other ideas at least."

"We will, but I'm not looking for a single campaign. If I like what they create for us, and how they operate, we could keep a person full time here with our marketing needs. Ridge Towers is a long-term thing, but we have the resort and other pokers in the fire." Bent stroked his lip thoughtfully. "The one company that has seemed to grasp that concept is The Gavin Group."

"Richard told me he had an entire campaign thought out already."

"I'm looking forward to hearing it."

"How about I arrange for video conferences from the other two at the start of the week? So we have something to compare when we meet with The Gavin Group?"

"Sounds good. Get Sandy to set it up." Bentley stood. "I'm out for the day. I promised Emmy I'd be home early tonight. We have wedding shit to plan."

Aiden laughed. "Wedding shit? Is that the technical term?"

Bent grinned. "Don't tell her I said that. I can't believe the details. I should have married her in Vegas like you did. Life would be simpler."

"You could fly down for the weekend."

Bent shook his head, a smile crossing his mouth. "No, if she wants a pretty wedding, she can have it. If I have to look at swatches and choose napkin designs to make her happy, so be it. It's a small price to pay to have her for the rest of my life."

He left with a wave.

Aiden and I shared a grin.

"I forgot to ask. How'd the ring go over?"

He smirked. "My wife was excited, shocked, and very . . . effusive in her thanks." He winked. "Very effusive."

I held up my hand. "TMI, bro."

He grabbed his phone and laptop. "I have to stop and get flowers and wine. We're going to dinner at Dee's new apartment. She's making fried chicken."

"I know. I was invited too."

He stopped. "Oh. I didn't know."

"Dee was a little emotional about it and asked me to come join you."

"Emotional? Over fried chicken?"

"Not over fried chicken, you idiot. She's having her sister and husband for dinner. *As guests.* Then you'll leave. I think it hit her how much life has changed. The fact that her little sister has a life of her own now. I'm going for support."

Aiden studied me, and I waved my hand, dismissing the thoughts I knew were going through his head. "Don't read anything into it. She needed a friend, and I'm happy to be there."

"A *friend.*"

"Yes," I huffed, impatient. "A friend."

"Right."

I stood. "A friend," I stated firmly. "You might want to mention to your wife that her sister needs a little TLC right now. I know you and Cami are on the happy train, but Dee is left alone at the station. It's an adjustment."

"One I am sure you're happy to fill."

"Don't be an asshole, Aiden. Dee is your family now too. Don't forget her."

I walked out.

I KNOCKED ON Dee's door, frowning when she yelled for me to come inside. The air was pungent with the aroma of dinner, the scent of spicy chicken making me hungry. Dee was in the kitchen, sliding a tray of chicken into the oven as I rounded the corner.

"You leave your door unlocked?"

She arched an eyebrow, brushing her hair away from her forehead. She had a pretty bow in her hair, an unusually girlie thing for her to wear, yet it suited her. Escaping strands kept falling in her eyes, the kitchen heat making them stick to her skin. I tucked the strands under her bow and tapped the frilly accessory.

"Pretty, by the way."

"Thanks. I knew you'd be coming soon, so I unlocked the door. I don't have my fancy lock yet."

"Reid will be here on the weekend."

"Okay, thanks." She sounded distracted.

She turned, moving things on the counter.

"Dinner smells wonderful."

"Hmm." She continued to look around, lifting and setting down items, not accomplishing anything.

"I brought wine."

"Good. Help yourself."

I frowned, setting the bottle on the counter. I glanced around the kitchen, realizing how chaotic it looked. I had seen Dee cook, been with her in the kitchen a few times at Bentley's. She was organized and neat. Focused. Like me, she cleaned as she went.

Today, it looked as if a bomb had gone off in the kitchen. There were streaks of flour on her face and splatters of food covered her apron. She was off. Distracted. Tense. Her thumb was red, and I knew she had been gnawing at it.

Was she that worried over dinner with her sister? I wondered.

I tested my theory.

"I became vegan today. Could you do me a salad?"

She opened a cupboard. "Sure."

I stepped behind her, covering her hand that was moving items around aimlessly on the shelf.

"Deirdre."

She stilled.

I wound my arm around her waist, pulling her body tight to mine. I lowered my mouth to her ear. "What are you doing?"

"Ma-making dinner."

"Why are you so distracted?" I ran my hands up to her neck, feeling the stiffness in her shoulders. "What is making you so tense? It's *dinner.*"

Her voice was thick. "It's her first dinner with me when she doesn't live here. I want it to be perfect."

I held her close. "*It's Cami.* She wants dinner with her sister. To feed her husband the best fried chicken he ever tasted. Zero expectations otherwise." I nuzzled her neck. "You need to relax."

"I-I can't seem to. I feel as if I'm going to explode!"

"What can I do to help?" I slipped my hand under her apron and shirt to her soft skin. "Do I need to fuck you hard and fast to get you to relax?" I bit down on her lobe, tugging on it with my teeth. "Would that help?"

"We don't have time. They'll be here in a few moments."

I plunged my hand down the front of her leggings, cupping her. "I know how to get you to calm down—fast." I kissed her neck, swirling my tongue on her skin. "I know what you need, baby." I slid my leg between hers, nudging them open. "Let me give it to you."

She whimpered as she pressed her head to my shoulder, lifting her arm, and wrapping it around my neck. "Please, Maddox."

I delved into her folds, finding her slick. "Oh, baby, you need me."

I flicked her clit, smiling against her neck as she jumped. "I'm going to make you come. Fast. Later, you're going to return the favor.

I want my cock down your throat, with those sweet lips wrapped around me, taking everything I give you, do you understand?"

"Yes." She strained against me. "Oh God, yes."

"Hold tight. We don't have much time, and I want to feel you."

I found her bundle of nerves, using her slickness to glide over her clit in hard, fast strums of my fingers. She pulled on my neck and turned her face. I captured her mouth with mine, kissing her fiercely. She bucked as I slipped two fingers inside her, using my thumb to rub tight circles on her clit. My tongue and fingers moved in tandem as I fucked her mouth and pussy, bringing her to an orgasm as fast as I promised. She shattered, screaming into my mouth, her body spasming, her pussy drenched. I eased up, letting the aftershocks settle before removing my fingers from her body.

As she watched, I drew my glistening digits into my mouth, licking them clean.

"Best appetizer in the world." I winked. "Dee."

She blinked up at me, offering me a lazy smile, her body relaxed. I kissed her nose. "Go get cleaned up. I'll start in here, and when Cami and Aiden arrive, try to enjoy the evening. Okay?"

She walked a few steps, then turned back, hurrying toward me. I was surprised when she rose up on her toes, flung her arms around my neck, and kissed me. "Thank you."

"Anytime."

"After—you'll stay for a while?"

"Stay?" I asked, shocked. Dee never asked me to stay. I had never even seen her bedroom. Sex was always at my place. Then she left. That was how our *relationship* worked—even if I wanted it to be something different.

"Stay. I owe you."

With a grin, I yanked her tight and kissed her. "You do. I look forward to collecting." I pushed her away, swatting her ass as she hurried away. "Go. They'll be here soon."

With a grin, I washed my hands, then turned to the mess in the kitchen. I needed to do something to take my mind off the way my cock screamed at me to follow Dee and fuck her fast before Aiden and Cami arrived. Logically, I knew we didn't have time, regardless of how desperately I wanted to give in and do exactly that.

The pleasure later would be worth the wait now.

At least, that was what I told myself.

⌒

"BEST FRIED CHICKEN in the history of fried chicken," Aiden declared with a groan, wiping his mouth.

"Are you sure?" I asked dryly. "You only ate eight pieces. Maybe you need to eat another whole chicken to be sure."

He glared at me. "I was being polite."

I laughed. "Right."

Dee patted his shoulder. "I'm glad you enjoyed it. I made enough so you could take some home."

I pouted as I swiped my napkin across my lips. I had to grin when Dee stood, picking up my plate and murmuring low so only I could hear. "Stop with the lip, Maddox. I saved you some as well."

I wrapped my hand around her thigh, squeezing the back of her knee in appreciation. It was awesome chicken.

Aiden slouched in his chair, patting his stomach. "How did you make it so juicy and spicy?"

She smiled as she took his plate. "I marinate it in buttermilk, spices, and hot sauce. I deep fry it fast, then finish it in the oven. Comes out perfect every time."

"I agree." Aiden thumped the table. "We should have it every week. You know, like a tradition."

"A tradition?" Dee asked, wrinkling her nose.

"Yes. We're a family. We should start our own traditions. Tuesdays are Mexican with our friends." He looked at me, one eyebrow raised. "We have a family dinner. Here."

Dee smiled, her eyes shining. I was grateful knowing he had listened to me. Dee shocked me again by patting my shoulder.

"Maddox is included in the dinner invitation."

Aiden's grin was wide. "Of course."

I shocked myself with my own words. "I don't think Dee should have to make dinner every week. What if we compromise and you come to my place sometimes?"

Aiden and Cami were almost dancing in their seats. "Great idea!"

I met Dee's gaze with a slight shrug. I had no objection to the four of us having dinner once a week. I liked to cook too, so it would be nice to be able to cook for more than just myself on occasion.

I thumped the table as Aiden had. "Okay, settled, then."

Dee and Cami laughed and finished clearing the table. I watched them work together, talking as they put away the leftovers, turning on the coffeepot, and tidying up. Not that there was much to tidy; I made sure of that. Once Aiden and Cami left, I had other plans for Dee.

Much bigger plans.

⌒

"WE SHOULD GET going," Cami said, standing. "I have a couple of assignments I need to work on."

Aiden stood with her, his arm going around her waist. "Okay, baby. Let me take you home."

I watched Dee's reaction to his words. A small frown floated across her face, but it cleared fast when Cami spoke again.

"Want to do something on Saturday?"

"What about Glad Rags? You're not working this weekend?"

"Oh." Cami looked embarrassed. "I, ah, quit."

"You quit?"

Aiden interjected. "She doesn't have to work so hard now, Dee. I asked her to give it up so she can concentrate on school—" he paused with a grin "—and me."

"Oh. You never mentioned it, Cami."

Cami looked apologetic. "I'm sorry. I forgot to tell you."

Dee's smile looked forced. "Of course. Not an issue. Saturday would be great."

Aiden glanced at me. "You coming, Mad Dog?"

"Nope." I lifted my mug. "I'm gonna finish my coffee. We're headed in two different directions anyway." I smirked. "I'm up, you're down. I'll see you in the morning."

He paused, seeming as if he wanted to say something. I arched my eyebrow at him in question, and he shrugged.

"Okay. Have a good night."

"You as well."

They left, and Dee wandered into the living room, sat down, and curled one leg underneath her. She lifted her mug, sipping the coffee.

"That upset you."

"Sorry?"

"Finding out Cami quit her job. It upset you."

"No." She hesitated. "I mean, I was surprised. I suppose I shouldn't be. I know Aiden is wealthy, and she doesn't have to worry about money anymore, so that's great. Less stress for her."

"It's okay, Dee," I assured her. "You've been responsible for her almost your entire life. Part of all her decisions. Being excluded from them all of a sudden is going to take some getting used to."

She looked thoughtful as she shifted, bringing her knees to her chest. She pulled off her socks, rubbing her feet as she mulled over my words in her head. I noticed her bright pink toenails, recalling they had been orange the other night.

"I like the color." I indicated her feet.

"Oh!" She laughed. "I change them a lot. Cami and I couldn't afford pedicures so we gave them to each other. I like to switch them up all the time. I paint them every few days." She wiggled her toes. "No one can see them but me most of the time, but I like them to be pretty."

"You hide your girlie side."

She tilted her head, studying me. "You hide your controlling side."

"Not from you."

"I like it."

I smirked. "I know."

She leaned back, running her fingers through her hair. "I think I owe you something," she murmured, her voice low and husky.

Looking at her, open and soft, I felt desire thump through my veins.

I stood, staring down at her. "Are you inviting me to your bedroom tonight . . . *Deirdre?*"

Her breath caught. "Yes."

I started down the hall. "I suggest you make sure the front door is locked and come join me."

HER ROOM WAS also a surprise. Glancing around, I saw another side of Dee. The real one—the person who went along with the sexy lingerie and the passionate woman she hid from the world.

Her room was everything I should have known it would be, yet didn't suspect. She had her bed piled high with jewel-toned pillows and fluffy blankets. Lace panels hung from the ceiling, draping along the sides of a white four-poster bed. They fell in pools of fabric on the floor. More lace was at the windows. A wingback chair covered in flowered fabric sat in the corner, and an antique dressing table, also painted white, adorned one wall. The main wall was painted in a deep red. Candles scattered around the room and a thick throw rug on the floor all gave it a feminine feel.

Dee's voice made me turn around. "I found the bed and table at a garage sale." She ran her hand along the top of the table. "They were in bad shape, but I worked on them for weeks, fixing and painting them."

"The room suits you."

She flicked off the light, and instantly the room glowed with small twinkle lights strung around various surfaces. The radiant glow reflected off the red paint, making the room sultry.

She lifted her chin. "It's my space. I don't have to be anything but Dee in here."

I stepped closer, ran my fingers up her arm, and let my hand rest on the nape of her neck, feeling her rapid pulse.

"You don't have to be anything else but Dee with me."

She swallowed. "I've never had anyone in my room."

"Never?"

"Never," she confirmed.

I bent my head, brushing her mouth. "I'm honored."

She slid her hands around my waist, burrowing them under my shirt. Her fingers clutched at my skin.

"You're so different tonight," I murmured, ghosting my mouth along her cheek to her ear. I tugged the lobe with my teeth. "I'm not used to seeing you this vulnerable, my Deirdre."

"I'm glad you're here."

"Tell me what you need."

"You," she responded. "I need you to be Maddox and take control. Tell me what you want."

Grabbing her hips, I pulled them flush to mine, grinding into her. "What I want is for you to take me in your mouth. Suck my cock until I tell you to stop. Then I want to toss you on your pretty, lacy bed and fuck you until you come all over me."

She shivered. "Yes."

"I'm waiting."

Her fingers fumbled with my belt, yanking down my pants fast. I stepped out of them and tugged off my shirt, then tore hers over her head.

"I want you naked," I growled. "Lose the rest."

In seconds, she was bare in front of me. The dim room didn't disguise her beautiful body—in fact, it enhanced it. It played over her dips and curves, highlighting her creamy skin. Her breathing picked up as I studied her, circling her. I traced a finger down the elegant line of her back, tracing her delicate vertebrae. I stepped closer, wrapping my arm around her waist and pulling her to my body. She moaned, pushing her ass into my erection.

"I want you on your knees, Deirdre. Now."

She spun, dropping in front of me. Sliding her hands along my thighs, she held my gaze as she lapped at the crown of my cock, teasing me with her tongue. Fisting my cock, I tapped at her full lips playfully. "Suck me."

My head fell back with a groan as she did exactly that. Her mouth was warm and wet, her tongue sliding around my shaft, heaven. She knew what I wanted and how I wanted it. She didn't waste time with small kisses or more licks to tease me. She opened her throat and took me deep—the suction and pressure amazing. Her tongue slid along the underside of my cock, her hands cupping and playing with my balls as she pleasured me. I fisted my hands into her hair, rocking forward into her mouth, groaning at the sensation. Our eyes locked.

"You look so sexy, Deirdre, on your knees with my cock in your mouth."

She hummed around me, making me groan again.

"This is turning you on, isn't it? Making you wet for me?"

Her hands curved around my ass, pushing my cock farther down her throat. I hissed in pleasure, my fingers moving restlessly in her hair.

"God, baby, I love your mouth. You're so good at sucking me off."

In a sudden blaze of possessiveness, I stilled her movements. "Me, Deirdre. The one person who gets to feel your mouth on his cock is me, do you understand?"

Her eyes widened, and she hummed again. Not satisfied, I pulled back, my cock screaming in protest at the loss of her mouth.

"Say it," I demanded.

"Only you," she repeated. Her eyes narrowed. "Only *me*." She guided me back into her mouth, her words equally possessive.

"Fuck," I groaned.

She swallowed around me, the sensation making me gasp. I had never been so deep in her throat. Her movements sped up, my orgasm barreling down on me like a freight train. There was no doubt about who possessed whom in the moment. She was staking her claim as vigorously as I had moments ago.

"Deirdre, baby, you need . . . I'm going to . . ."

I exploded, coming in heavy spurts down her throat, cursing and shouting her name.

Breathing hard, I stepped back, my cock falling from her lips. She smiled at me impishly. Wordlessly, I studied her for a moment, then leaned down, lifting her under her arms and tossing her on her bed. Cushions fell over the side as she bounced, gasping.

"I think I said you had to stop when I told you, *Deirdre*."

She lifted her arms, her legs falling open. Her sex beckoned, pink and glistening. "I didn't hear you. Sorry."

I crawled up the mattress like a lion going after its prey. "I don't think you are." I grasped her knees, spreading her wider for me. "I think you enjoyed unraveling me."

"Is that what I did?"

"You know you did."

"You didn't like it?" she asked, her voice breathy and soft.

I crouched between her legs, nuzzling her thighs. She squirmed at the feel of my scruff on her skin. "I did," I admitted. "But I'm not sure if you need to be rewarded or punished."

"Maybe some of both."

I dragged my lips to her apex, barely touching her with my mouth. "Oh baby, you are soaked."

She fisted the sheets, twisting them in her hands. "Please," she whimpered.

I dove in, not wanting to deny her or myself any longer. She cried out when my lips met her core. She was hot and wet, ready for my tongue, my fingers, and my cock.

So I gave them all to her.

She moaned loudly as I teased her. Lapping at her with long, heavy swipes of my tongue.

"You taste so fucking good, Deirdre."

I added my fingers, one, then two, stroking hard, hitting that place that made her shake and whimper.

"That's it, baby, feel me," I urged.

I nipped at her, drawing her clit into my mouth and swirling my tongue on her hard bud. I fucked her with my fingers until she was a writhing mass under me. Then I lunged forward, covering her torso with mine. I stopped long enough to roll on a condom, then buried my cock deep inside her with one thrust.

"You wanted me? Take me. Take all of me," I demanded.

I set a punishing tempo, frantic and harsh. She met my movements, her gasps and pleas heightening my passion. She clutched at my shoulders, her nails digging into my skin. Her feet pushed on my ass, and she matched my rhythm, our bodies in complete synchronization. Our mouths fused together, our tongues dueling for control. Her breath was hot and heavy in my mouth. Our sweat-soaked skin glided together, the friction and damp welcome.

"With me, Deirdre. I want you coming with me."

Her nails dug deep, the pain burning in my skin. I shouted, slamming into her once, twice more, as she moaned out her release.

I collapsed on her, unable to move, to feel my body as I drifted in ecstasy.

CHAPTER 5

MADDOX

I COULDN'T PINPOINT the exact moment I fell in love with Deirdre Wilson. Thrown together by mutual friendships, I was drawn to her intellect, enjoyed her quiet wit, and I respected her intense drive. It didn't take me long to realize we were very similar in our views on sex, relationships, and life. Neither of us wanted to depend on another person for anything. We had learned to rely on ourselves, and we were beholden to no one.

The main difference between us was her nurturing side. It was fierce when it came to her beloved sister, Cami, and it extended to Emmy. She was their mother figure, and she watched over the girls with a tenderness and devotion she showed few other people. As our odd group grew closer, she extended that caring toward Bentley, Aiden, and me.

Except with me, there was the addition of the physical pull between us. Once we allowed it to take hold, it became a living, breathing thing we shared passionately.

Somehow, between the tacos and bowling, the Sunday brunches, the laughter and camaraderie we shared, something changed. The affection I felt for Dee morphed into something I had never experienced, especially after the scares of Emmy's kidnapping and Cami's stalking incident. I found myself thinking about Dee's safety, wanting to spend time with her alone—and not only to fuck her. Random texts became daily, which led to phone calls that lasted hours. After having her, I wanted more. I wanted her to stay, to hold her, to know how she was feeling, to delve into her clever mind and understand what she was thinking. To break down her walls and get her to admit she was feeling the same way about me.

When she went out of town on a business trip, I was lost. For the first time in my life, I missed another human being. When she came home, she allowed my comfort at the airport, stressed and anxious over the recent scare with Cami. I had hoped we would move forward, but her walls returned, and again, I was Maddox—her fuck buddy.

I hated it, yet nothing I tried seemed to change my role. Her walls were solid and so high I wasn't sure I would ever break them down. However, I wanted to. She had effectively disassembled my control without trying, stripped away my defenses, leaving me vulnerable to her. The feelings I had for Dee caused me turmoil and chaos. They were feelings I had avoided all of my adult life. I craved being close to her—a first for me. Never one for much physical contact, I wanted to touch her all the time. The detachment I had created so vigilantly vanished when it came to her.

And I was powerless to get it back.

She stirred in my arms and I held my breath, hoping she didn't wake.

After we had calmed, I had lifted myself from her, disposed of the condom, and returned to her bed, expecting she'd dismiss me.

"I hate those things," I muttered.

She shocked me when she patted the mattress and smiled at me sleepily. "We can talk about that later. Come to bed."

I didn't need to be asked twice. I slid in beside her and pulled her into my arms, letting her curve around my body. She fell asleep right away, and I tucked an arm under my head, trying to adjust to the new development.

It was another first for me. I had never once slept in a bed with someone. I liked the feel of her pressed close. Her breath was warm on my skin, and her hair was soft under my chin. I drifted, ever conscious of her beside me.

Fingers running over my chin startled me, and I opened my eyes to meet her soft, green gaze.

"We fell asleep."

I smiled. "We did."

She glanced behind me. "It's two a.m. Late."

I held my breath. "Are you kicking me out, Deirdre? Making me do the walk of shame in the middle of the night?"

"Do, uh, do you want to go?"

"No," I said, surprising myself. "I don't. I'm quite comfortable."

She snuggled closer. "I am too." Her hand drifted over my stomach, teasing. I captured it, kissing her palm regretfully.

"Don't get any ideas. I only brought one condom with me. I hadn't expected to use it, to be honest."

"You really hate them?"

I had never given it much thought. They were necessary, and I never went without one. Ever. But things had changed for me, even if I couldn't admit it. Since she was asking, though, I was truthful.

"Lately, yes."

She laughed, low and husky. I loved the sound of her laugh and her voice. Both turned me on.

She didn't say anything for a moment, then sighed, the air drifting over my chest like a kiss.

"I haven't been with anyone else since we, ah, started this, Maddox." She paused. "Or for a long time before, if I'm being honest. I know I'm clean."

"Neither have I. I'm clean as well."

"I get the shot."

My cock twitched at her words. "Are you saying we can go without condoms?"

"If you wanted, yes."

If I wanted?

My cock wanted. In fact, he wanted to go for it right now. From the heat of her body molded to mine, she wanted it as well.

Still, I wanted something more and knew how to get it. I had to seize the moment when Dee's defenses were down and she was oddly vulnerable.

"I meant what I said earlier, Deirdre."

"Which part?"

She knew damn well which part. "That it's me. My cock. My body. If we're together, then it's only me."

She lifted her face, and I met her gaze in the dimness.

"What if I said I expected the same of you?"

"You already have it. I would never be with someone else. That's not how I work."

She frowned. "I'm the same way, but I don't do relationships, Maddox. You know that."

"Stop fooling yourself, Deirdre. We're in a relationship."

"I don't date," she insisted, stubborn as a child being told something they didn't want to hear.

I scrubbed my face. "I hate to break it to you, my lovely. We've been dating the past few months."

She sat up, clutching a pillow in front of her like a talisman. "We have not!"

I sat up as well, grabbing her shoulders. "Listen to me. We've been having dinner, meeting with our friends, talking on the phone, texting. Having sex." I dropped my voice. "Amazing, crazy sex. Neither of us is seeing anyone else. Now we're talking about unprotected sex because it's the next natural step. Whether you like it or not, we're in an exclusive relationship."

She gaped at me, making me laugh. I ran my fingers over her cheek.

"Relax, Dee. I'm just pointing out the facts."

"I don't—"

I held up my hand, interrupting her. "I know, you don't believe in love. I don't either," I lied. "However, there is nothing wrong with admitting we're together." I warmed to my plan. "In fact, it would have a lot of advantages."

"What are you talking about?"

I leaned against the headboard, trying to appear casual.

"You know, you're not the only one struggling with Cami's sudden marriage. I know she's worried about you as well."

"What does that have to do with your sudden revelation we're in a relationship?"

I leaned forward, grasping her neck and kissing her hard. "*We are,* Deirdre. Maybe not a conventional one, but to us, it is a relationship. It's our own version. Now shut up and listen to me."

Her mouth formed an O at my words, but she didn't say anything.

"Bent and Emmy are engaged. Cami and Aiden are married. They're all in that stage where they think love is the answer to everything. They're constantly trying to throw us together. And it's going to get worse. So let's beat them to it."

"Beat them to it?"

"Let's date. Openly."

"I. Don't. Date," she hissed out through tight lips.

I waved my hand. "Nothing changes. We see each other. We fuck. We text. We simply let them see it now—well, maybe not the fucking part." I winked. "If they think we're following in their footsteps, they'll stop trying to interfere."

She huffed out a long breath. "That sounds dangerous."

I shrugged. "Nope. The added bonus is that it will comfort Cami, thinking you are happy. She can relax a little."

She flopped against the pillows. "So, what, you want to walk into Bentley's place and announce we're dating?"

"No." I chuckled. "We can be subtle. A kiss here, a look there. When they ask, which they will, we can say yes, we're seeing each other."

She was silent for a minute, her fingers worrying the fringe on a pillow.

"I don't believe in love, Maddox."

I gritted my teeth to stop the words, "You will soon enough," from coming out.

"No one said anything about love, Dee. I am simply asking you to be faithful to me, and I will to you. If we're exclusive, then why not call a spade a spade? It's not as though I'm asking you to marry me."

She shuddered visibly. "That isn't something I can ever see happening for me."

"I know," I snapped, unable to keep the bitterness from my voice. "You've said so many times."

Her brow furrowed. "Why do you want to do this?"

"I like you," I stated honestly. "You get me. You make me laugh." I drifted my hand over her shoulder, stroking her smooth skin. "Sex with you is fantastic. The best I've ever had."

"The best," she whispered, nodding in agreement.

"We get along well, Dee. Whether you admit it or not, we're already involved. Call it what you want in private. Fuck buddies, friends with benefits, booty calls—I don't much give a fuck. I still want to call it dating in the real world."

"What if I decide I don't want to?"

My heart skipped a beat and my neck broke out in a sweat, but I couldn't tip my hand. "Then we call it off."

"So we're at a standoff?"

"Are we? Is the idea of holding my hand or saying the words 'my boyfriend' so abhorrent to you that you would rather walk away from a good thing?"

Her voice rose. "You want me to call you my *boyfriend*?"

Her reaction amused me. I fell back on the bed, laughing. "Of everything I said to you, that's the thing you react strongest to?"

She grinned, looking abashed. "Sorry. This has come out of left field."

I pushed up on my elbow. "No, it hasn't. It's been simmering below the surface for a while." I swallowed. "I'm not asking you for a lifetime, Dee. I'm asking for right now. Knowing we're together, as lovers at least, would help me."

At least, for now. I didn't add.

"How?"

"I like control and order. All the undercover stuff is wearing."

"You *are* very controlling when we're in bed."

I kissed her bare shoulder. "You like it."

"I like order too."

"I know."

She narrowed her eyes. "Nothing changes except a label, right? You aren't suddenly going to expect me to be at your beck and call? Or tell me what to do?"

Those questions I was able to answer honestly. "No—I have no desire to change you, or us. I don't expect you to put restrictions on me either. The one thing I expect is for us to be exclusive."

"What about when it ends?"

The urge to inform her it wasn't going to end was strong. Again, I bit my tongue and lied.

"We know it's only sex. What our friends think, what the world thinks, is another matter. One we won't concern ourselves with right now. As for the future, we'll take it as it comes." I held out my hand. "So, girlfriend?"

She looked at my extended hand and slowly raised hers, letting me grasp it tight. "Boyfriend."

"Excellent."

"Can we fuck now?" She grinned widely. "Bareback?"

I was over her in a second. "Fucking right we can, *Deirdre*."

⁓

I DRIFTED AGAIN, Dee draped over me. I liked it and decided it was going to be a fringe benefit of our new arrangement. It would be one of my favorite parts. That, plus fucking her without a condom.

Messier, but holy hell, it felt incredible.

Her warmth. The feel of her tight pussy holding me snug. The slickness and softness of having my cock buried inside her. The intensity of *feeling*, really feeling, her muscles gripping me.

I had never known anything like it.

Judging from her reaction, neither had she.

It had been fast and hard. My control was lost the second I slid inside her, and I didn't give a flying fuck.

It raised fantastic to an entirely new, mind-blowing level.

Her voice startled me.

"Can I ask you questions now that you're my boyfriend?"

I peered at the clock to see it was after four. Neither of us was getting much sleep tonight.

"You can ask me anything."

"Why is control so important to you?"

All the breath left my lungs in a fast exhale. Of all the things she could have asked, that was the most personal. I contemplated telling her to ask something else, but I realized if I wanted a relationship with her—not the pretend-for-the-world one I told her we should have—but the real, committed kind of relationship, she had every right to know. At least part of the story.

"It stems back to my childhood, Dee."

She shifted, gazing at me. "Can you tell me?"

"My father raised me. He wasn't a kind man. He drank and was bitter that my mom was gone."

"When did she die?"

I sighed, pressing my lips to her temple. "Let me tell the story, okay?"

Her thumb went to her lip the way it did every time she was upset. I pulled it away before she could worry it with her teeth. I wrapped my hand around hers, holding it tight.

"When I was younger, my father was distant but all right. He wasn't prone to hugs or cuddles. My mom, on the other hand, loved both. She hugged me all the time. At night, we'd cuddle. She'd read to me and stroke my head."

"What happened?"

"I was always an odd child. My father called me difficult. I needed order and quiet. When things were chaotic and loud, it bothered me. I preferred a book and my own company to other kids. My mom got that—my father hated it. He constantly tried to push me into sports or group activities at school. I failed miserably every time. They would argue, and he would storm away. My mom never left, though. She always stuck up for me. She knew what I needed. I kept my room neat. My toys tidy and in their places." I paused, lost in memories. "My father thought I was 'challenged'—his word. My mother said I was simply unique. Either way, I caused a lot of trouble."

I pressed her face to my chest, not wanting to meet her gaze anymore.

"When I was seven, my mom died in a freak accident. She fell down the stairs and broke her neck. When I came home from school, I found her."

"Oh, Maddox."

"My father didn't handle it well. It turned out, he had never wanted kids, but he let my mother talk him into having one. Me. I was nothing but a disappointment, and he blamed me for her death."

"How? You were seven and at school!"

"She was making me a surprise—my favorite cake—and was carrying it down to the extra refrigerator in the basement when it happened. I remember there was icing all over the stairs. I think it fell from her hands, and she slipped trying to save it or when she went down to clean it up."

"Not your fault," she insisted.

"No, I know that. But my father disagreed. After that, he gave up pretending to like me. It was as though he made it his mission to make me miserable. He knew I needed order and quiet." I sighed as I thought about it. "He made sure I never got it. We moved all the time. He liked to throw out things I liked, so I learned never to show emotion. He would move furniture around to upset me. He kept the TV or radio on all the time. Loud. He tossed out books and mementos to upset me. There was never any peace."

"What an awful man."

"I will never let someone have the sort of power over me again that he had. He knew how to hurt me, and he did it as often as he could. He enjoyed it. If he knew I disliked yellow, he'd paint the walls that color to upset me. If he knew I liked apples, none was ever in the house. I hated dirt—being unclean, or the place we lived in filthy. He'd go for days without showering, knowing how much it disgusted me. He never once cleaned anywhere we lived. Either I did it, or it didn't happen. He loved to mess it up because of the way I reacted, even though I tried not to." I shook my head at the unpleasant memories. "I slept on the floor for so long, I'd forgotten what it was like to sleep on a bed. I had to hide anything of value or that I loved. He would even destroy a book if he thought I liked it." I blew out a long breath. "And he lied all the time. At first, I believed him. He would trick me into things. Lie about why there was no money or food. Where we were going. Why my toys were gone. Why he lost another job." I lowered my voice. "Why I deserved it when he hit me and told me I was the biggest mistake in the world and he'd trade me for my mother in an instant. He said he wished I had died that day, not her."

She stiffened and I felt the wet of her tears on my skin.

"Every place we went, I had to adjust. Find a pattern and routine. As soon as I did, he would yank me away, and we'd start again. His drinking got worse, the jobs paid less. We went from houses to apartments, then to rooms. Those were the worst. I had no way to get away from him, except to hang out at the library. There, I could lose myself in books, work on homework. It was my only peace."

"How did you survive it?" she asked, her voice choked.

I shrugged. "I just did. When I was old enough, I got a job cleaning in a store after school. I found my birth certificate in a metal box he always took with us wherever we moved, and I went to the bank and opened an account in my own name. Every penny went in there so my father wouldn't know. He didn't care where I was as long as I wasn't there. I learned to rely solely on myself. I knew I had to be the one to get away from him—from the hell he made my life."

She looked up, her eyes glassy and sad. "And you did?"

"When I was fifteen, he got too decrepit to push me around. He could still be verbally abusive, but he could barely get out of his chair anymore. I would go to school, to work, and I would study hard every day. Every weekend. I stayed as far away from him as I could. Most nights, when I could, I would sleep under the bleachers in the gym or hide in the library and sleep there. I did everything I could to stay away, going back occasionally to check on him. I graduated early, and I left that little town and that poor excuse for a father behind me."

She laid her head on my chest, tracing a finger over my skin. "You came here to Toronto?"

"Yes. I could lose myself here. No one cared where I came from or my history. I found a bookkeeping job, a small place where I could sleep and eat, and I worked my ass off. I got a scholarship to university, and not long after that, I met Bent and Aiden." I drifted my finger down Dee's arm. "I don't know where I'd be without them.

"All my life, I learned to control things, Dee. My emotions, my mouth, my brain, my instincts. I never showed emotion because it egged him on. My happiness had to be eliminated. My fear made him happy. My tears were his victory. So I stopped showing anything but indifference. I learned, by controlling my environment, I was calmer. When I surrounded myself with order, I could think clearer. I think that's why I was drawn to numbers. They make sense. They never lie. I control how they work, how they are arranged, and the outcome."

"And your personal life?"

I smiled. "Yes, I like to control that too. When I was in university and that side of my life opened up, I found it overwhelming. It took me a long time, but I discovered when I was in control there, I enjoyed sex and it was a great release for me. I went through a few phases and I dabbled a little, but I found my place."

"Dabbled?"

I didn't want to get into that part of my life or relive memories I had buried. Telling her wouldn't do any good. It was over.

"Just a figure of speech. I think we all dabble until we find what is good for us. I've been with women who don't like my control and some who do. Everyone has a different version of what works for them. Control is part of me. Part of who I am."

She traced lazy circles on my chest, her touch light. I realized it was the longest we had ever talked about anything so personal, and the longest time we had ever stayed together after having sex.

"I like your control."

"Good thing. Especially now we're dating."

She smacked my chest. "I know what you're trying to do."

"Oh?"

She lifted up on her elbow, meeting my gaze. The intensity of her look took my breath away. "I know you don't want to hear this, but I'm sorry your father was so horrid. I'm sorry you lost your mother and you struggled all your life. It's unfair and appalling."

"It is what it is. It made me who I am today."

"I like who you are." She inhaled, then sighed out a long breath. "I like having you here with me."

I knew that was a huge concession for her. I cupped her cheek. "Thank you."

"Is your father . . . ?" She let her question trail off.

"He died not long after I left. He died of a stroke in his chair. Without me checking on him every so often, he wasn't discovered for a while."

"Gruesome."

"Fitting."

I stared at the ceiling. "Bent and Aiden helped me loosen up. They gave me my first real home and a place to simply be Maddox. We became each other's family. I learned to laugh and relax. To be part of a friendship—a team. They accepted me, faults and all, and I accepted them the same way. We respected each other's boundaries. Even with my best friends, however, I can only give up so much control. I will always need some form of it in all aspects of my life."

"I understand."

I rolled, facing her. I wiped away her tears. "Please, don't." I hated to see her cry. It happened so rarely that when it did, my heart split in two.

"Have you ever told anyone else?"

"Aside from Bent and Aiden? No."

"Thank you for telling me."

My stomach chose that moment to growl. It was loud and long, and Dee giggled.

Giggled. Like a schoolgirl. It was short and high-pitched, and it amused me. I chuckled at the strange sound.

"Hungry?" she asked, the sarcasm evident.

"So it would seem."

"I have cold chicken."

"Lead the way."

We sat on the sofa, a plate of cold chicken between us. Apparently, I had turned into Aiden since I had wolfed down three pieces of chicken, while Dee nibbled on a drumstick. I decided I had built up an appetite with all the sex and the talking. I needed to replenish my dwindling energy.

It was still dark out, but I knew, all too soon, dawn would begin and our night would end. I wasn't sure I would get another night like the one we had. Dee had been unusually defenseless, and I had taken full advantage of it.

And I wasn't done yet.

"Since it's obvious neither of us is going back to sleep and we're being all honest, I have a question for *you*, girlfriend of mine."

She narrowed her eyes. "You can stop calling me that."

"Nope. You agreed."

"What is your question?" She huffed, tossing down the drumstick and wiping her fingers.

"What about your childhood, Dee? I know you didn't have it easy."

"No, I didn't. All my parents did was argue. My mother was unstable, and my father was absent a lot—even before he left. I tried to protect Cami as best I could."

"Who protected you?"

"No one, I guess."

I wanted to tell her I would protect her for the rest of her life, but she wasn't ready to hear those words. I took the plate between us, placing it on the coffee table. I shifted closer, our knees touching, and entwined our fingers. I liked being able to touch her that way.

"Why are you so adamant about never falling in love?"

I expected her to tell me the subject wasn't open for discussion. Even to push away from me and tell me it was time to leave. She didn't, though. She frowned, lifted her thumb to her mouth, and nibbled on it absently.

"My mother was obsessed with my father. Everything revolved around him. How she dressed, the way she decorated the house, what she cooked. Always his favorites. The colors he liked. When he got home, she pushed us aside. She fed us early. We were bathed and put in our rooms so she was free to be with him." She gnawed on her thumb harder, and I pulled it away from her mouth with a shake of my head.

She grimaced, tugging her hand away, but not biting at her thumb. "She smothered him. When she'd have one of her episodes, it became worse. There'd be crying and screaming. Fights. She'd accuse him of having an affair. He'd beg her to take her meds. It was a vicious circle."

"Then he left."

"Yes," she acknowledged. "He walked away. It had been getting worse. The fights, him staying away, her acting out, not taking her pills. It was horrible. Then one day, he was gone. He packed a bag and walked away. She literally grabbed his legs, begging him not to go. He told her he was done and shook her off."

A tear rolled down her cheek. "Poor Cami watched, confused, not understanding what was going on. She called out and asked him to take us. He looked at her and said he couldn't. He left us all." She sighed and swallowed audibly. "You know what happened. My mom never recovered. I looked after Cami, hoping Mom would straighten up, but she never did. She became ill with cancer and refused treatment. She died and left us alone."

"I think you were already alone, Dee."

"I suppose we were."

"So your parents turned you off love?"

She hesitated, and I shifted closer, rubbing her thighs in comfort.

"You really want to know?"

"Yes."

"I had a few relationships as I got older, but none I was particularly invested in. I had seen what love could do to a person and I wasn't overly interested. At the time, I thought I was simply incapable of truly loving anyone. I decided I was like my dad—unfeeling."

I scowled at those words but remained silent.

"When I finished school, I got a job with a large firm. I was low woman on the totem pole, so to speak, and I was assigned all the smaller and less desirable tasks. But I worked hard. One night, I'd stayed late and a lawyer came into the library looking for something. I helped him find it since I had been looking for similar cases a few days prior. We sort of hit it off, and he started dropping by more often. Eventually, we started having an affair." She sighed. "I thought I was in love."

I was shocked to discover my hands locked in fists by her legs. The thought of another man touching her, loving her, drove me crazy. I forced myself to relax, loosening my hands, and crossed my arms across my chest.

"He was married, I take it?"

"No. Todd was young, ambitious—working his way up the corporate ladder. He was being fast-tracked for partnership. He told me he wanted to remain private. He didn't want the partners to think he was concentrating on anything but the firm. I believed him. I didn't tell a soul."

I arched my eyebrow. "Not even Cami?"

"No. No one. We met in secret. It added a layer of naughtiness to the relationship. Trysts in the library. A hotel. He made me promises about when he became partner. Our life together. How he'd take care of me. I helped him in secret with every case he had. Dug up facts, cited cases, anything he needed. I thought we were an amazing couple."

I had a good idea where her story was going, but still, I asked. "What happened?"

She laughed, sounding bitter. "Todd announced his engagement at a function at the office. To one of the partner's daughters. I wasn't supposed to be there that night, so I think he thought it was safe. I was so shocked that I stumbled out of the room and into the library to try to gather myself. I sat there for a long time to calm down, and when I left to go home, I heard him in another office down the hall talking on the phone—about me—bragging about how he had the best of both worlds. A slut to suck his cock whenever he wanted, help him with his job load, and a beautiful wife to show off on his arm and boost his career. He figured he'd make partner in a few months and eventually run the practice since her father held the majority shares."

Rage tore through me.

"What did you do?"

"Confronted him. He told me he had to marry her, but he loved me not her. However, when I told him I'd overheard him in the office, he knew it was pointless to pretend. It got heated and ugly. I kicked him in the nuts and left."

"Good girl."

She shook her head. "The next day, I was fired for sexual harassment against *him*. I tried to fight back, to deny it, but it was his word against mine. No one had ever seen us together, and he was smart enough never to say who he was fucking to the other lawyers." She scoffed. "I didn't know what to do, but I got a call from the office where I work now. One of the lawyers used to work at that firm and knew how they operated—the whole 'boys club' attitude. She believed me—every word. She offered me a new job, and I've been there ever since. After much thought, I decided not to go after him." She ran a hand through her hair. "He was caught screwing another lawyer, his marriage failed, and he was fired, so there's that. The last I heard, he was an ambulance chaser when he was sober enough to go into the office."

"He got what he deserved."

"I suppose. I don't spare much time thinking about him. I learned my lesson, though. Like you, Maddox, I swore I would never again allow someone to have that much control and power over me. He never loved me—he used me—and I let him. I realized what I had been feeling for him was lust and not love, but it was enough to prove to me how dangerous love was to people. I watched it with my parents, I witnessed it at work, and I still let the thought of it swallow me up. I swore I would never again let anyone control my life, except me. I swore off it."

"You are capable of love," I insisted quietly.

"Yes. The lesson came with a benefit. I realized I wasn't unfeeling like my father. I do love Cami—with all my heart. I'm very fond of Emmy. Even Bentley, Aiden—" she reached out her hand, squeezing my arm "—and you. I am capable of feeling love. Just not romantic love. Never again."

Her tone held finality.

"He was at fault, not you."

She stood, brushing off her silky robe.

"Regardless, it showed me how easy it was to fall into the trap. I like men. I enjoy sex. Still, it doesn't mean I have to fall in love—they are not inclusive."

"Some would say the best sex is with someone you love."

"Well, we prove them wrong, don't we?" She leaned down and brushed my lips. "Enough sharing. I have to get ready for work, and so do you. You can let yourself out, yes?"

"Yes."

She hurried away, and I sat lost in my thoughts for a while.

Love had burned her. Her father's desertion, her mother's rejection, and the asshole that used her. They all made her think she was incapable of the depth of that emotion.

I knew better. I had seen her with her sister, with Emmy, and even the way she treated Bentley and Aiden. Me. Her capacity for love was deep, but she was too frightened to relinquish control for fear of getting hurt again.

I knew how she felt. She was the one who had changed my mind about love.

I would have to prove to her the reward was worth the risk.

Because the reward of *her* was worth it to me.

CHAPTER 6

MADDOX

DEE OPENED HER door on Sunday morning, looking decidedly nervous.

I indicated the new keypad feature on her door. "I see Reid was here. Is the system not working? You didn't use the remote."

"Oh yes, but I was right here. No need for the fancy gadgets."

"You should check to make sure who is at the door, Dee."

She rolled her eyes. "I heard the elevator. I know your footsteps, Maddox."

I wanted to grin at that intimate piece of information.

"Use the system, Dee. We need all the feedback we can get."

"Fine. I need to grab my coat."

She was out of sorts again and tense.

"Sure."

I helped her on with her coat, rubbing her shoulders lightly. I lifted her hand, inspecting the fresh nail bites on the pad of her thumb.

"What's going on, Dee?"

"I don't want you to tell them we're dating," she blurted out.

"We agreed. We are."

"No. You agreed. We're just having sex. I'm too old to be dating."

Taking her arm, I escorted her to the elevator, studying her as we descended to the parking garage. "I am going to say this once. I know you're three years older than I am. It's nothing. Get over it."

"It's not that—well, not only that. The term dating in general for me . . . I don't like it. I'm not comfortable with it."

I crossed my arms. "Fine. We're in a relationship. How's that?"

"Better than dating. It still feels like a lie, though."

I took her shoulders, meeting her gaze. "Again, this is the last time I'm going to repeat myself. What we call a relationship and how others view it, is *not* our problem."

"But—"

I interrupted her. "Are you having sex with anyone else?"

"No."

"Are you having sex with me?"

Her lips curled into a smirk. I found it rather sexy.

"Yes."

"Do we have dinner together? Talk? Call and text each other?"

She rolled her eyes. "Yes."

"Then it's a fucking relationship. End of story. And today, we're telling our friends."

"But . . ."

I kissed her hard. "Shut up, Dee. For once, just shut up."

Twice, I pulled her thumb away from her mouth at Bentley's place. She was jumpy and edgy. Even Bentley noticed her odd behavior, arching his eyebrow at me in silence. Finally, I decided just to lay it out there. I cleared my throat, getting everyone's attention.

"So, Cami, your sister and I are in a relationship. Are you okay with that?"

Dee grabbed my knee. Cami's fork froze partway to her mouth, and she gaped at me. Emmy looked shocked. Bentley smirked. Aiden smacked the table.

"I knew it."

"You're dating?" Cami gasped. "For real?"

Dee tensed, and I placed a calming hand on her shoulder.

"Dee doesn't like the word dating. We're in an exclusive relationship. With each other."

Cami's gaze bounced between Dee and me. "And you're asking my permission?"

"No," I replied easily. "I was being polite." I tugged Dee closer, trying to get her to relax. "We wanted to share."

"I think we need to talk," Cami whispered, looking at Dee.

Dee stiffened more. "Nothing to talk about. You're not the only one moving on with your life. Maddox and I are together. I doubt it's a huge shock, and although he was being funny, if you're not okay with it, that's your problem."

The whole table stilled.

I dropped my lips to Dee's ear. "I think she's a little worried, Dee. Don't get defensive."

"As long as you're happy, of course I'm okay with it," Cami insisted. "You didn't say anything the other night at dinner. You just surprised me."

"Like your wedding surprised me," Dee shot back. "Or the fact that you quit your job and never mentioned it."

"Oh boy," Aiden muttered. "Here we go."

It was my turn to gape.

Holy shit. I was beginning to be sorry I said anything.

Cami flung down her napkin. "Excuse me."

She hurried away, and after a few seconds, Dee followed her.

Aiden glared at me. "Nice."

"All I said was we are dating—I mean, in a relationship!"

Bentley sighed. "I think you've been taking tact lessons from Aiden. You should have done that in private."

I jerked my head toward Aiden. "Like those two did when they announced to the table they got married? Fuck that. Dee and I are adults. If we want to see each other, we will." I yanked on my hair. "You've all been pushing it anyway. What's the goddamn problem?"

Now Bentley glared at me. "Don't bitch at me because you screwed this up."

Aiden nodded, seeming pleased. "Yeah."

Bentley snapped his head in Aiden's direction. "You zip it."

Emmy stood, slamming her hand on the table, startling us. "Shut up, all of you!"

We stared at her.

"If you don't understand this, let me explain. What happened has been simmering since you and Cami got married, Aiden. Whether she admits it or not, Dee was hurt. So was I. We would have loved to be involved in your wedding." She redirected her gaze to me. "So your little announcement, Maddox, brought it to a head. Finally. Now, I am going to go and make sure they work this out once and for all." She stalked away, turning at the foot of the stairs. "And for ruining brunch, you three are doing the cleanup and dishes. So get to it."

Aiden huffed. "Way to go. I'm still hungry."

"You're always fucking hungry," Bentley growled.

"Bottomless pit," I added, looking at the dishes. There were a lot of them.

"I had nothing to do with the situation, and I still got in trouble. Thanks, Maddox," Bentley snapped.

"Happy to have included you in the debacle."

"Shut up, both of you." Aiden shook his head, reaching for the platter of pancakes. "I'm eating first, then cleaning."

I looked at my half-eaten plate. "Good idea. Maybe we should cover the girls' plates, and they can warm them or something."

Aiden looked over his shoulder. "Do you think they're fighting?"

"Talking," Bentley said. "They talk." He sighed. "They talk a lot."

"I hope Cami is okay," Aiden said with a groan. "If I have to beat you for this, Mad Dog, I will—but I'll try to be gentle."

"Whatever," I snorted. "I can take you, big man."

"You think so? I could snap you like a twig."

"I'll throw a couple of lemon Danish at you and run. You'll be so busy trying to catch them, I'll be fine."

He frowned and started to laugh. "That would work."

We all chuckled. Aiden started eating, and with a shrug, I joined him. The food was too good to waste. When we were done, I laid down my fork.

"I didn't mean to start anything. I just wanted it out there before Dee changed her mind."

"What do you mean?"

I wiped my mouth. "Let's say Dee isn't as far into this relationship as I am and leave it at that. I'm trying to be patient." I slouched in my chair. "I need you two to be supportive."

Bentley rested his elbows on the table, studying me. "Are you serious about this relationship?"

"As a heart attack."

"And Dee is . . ."

"Skittish, to say the least."

"Okay."

Aiden frowned. "Are you forcing her into something? As her brother-in-law, I think I need to stop you."

"You really think I could force Dee into anything? All I've done is move us along a bit. Once she is comfortable with us being a couple, we'll go from there."

"Do you ever do anything like a normal person?" Aiden huffed.

"Like you, you mean? Push the woman I love away, then turn around and marry her on a whim? Yeah, so normal."

Aiden and Bentley gaped at me, making me realize what I had said.

"You love her? I thought you didn't believe in love."

I shifted in my chair. "Well, I'd never met Dee."

Bentley smiled. "Maddox, that's great. I'm happy for you."

"Don't be too happy yet. I have to convince the lady."

"You will."

Aiden grunted. "You hurt her, I will hurt you. She's my family."

I met his gaze, serious. "If I hurt her, I'll let you. She's everything to me."

His eyes softened in understanding. "I hear you."

We heard the sound of footsteps, and we all stood, grabbing plates.

"Enough sharing. If we aren't busy when they get down here, we'll all be in shit," I ordered.

Bentley winked as I grabbed a platter.

"Welcome to couple-hood."

～

DEE AND I were alone and quiet in the elevator.

Aiden and Cami had left not long after the girls joined us in the kitchen. They rolled their eyes at our efforts and helped us clean up, so we finished the task quickly. They seemed fine, although they all had red eyes and weren't as chatty as usual. They did appear better when we sat down with fresh cups of coffee and discussed plans for the wedding. We left as soon as I drank my coffee.

I glanced over at Dee. "Everything okay?"

She met my gaze. "Nice announcement. You're like a bull in a china shop."

"I said I was going to tell them."

"You said we'd be subtle."

I scratched the back of my neck. "Yeah, I forgot that part." I took the chance and slipped my arm around her shoulders, pulling her close. "Are you and Cami okay?"

She sighed, leaning into me. "We will be. We cleared the air, I think. I told Cami how hard I was struggling not being her first to confide in anymore. She admitted she feels overwhelmed at times, and because we're not living together anymore, feels as if she shouldn't bother me." She smiled at me, her eyes watery. "We'll work it out."

The elevator door opened, and we walked outside to the car. "Good. Did you address the marriage part?"

"Nothing much to be done there. They're married, end of story. It was impulsive on their part, but it was their decision. She and Aiden are happy, and that's what really matters."

"Are you sure about that? I think you're still upset about not being involved."

"I'll get over it. We have Emmy's to plan, and one is enough. Simple as it is going to be, there are still lots of details."

"So Bentley tells me."

"Cami has a friend who helps out brides. Emmy is going to go see Jen. It will take a lot of stress off her so she can concentrate on school and enjoy her wedding."

I pulled into traffic. "Good. Now let's go home. I'm going to pull rank as your boyfriend and demand sex this afternoon." I glanced her way. "In your frilly room, with you naked and spread out on that fancy bed of yours."

She rolled her eyes and looked out the window. "Stop with the boyfriend comments."

I was certain she smiled, though.

DEE

I OPENED MY eyes, my body warm. I shifted, the weight of something pinning me down. For a moment, I began to panic, then realized it was Maddox. He was asleep, his arm flung across my waist and his head buried next to mine on my pillow. He had one leg wedged between mine, effectively holding me prisoner. His silver hair was bright against the deep red of my pillowcase, and his scruff tickled my shoulder. I had to suppress a smile. Considering he wasn't someone who liked being touched, he certainly seemed to like touching me. Thank goodness he was on the same page when it came to PDA. It didn't bother me to watch Emmy and Bentley, or even Cami and Aiden, snuggle or kiss, but I preferred to keep that side of my life private and Maddox agreed.

At least he hadn't changed the game rules there.

His sudden declaration that we were in a relationship and wanted to announce it had shocked me. While his thoughts made sense, hearing the words he used filled my head with warning bells.

Dating. Boyfriend. Exclusive. Relationship.

Broken down, none of the words frightened me by themselves. Used together, they scared the shit out of me.

However, he wanted the words, and the entire time we had been involved, he never once asked me for anything else. To my surprise, I found I wanted to give in to him. To please him.

From the moment we first had sex, it was intense. He was exactly what I needed in a lover: demanding, passionate, and controlling. He issued directives I followed without question; I had complete trust in him. No matter what, there was a quiet sense of respect, even when he had me on my knees in front of him. Regardless of the demands he growled in his low voice, his eyes were always warm, his hands handled me with care, and his body drove me to the highest pinnacles of pleasure. We were electric together.

The first time I met him, I had been attracted to him. Tall and lean, he looked older than his thirty years because of his prematurely gray hair. Some of the strands were so light they shone silver, and his scruff was the same. He kept his hair short on the sides, but longer on the top, the waves carefully disheveled. He had a toned and muscled body, his legs long and sinewy. He dressed with care and looked every inch the modern business executive.

He shifted, his hold tightening. Taking advantage of his closeness, I stared at him. In repose, he lost the tightness around his eyes, the skin smooth. His jaw was sharp, the silver scruff soft under my fingers. His eyebrows were still dark, highlighting his light blue eyes. The glasses he wore, simple, with heavy black frames, accentuated the amazing color. His normal expression was somber—serious and contemplative—older than his years. With those he cared for, he showed his humorous side. His smile was easier, and the constant worry lines on his forehead smoothed. His laugh was contagious, and I had noticed it ringing out more lately. When we were alone, another side of his personality shone through—one I knew not even his closest friends saw. A gentle, compassionate side that made me feel protected and safe. He was open and honest with his thoughts, and I loved our discussions about books, movies, and whatever other subject came up.

I was surprised at how natural it was to have him sleep beside me for the first time. To feel his strong form close when I woke. My body's reactions to him were vastly different from the swirling thoughts constantly in my head. I felt as though I melted into him once I was in his arms. When he touched me, the chaotic thoughts dimmed. I felt myself drawn to him—every brush of his lips or caress from his hands easing me. Doubts evaporated and only the rightness of being close permeated my soul.

He worried over small things: the lock on my door, how often I took the subway, if something stressed me out at work, or lately, Cami. His introspective nature made him quieter than most people, but his eyes saw everything. His understanding of my feelings, his patience in letting me talk, to try to help me come to terms with it, made me care for him even more.

And I did care.

I simply couldn't love him.

I would never allow that intense connection. It destroyed my mother, and the one time I allowed myself to feel it, almost did the same to me.

Still . . .

At times, I found myself wondering how it would feel to love Maddox. To have his love in return.

I shut those thoughts down as quickly as they surfaced, because it wasn't going to happen.

That was the one hard rule we both agreed on.

Exclusive sex? Yes.

The inevitable failure of love? No.

My thoughts were too overwhelming. Suddenly uncomfortable, I shifted, easing myself away from Maddox. He stirred, his eyes opening, and he frowned.

"Where are you going?" his sleepy voice asked.

I grabbed my clothes strewn around the floor, pulling a shirt over my head, needing its cover. I had to hide away from his penetrating gaze, so I bent again to grab my skirt. He had been impatient to fuck me when we arrived, and there was a path from the door leading into the bedroom of discarded fabric. "It's almost five in the afternoon. I need to do some laundry and get ready for work tomorrow."

He sat upright, leaning against the headboard, and stretched, resting his large hands on his lap. I tried not to think of how easily they encompassed my waist when he yanked me close. He looked so masculine in my frilly bed. He had one leg draped over the edge of the mattress, the muscles taut. When he was dressed in one of his stylish suits, he was handsome. Naked in my bed after our afternoon nap, his hair in disarray, he was devastating. I had to drop my eyes from ogling him.

He slid from the bed, not concerned with his nakedness. His semi-erect cock jutted out, and he smirked as he grabbed his pants. "I see that flush, Deirdre. Laundry isn't what's on your mind at the moment." He stood, slowly tugging his pants up his thighs, leaving them open at the waist. He rested his hands on his hips, the bulge at the front growing. "You know, I rather like this no-condom thing. We can be spontaneous." He stepped closer. "I can have you anytime, anywhere, *anyway,* I like."

His words were small bombs of heat hitting me right between my legs. The feel of him without a barrier was mind-blowing—steel encased in silk. When he was buried deep in me, it felt as if his cock was made for me and me alone. It was heady and powerful.

"You like Sunday evenings to yourself," I reminded him, biting on my thumb. Maddox liked order and schedules. "I'm sure you have things you need to do as well."

He stepped even closer, cupping his erection. "Right now, the one thing I have to do—is you."

"You already did that—twice," I protested weakly, knowing it was useless.

His laughter was low. Deep. That of a man thoroughly in control.

"Third time's the charm, Deirdre." He tugged my thumb from my mouth, drawing it into his and swirling his tongue on the flesh.

I whimpered at the sensation, feeling the dull ache build between my legs that only he could create.

His eyes darkened, his voice quiet in the room. "Ask me to stay."

There was no choice.

"Stay."

CHAPTER 7

MADDOX

MONDAY EVENING, I examined the latest figures, satisfied with what I saw. Our footing was solid—even more than I had envisioned. Our bank accounts were full, our investments strong, and everything pointed toward another massive success with Ridge Towers.

I picked up my mug, frowning when I realized I had drunk the contents already. I wasn't sure how many cups I had downed today. I'd come in early, knowing it was a crazy week ahead. Yesterday, I had left Dee's place late, somehow unable to tear myself away. I'd had her repeatedly, needing her with an intensity that surprised even me. She was asleep when I left her, curled up in her frilly bed, sated and at peace. I hated to see her upset, but I hoped that since she and Cami had cleared the air, she would be able to move ahead.

With me.

I shook my head to clear my thoughts. I needed to put Dee aside and concentrate on work.

Earlier, I had remembered my promise to Dee about the surplus office furniture, and I checked out the storage room, finding the set I had thought about. Light wood, clean lines, with a modern feel, I knew Dee would like it. There was a desk and credenza, along with the set of shelves which I knew would fit in the space. It had been in an office we kept for visitors, but when we added the legal department, the décor had been changed to something more masculine.

I snapped a couple of pictures and sent them off to her, then asked Van to arrange the delivery without waiting for her reply. I knew she would love them. When her reply appeared a short time later, I let her know they were already hers. Her one-word response made me laugh.

Bossy.

I pulled a folder to me, flipping it open. We'd had our first video conference for the marketing of Ridge Towers with both Advance and Zip, which took most of my day, and I was rereading my notes. Both companies had been professional and bright but lacking in their grasp of what we wanted when it came to Ridge Towers. I hoped The Gavin Group had a better handle on it.

Bentley walked in, briefcase in hand. He sat down, crossing his legs with a sigh.

"What did you think?"

I knew what he was asking. I shrugged. "Good concepts, but not what we wanted."

He ran a hand through his hair in frustration. "I want more than pushing a new condo tower and all the amenities. I didn't like the one slogan, and Zip made the place sound elitist."

"I agree."

Aiden wandered in, a muffin in his hand. He flung himself onto the sofa, kicking up his feet as he chewed.

"'The best instead of the rest'?" He snorted. "That was lame."

"Hopefully, The Gavin Group will step up to the plate," Bentley mused. "I spoke with both Graham and Richard. I liked what they had to say."

"I did too."

"I have a good feeling about them," Aiden said, swallowing the last bite of his muffin.

"Seriously, are you ever without food?"

"Dude, have you met me? I need constant sustenance." He flexed his arms, the muscles rippling under his shirt. "It takes a lot of fuel to keep this temple going."

I rolled my eyes. "Don't you have a wife to get home to?"

He grinned. "She's having dinner with her sister so they can talk more." His grin widened. "Your *girlfriend*."

"Shut up."

"What about you, Bent?"

"I'm free. Emmy is meeting with a consultant."

"Oh yeah, Dee mentioned her."

Bentley nodded. "She'll help Emmy figure out what she wants, then handle the details. Emmy's crazy with school and her work here. I don't want our wedding to stress her out." He grinned. "Still, I want to marry her as fast as possible. If Jen can speed things along, even better."

Sandy bustled in, always efficient. "I booked a table for Thursday's dinner at Stables for ten people at eight o'clock. It's business casual, and before you can ask, yes, Reid's suit is clean and in his closet."

I chuckled and met Aiden's amused grin.

"The boardroom is set up, their hotel is confirmed, and as you requested, lunch is ordered for Wednesday and Thursday. Friday, they will be at your disposal—their words, not mine—until they leave for the airport for their afternoon flight. I've arranged with Frank for them to be picked up at the airport, and for their return journey."

"Excellent. Thanks, Sandy." Bentley beamed at her.

I had asked Dee to join us for dinner on Thursday before I left her last night. Cami and Emmy were coming and I wanted her included. She had hesitated, but she finally agreed when I informed her since we were in a relationship, our friends would expect her to accompany me.

She had slapped my arm, told me off about taking advantage,

and told me to stop using the word "relationship" so often.

Still, she was coming, so that was all that mattered.

"I listened to the pitches today. They were both crap," Sandy announced, pausing in the doorway. "Let's hope this group does better. They certainly seem to be more on the ball."

Aiden guffawed from the sofa, his head reclining on the cushions. Bentley shook his head, but his lips quirked at Sandy's declaration. I knew she'd been hovering during both presentations. We welcomed her input. She was honest to a fault and had no problem telling us what she thought.

We all adored that about her.

"You heard the woman." I chuckled. "Crap."

"Really. That one man, Bruce"—she shook her head—"he was such a pretentious asshole. He makes Bentley look like a laid-back hippie. The pole he has shoved up his backside must tickle his throat."

Aiden's laughter exploded and echoed in the room.

Bentley blinked, and a wide grin split his face. "Okay, well, on that note, I'm going to get ready and go. I want to head to the commune early and see my chick," he deadpanned, holding up his fingers in a V formation. "She's groovy."

Aiden rolled off the sofa.

I snorted, unable to stop myself from joining in the laughter. "Peace, brother."

For a moment, all we could do was laugh. It felt good and broke the tension of the day.

Bentley stood, his shoulders still shaking with amusement. "I hope The Gavin Group pleases her, or they'll get an earful."

"She might as well sit in on the meeting since she is going to eavesdrop anyway," I stated loudly, knowing she would be in earshot.

Sandy poked her head around the doorway. "I planned to," she quipped. "You need me."

None of us argued as she spun on her heel, clearly smug.

"This week is going to be interesting." Bentley brushed off his suit. "I'm looking forward to it."

Given the new role I was playing in the process, I was as well.

⌒

WEDNESDAY MORNING, THE Gavin Group arrived.

Graham Gavin was a true professional—polite, courteous, with an old-fashioned charm that spoke of class. His handshake was warm and his gaze direct.

Richard VanRyan was a force unto himself. He was confident, assured, and dynamic. He was at home in the boardroom, ready to impress, never doubting his ability to do so. Yet, his bravado suited him. He possessed an underwritten cockiness and an easy composure I liked. He and Graham were obviously close, sometimes finishing each other's thoughts.

With them was a young, attractive woman with deep brown hair, whom Graham introduced as Rebecca Holden. She was petite, dressed in a smart suit, her hair twisted into a knot on top of her head. Her eyes were a bright blue, kind and intelligent, and her smile somewhat shy.

I shook her hand, smiling. "Nice to meet you, Rebecca."

"Becca, please."

"Becca."

We sat down after collecting coffees and pastries from the trays Sandy had provided. Before we could start, the boardroom door opened, and Reid stumbled in. His face was creased, his hair all over the place, and his sneakers undone.

"Good God," Bentley muttered. "I thought his suit was in his closet. Did he forget to open the door?"

Aiden and I shared an amused glance. Reid's torn jeans and wrinkled T-shirt were his standard office uniform. While we were used to them, I still wanted to cringe at times.

"Sorry," Reid rasped. "I was here all night working on some code. I guess I fell asleep and . . ." His voice trailed off, and he swallowed. His gaze was locked on Becca, who smiled and dropped her gaze to the table. He cleared his throat, pulled off his glasses, and rubbed his eyes. "Yeah, sorry," he finished, seemingly at a loss for words—a rare thing for him.

I glanced at Bentley, unsure how to handle the situation. He half shrugged, then addressed the table.

"This is Reid Matthews, head of our IT department, resident genius—" his lips curled into a grin "—and fashion guru."

Everyone laughed, the tension draining from the room. Reid shook everyone's hand. I noticed he lingered over Becca's a little longer than acceptable. I elbowed him. He dropped her hand and turned to grab a coffee and fill a plate with pastries.

"Hungry?" Richard asked, amused by the plateful.

"I forgot to eat again," Reid responded. He pulled out a chair across the table from Becca, almost missing it with his ass because he was so busy staring at her. Aiden was fast and pushed the chair forward. Reid flushed at Becca's soft laugh and shoved a Danish in his mouth, avoiding her gaze.

"I think we're all settled now," I announced dryly. "Richard, the floor is yours."

Richard cleared his throat. "We're very excited to be here. Based on our conversations, I've come up with some ideas for Ridge Towers."

"I'm anxious to see your vision," I said. "We all are."

He stood. "This is my concept. Remember, it's still in the infancy stages, and we can tweak, change, or scrap it and start again." He paused. "You're the client, and we want you happy." His eyes twinkled with suppressed humor, and he winked. "I think you'll find I've nailed it for you."

We all laughed.

I wasn't laughing a short time later. Richard had every reason to be confident. He *had* nailed it. The other two companies had concepts, a tagline or two, and stock visuals with promises of more when we approved their ideas and moved forward.

Richard wasn't waiting for us to move forward. He was already at the finish line, with an entire plan.

His presentation was slick and detailed. His keywords bang on.

His marketing idea revolved around family. Home. Life. Exactly the direction we wanted for the project. He had numerous slogans and taglines, but they all came down to the same theme.

Home. Ridge Towers. You've found it.

I glanced at the sample boards. Bright, vibrant. Eye-catching. The images were sharp, the vision clear. The logo they had created was clean and went well with the overall design concept.

I knew Bentley was impressed. They responded to every question with a thoughtful answer. Graham and Richard each had input, although I noticed Richard took the lead on the majority of the responses. Becca added her thoughts, showing she knew the campaign as well as her coworkers did.

She was intelligent, often referring to Reid on technical points of the project. He answered her directly, but his replies were unusually slow, and he cleared his throat often. Most of the time it was like a private conversation with the technical jargon they used, but it was interesting to watch. He rarely took his gaze away from her as he spoke, even as he searched for words. The boy seemed to be off his game today, and I wondered how much of it had to do with lack of sleep and how much had to do with the pretty girl across from him.

Becca had a lot of queries for us, and she took constant notes. I had the feeling they wanted to know as much about us as we wanted to know about them in order to work as a team. I liked the idea, and I liked them as a whole.

Sandy sat at one end of the table, taking notes. She nodded frequently, looking pleased. There were no pretentious assholes in the group. I could tell she approved of Richard, his cocky attitude and all.

After lunch, we spoke briefly, and they departed. I sat at my desk, inspecting the boards, jotting down some notes.

Bentley wandered in, sitting down in his favorite spot. I waited, knowing Aiden would join us any second. After he appeared, settling on the sofa, I looked up.

"That was impressive."

Bentley nodded in agreement. "Blew me away, to be honest. He got it."

Aiden spoke up. "Cocky bastard. Yet, I like him."

I chuckled. "He is. Let's face it. We want that working for us, right?"

"Absolutely."

"I liked the way he rolled with our suggestions and comments," Bentley added. "He might be cocky, but he's not arrogant enough that he refuses to listen."

"I agree."

"Rebecca is bright. I think she'd be good to work with in the office."

"Reid was strangely quiet," Bentley mused. "He usually jumps right into our meetings."

Aiden chuckled. "What was with his behavior today? He was like a cat on a hot tin roof, all jumpy and edgy."

"I think Becca had something to do with that."

Bentley frowned. "Is that going to be an issue? Them working together?"

"No. Reid will be fine," I assured him. "He was a bit off his game at first, but he settled in. He needs to stop pulling these all-nighters."

"And get some new clothes. He looked like he rolled out of a trash can today."

"Ease up, Bent. I'll take him shopping. To their credit, I don't think they gave it another thought. Once he started talking about what he was bringing to the project, and all the things he handles here, they didn't care what he was wearing." Aiden defended Reid.

Bentley raked a hand through his hair. "Make sure he wears his suit at dinner."

"Yes."

"Okay then, fine. Can you at least get him some new T-shirts? Ones without holes?"

Aiden smirked. "On it."

"And a haircut."

"He's a grown man, Bent. I can't force him to cut his hair."

"Suggest it. Offer him a bribe."

Reid walked in. "A new wall of hi-def monitors would work. Eight of them. I'll even wear a dress shirt once a week to show my appreciation."

Bentley's eyes narrowed. "Every day. Pants too."

"Twice a week. Not on weekends."

"I want you in here for normal hours. No more sleeping on the floor of your office."

"Not happening. I do my best work at night." Reid tugged at the hem of his shirt. "And that happens in these T-shirts." He huffed out a long breath. "I like it in the office. It feels like I belong here. I'm zoned in. My apartment stifles me."

Bentley's gaze met mine. We knew Reid had a rough time before he started working at BAM. He rarely talked about it, but on occasion, his comments spoke volumes.

"Three times a week."

Reid held out his hand. "Deal."

Bentley stood and shook his hand. "Order whatever you want. After you get your hair cut." He walked out.

Aiden whistled. "You worked that angle well."

Reid sat down with a grin. "I would have gone as high as four days. The old broad bought me some nice shirts. I like them." He waggled his eyebrows. "I look smoking hot in them."

I chuckled at his antics and his nickname for Sandy. Only he could get away with it.

Reid cleared his throat. "So, ah, Becca . . ."

I raised my eyebrows. "Yes?"

"She is going to be here, right? In the office?"

"If we sign a deal with them, yes." I pointed to the left. "The office beside mine."

"Oh. Across from me."

"She'll be your coworker, Reid," Aiden admonished him.

"I checked the company policies. There is no non-fraternization policy."

I folded my hands on top of my desk. "She'll be here as a liaison between us and The Gavin Group. As such, she'll be a valued member of the staff and under my direction."

He shifted. "I'm not going to bother her. I was only asking. Maybe I can help her find her way around. I know Toronto well, and I can help her get settled."

"Reid." Aiden sat forward with his elbows resting on his thighs. Reid looked at him.

"Tread carefully. This is huge for us. Don't make me regret hiring you."

Reid shook his head, his tone uncharacteristically serious as he spoke. "I would never do anything to jeopardize your trust or make this company look bad. You all mean too much to me. I thought she was cool, and I liked her vibe. She knows my language, and I think we'll work well together. I thought she'd like a friend in a strange place. That's all."

Aiden sat back. "Okay then. As long as we're clear."

Reid stood. "I have a wish list to compile so Bentley can approve it." He stopped at the door. "I should look into new equipment for Becca, I suppose. I imagine she needs some major software for graphics and a couple of monitors."

I shrugged. "You'll have to ask her."

His face lit up. "I'll do that. I'll start investigating what's out there. She needs the best."

He hurried out of the office. Aiden and I shared a glance.

"Friends, my ass," I snorted. "This is going to be interesting."

Aiden shook his head. "I think I'm too old for this shit."

"You and me both, Aiden. You and me both."

CHAPTER 8

MADDOX

THE NEXT MORNING, Reid sauntered into the boardroom, his typical swagger in place. I hid my smile as he grabbed some coffee and food, then sat across from Becca, smiling widely at her.

"Morning, Becca. How was your night?"

I met Aiden's amused glance with one of my own. Reid had stepped it up today. He'd replaced his jeans with khakis, still casual, but wrinkle-free. He had on a black T-shirt, free from any band logo, and an open red and black plaid shirt over top, with the sleeves rolled up. He'd had his hair trimmed, and although it was still in disarray, he looked much more put together than normal. I leaned back, glancing at his feet.

New sneakers.

Yep. The boy had dressed to impress this morning.

And it wasn't for us.

Becca offered him one of her shy smiles. "Great. We went to

dinner, and I walked around Eaton Center."

Bentley entered the room, the atmosphere changing. It always did when he showed up. His natural leadership and presence made everyone sit up and take notice. He placed his laptop at his usual spot at the head of the table and greeted everyone. His eyebrows raised a little as he looked at Reid, a grin making his lips turn up. He met my eyes with a subtle wink, then grabbed a coffee.

We spent the morning going over the tweaks Richard had made, discussing timelines and concepts. After lunch, we sat with Graham and Richard alone, laying the groundwork and hammering out details of the contract and Becca's placement in Toronto. We had no doubts they were the company for us. There were hundreds of details to work through and contracts to finalize, but I was confident we would reach an agreement.

I tilted my head, curious. "Can I ask why Becca wants to move here? Or even more important, why you want to let her go? She seems to be a big part of your team."

Richard swallowed the last of his coffee. I had noticed he drank as much of it as we did. "Becca *is* a huge part of the team. She came to us on an internship the first year she was at university. She was a natural. She started working part time for us, and we hired her as soon as she graduated." He winked. "I've been her mentor the whole time, which is one of the reasons she's so amazing."

We all chuckled at his comment, and he continued. "Becca loves the big city. She loves to travel and explore, and she finds Victoria a little sleepy for her tastes." He chuckled. "She makes me feel old sometimes."

"Toronto is a great place if she likes the bustle of a big city. It's a great travel hub as well," I said.

Richard tugged on his hair. "I got to know Becca personally. My wife, Katy, met her at the office, and they grew close. She became part of my family. She's shared holidays with us, babysat my kids. Katy has been her sounding board about guys." He lifted one shoulder with a smirk. "I've scared a couple of them off myself. She's more than a coworker. I hate to lose her, so does Katy, but we want her happy."

Graham spoke. "When your request came to us, her hand was up before I had even finished telling the group about what you were looking for. As much as we hate to lose her, we thought this was the best of both worlds. She'll still be part of our team, but she'll be in a place where she is happier." He shrugged. "We knew we would lose her eventually. She had always been open about wanting to be in a bigger city, so this seemed like the right fit."

He met my gaze. "My company and staff are family to me. Normally, Richard would come by himself to do a presentation." He grinned as he clapped Richard on the shoulder. "He can handle himself pretty well in the boardroom."

Again, we chuckled and he continued. "I wanted to meet you first, so I would know Becca would be a good fit and that she'd be treated well."

"I hope we've laid your fears to rest," Bentley said.

Graham smiled. "I checked you thoroughly beforehand. Your company is first-class. I like your values and the way you treat your business affairs, especially your staff. What I've seen since I arrived has strengthened my opinion. I think Becca will do well here with you, and together we can create some magic." He draped an arm over the chair, as confident as Richard. "My team is brilliant, and I have no doubt we'll deliver."

I knew Aiden, Bentley, and I all agreed. We exchanged a brief glance, and Bentley tilted his chin.

"I think, gentlemen, we can call tonight's dinner a celebration."

Graham stood, extending his hand. "We look forward to working with you."

⌒

I CALLED DEE later in the afternoon. I had been so busy I hadn't spoken to her since I left her place in the early hours of Monday morning, only communicating through texts. I wanted to hear her voice.

"Hey," she answered.

"Hey, yourself. Calling to check you're still okay for tonight's dinner," I responded.

I felt my body relax when she assured me she was looking forward to the evening. She was coming straight from work, meeting us at the restaurant.

"I'm wearing a new dress tonight."

"Nice." I dropped my voice, teasing. "What's it like? Tight, red, and held together with safety pins? Easy for me to rip off with my teeth?"

There was silence, and I started to laugh.

"Relax, Dee. I was teasing. I have no doubt you will be beautiful."

"That's stretching the truth. I won't shame you, though."

I frowned into the phone. "You *are* beautiful."

Had I never told her that?

"Hmm," she hummed, unconvinced. "Okay."

"You are," I insisted. "Have I ever been anything but truthful to you, Dee? I think you're incredibly beautiful, and if I've never told you that, then I have been remiss. That's on me, not you."

"Wow," she whispered.

"You're also as sexy as hell, smart, and feisty. It's a remarkable combination."

"Maddox, if you're trying to butter me up, let's get one thing straight. I'm a given. I'm going home with you tonight and you're going to fuck me. No need to go overboard."

Her husky voice turned me on.

I glanced toward my door, making sure no one was hovering in the hallway. I lowered my voice, my lips pressed close to the phone.

"Listen to me, Deirdre Wilson, and listen well. I am not buttering you up. I'm telling the truth. You are incredibly beautiful and sexy. As for fucking you, you bet your sweet ass I'm going to do exactly that. I'm going to fuck you so hard you'll forget your name. You'll forget everything but me and my cock inside you. I'm going to fuck you until you believe how beautiful you are." I growled. "And you know who you belong to. Understand?"

The sound of her sharp inhale made me smile.

"Maybe I'll butter something else up later and teach you how beautiful that part of you is as well," I promised with a dark chuckle.

"You-you can't say things like that over the phone."

"I can and did. Now go back to work and remember what I said. I'll see your beautiful self at the restaurant."

"O-okay," she stuttered.

I chuckled. "Deirdre?"

"What?" she whispered.

"Are you wet for me now?"

There was a pause before she answered, "Yes."

She hung up.

I set my phone on my desk and shifted in my chair, thinking of her. Thoughts of what I wanted to do to her took over my mind. Remembering how she moved under me, how it felt to be inside her, made my cock swell against the confines of my dress pants. Only she had that effect on me.

It was always her.

I grinned. I affected her as well. I had no doubt she was sitting at her desk right now, squirming and wet. I could picture her gnawing at her thumb, distracted, and thinking of me.

I picked up my phone and sent her a text.

You have no idea what I'm going to do to you tonight, Deirdre.

I waited until she replied.

I'm yours.

My response was fast.

Yes. Remember that.

I turned over my phone before I gave in and called her again or started sexting her.

The wait would be so worth it.

⌒

I ARRIVED FIRST and chose to wait out front. Aiden and Cami showed up shortly after, followed by Bent and Emmy. When Dee's cab arrived, I was waiting. I opened the door, helping her out of the back seat. I thrust some bills at the cabbie, never taking my eyes off her. I had never seen her so elegant. Her dress was a dark green, complementing her coloring perfectly. Her strawberry-blonde hair had grown over the past months, brushing against her shoulders. Lace trimmed her neckline and sleeves—a hint at her love for girlie things. Her makeup was light, but her eyes seemed larger and darker than normal. Her mouth was rosy, and all I could think of was kissing her until she was breathless. Except, I disliked PDA and preferred to keep my affection private.

Our eyes locked and held, and I saw a glimmer of my own desire reflected at me.

So I did it anyway. I bent down, ignoring the fact that our friends were watching, and I kissed her. I held her tight to my body and claimed her in front of everyone.

When I drew back, her eyes were shocked and her lips swollen. "What was that for?"

"Because you wanted me to."

She rolled her eyes, but she didn't deny it.

I crooked my arm. "Shall we?"

She reached up, wiping my lips. "I don't think you need the gloss."

I captured her hand, kissing her delicate fingertips. I tried not to smirk as we went past our shocked group.

I failed.

⌒

BY THE TIME Richard, Graham, and Becca arrived, we had been seated and ordered wine. The last one to join us was Reid. I tried not to laugh at the look of delight when he saw the one empty seat was beside Becca. He wore his suit, a white shirt, with a wildly patterned tie.

He worked the table, shaking hands and kissing the girls. When he reached Becca, he bent over her hand, kissing her knuckles with a flourish and making her laugh. He sat beside her and winked at Bentley.

Bentley sighed with relief.

Becca leaned over, patting Dee's hand. "Your dress is gorgeous. You must tell me where you got it. I have to find all the good places in Toronto to shop."

All our girls looked lovely tonight. Emmy was in Bentley's preferred shade of blue, Cami in her favorite purple, and Dee rounded out the jewel tones in her green. She was the most beautiful in my opinion.

Dee smiled, touching the lace on her sleeve. "Cami designed and made me this one."

Becca's eyes widened as she looked at Cami. "You designed it?"

Cami nodded, her cheeks pink. "Yes."

"Your dress too?"

"All of our dresses," Cami admitted. "I take fashion design, and I did these as part of a presentation. Dee is my sister, and Emmy is my best friend. They're my go-to guinea pigs."

Becca clapped her hands. "If you need a fourth anytime, I'm your girl. You are so talented! I love these dresses."

Aiden beamed with pride, sliding his arm around her shoulders and dropping a kiss to her head. "That's my wife. Talented."

Richard lifted his glass. "Here's to talent. I think this table is filled with it."

I raised my glass in agreement.

⌒

I SHOOK RICHARD'S hand. "I'll see you tomorrow."

"Looking forward to it."

I wished Graham a safe trip home. He was catching the last flight out, heading back home to BC. Richard and Becca were staying one last day to go through some more details. At dinner, Becca had asked for advice on where to live, and I offered to show her an apartment I knew was coming up for rent shortly which coincided with her arrival.

"It's close to the office—a few blocks away. The building is older and it's one bedroom, but it's clean, secure, and a decent size for Toronto. The rent is reasonable for its location."

"Is the landlord nice?"

I chuckled. "He's okay."

Becca's eyes narrowed. "Is it you?"

"Yes. I lived there when we were first starting BAM. I bought it as an investment. My tenant is moving, so this would work. No pressure, but you can have a look," I explained.

"Sounds good."

I watched their taxi pull away and waited for the valet to bring my car. I tugged Dee close.

"You were wonderful tonight. Thank you."

"I like Becca." She laughed. "So does Reid. He barely took his eyes off her."

"I noticed."

"I think she did as well."

"I hope it doesn't cause problems."

"They're both adults. I'm sure they can act accordingly."

"Given Reid's, ah, goals, I hope so."

Her brow furrowed. "His goals?"

I lowered my lips to her ear. "Reid's a virgin. He doesn't want to be one anymore."

Her mouth formed a small O. "Maddox Riley—*that* is personal. You shouldn't be telling me such things!" she scolded, dropping her voice. "Really, though, at his age—he's a virgin? How do you know that?"

I chuckled, resting my chin on her shoulder. "You little gossip-lover. He told Aiden and me he was a virgin when we interviewed him."

"What? He said that in an interview?"

"Yep. We asked him to tell us 'all' about himself, and he dropped that tidbit in." I recalled the look Aiden and I had shared when he informed us of his unwelcome . . . *situation.* "He keeps us updated on his status."

"Oh my God."

"Aiden informed him he is never gonna lose it if he spends all his time in the office lying on the floor writing code."

Dee nudged me with her elbow. "Maybe he will now." She waggled her eyebrows suggestively. "I like it on top. Maybe Becca does too."

I threw back my head in laughter, hugging her close to my side. Dee looked sexy, relaxed, and I loved it when she was being funny. I didn't see that side of her often enough.

"Let's get you home. I think I want you to show me just how much you like riding me." I wrapped my mouth around her lobe, tugging on it.

"Yes," she breathed out.

Unable to resist, I kissed her. It was long, slow, and deep—the exact kind of kiss I would never give in public. And for the second time of the night, I didn't care.

My car pulled to the curb, and I helped Dee inside, shutting the door. As I walked around to the driver's side, a car pulled past me. It was moving slowly and was too close to my side of the driveway. Unable to move, I pressed against the door, waiting as the car crawled past. I glared at the driver, my body suddenly frozen on the spot when she turned her head and I met the eyes of the woman behind the wheel.

Cold, icy blue eyes I recognized.

My heart rate sped up, and I grasped the handle in shock. Memories, ones I had buried and refused to think about, tore through my mind's eye.

In a split second, the connection was broken, and the car sped up, tearing out of the driveway, cutting off another vehicle. The blare of a horn startled me back to the present, and I blinked and shook my head.

I slid into the car, still staring toward the road. My car was running, the heat blasting from the vents, yet I felt a long shiver race down my spine.

Dee laid her hand on my arm. "Maddox? Are you all right? That car was awfully close!"

Turning my head, I met her gaze. Her green eyes were warm and concerned—nothing like the frosty look of hatred I had seen a moment ago.

I looked to where the car had been. It couldn't be. I'd either imagined it or read more into the glance than there had been. Lots of women had icy blue eyes. It was similar because of the glare. She obviously felt I was in her way instead of the other way around.

That was all it was. I was certain of it. I forced the memories from my mind, locking them away where they belonged—the past.

I patted Dee's hand. "Sorry. I thought she was going to hit the car. She startled me."

"I thought she was going to hit *you*."

"She looked . . ." I shook my head and laughed self-consciously.

"What? She looked what?"

"Like someone I knew at university. Impossible, probably."

"Someone you were close to?"

I swallowed heavily. "No. Just a girl. No one special. I'm sure I was mistaken."

I clicked my seat belt into place and pulled the car out into traffic. "Let's go home."

Luckily, she dropped the subject. "Mine or yours?"

I made a fast decision. "Yours."

"Okay."

DEE'S HAIR SHIMMERED in the moonlight that streamed in the windows. She arched, bending so far backward, her hair brushed my legs. She moaned low in her throat, her muscles constricting around me.

"Oh *God*, Maddox. You feel so good."

I gripped her hips, thrusting up hard. I was desperate to feel, to lose myself in her. I tried to focus on her sounds, the way she looked riding me. Her breasts were full, nipples glistening and red from my mouth. Her neck and collarbones bore patches of pink from my scruff where I licked and nipped at her skin. Her pussy was drenched with desire, filled with my cock, and milking me.

Icy blue eyes kept distracting me.

With a roar, I sat up, winding my arm around Dee's waist and tipping us over. We fell into the mattress, my weight pressing her down. I wrapped my hand around her wrists, raising them over her head. Her legs went over my shoulders, and I sank deeper inside of her.

She gasped, her neck straining as pleasure tore through her body.

"Who do you belong to?" I snarled, pounding into her. "*Who?*"

"You."

"I take you *how* I want. *When* I want," I commanded.

"Y-yes," she whimpered, pulling at her hands, arching under me.

I stilled suddenly, looking down at her, a strange feeling tugging at me. My chest heaved, needing oxygen. My mind raced, needing peace. My body ached, needing her.

But in a different way.

Not commanding, not taking.

Giving.

She widened her eyes as I leaned down, covering her mouth with mine. Releasing her hands, I wrapped my arms around her back, tugging her up to me. Smooth, languid strokes of my tongue on hers made her groan. I explored her, fusing our lips together as I began to move again. I immersed myself in her. Her touch, her taste, her heat. I rocked into her, the motion slow and easy. I brushed kisses over her face, down her neck, kissing and caressing all of her. Adoring, loving her the one way she would accept it. I slid one hand between us, finding her clit, stroking it until she stiffened and cried out, shattering around me. My orgasm rolled through me, long, lazy tendrils of ecstasy rippling down my spine, tightening my balls, making me bury my face into her neck as I released into her body, her name a kiss on my lips.

Once we were spent, I rolled, keeping her with me. I pulled her to my chest, needing to feel her. To know she was real and what happened earlier was nothing. A mistaken identity and nothing more.

I sighed, my breath stirring her hair. She ran her fingers through my hair as I stroked her back. Aimless brushes of my fingers up and down, tracing her spine, touching her skin.

"Maddox?"

"Hmm."

"Are you all right?"

I kissed her head. "Yeah, I'm good."

"You seem . . . off."

I knew she was right, but I refused to admit it.

"*Off*, Deirdre? That wasn't good for you?"

She lifted her head, her eyes sleepy. "It was amazing." She traced my jaw with her finger, teasing my scruff. "It was different for you." Her brow furrowed. "Tender."

I captured her finger in my mouth, teasing it with my tongue. I kissed the end, letting it drop to my chin.

"I was changing it up, Deirdre. Give me ten, and we can go again. Hard."

She snorted, cuddling closer. I liked it when she did that since it didn't happen often. "Ten. You're not seventeen."

"Is that a challenge?"

"Maybe," she mumbled, her voice heavy with sleep.

I didn't reply, staying still, and let her drift off. When I knew she was out, I carefully moved away from her, tucking the blankets around her shoulders.

I dragged on my pants and shirt, picking up my shoes and jacket. It was late, and I knew no one would be on the elevator with me. I paused in the doorway, looking back, a sense of foreboding filling my chest.

I let myself into my condo, the silence too loud. Tossing my jacket over the sofa, I poured a generous whiskey and stood at the window, gazing out into the city. I noticed the red light of my answering machine blinking with a message. I hesitated, the glass partway to my lips. I had no idea why I kept my old home phone and number. I'd had it for years and never canceled it, even though most of my calls came on my cell.

I pushed the play button, the haunting voice filling the room as clear as if she were standing in front of me.

Jill.

"Hello, Maddox. Fancy seeing you again. I think we should talk. I'll be in touch."

The call ended.

My glass of whiskey hit the floor, exploding into thousands of shards, the liquid spraying my pants and feet.

I dropped my head.

I hadn't imagined it.

It wasn't a case of mistaken identity.

My biggest regret had found me.

CHAPTER 9

MADDOX

I SPENT THE night prowling my condo, the oblivion of sleep eluding me. I was in the office early, desperate to lose myself in work. Anything to stop the barrage of thoughts and squelch the sense of dread in my stomach remembering her words.

We should talk.

I had nothing to discuss with her. I never wanted to see her again.

I went through the motions all day. I showed Becca and Richard the apartment. She was pleased with the unit, especially when I promised fresh paint and refinished floors prior to her arrival. The kitchen and bath had been updated a couple of years prior, and it was in great shape. As she looked around, I leaned on the counter in the kitchen, unable to keep my fingers from drumming restlessly on the edge.

"You okay, Maddox?" Richard asked, concerned. "You look tired today."

I waved my hand, keeping my face impassive. "No, I'm fine."

"If you say so."

Becca came into the kitchen, interrupting us. "I think this will do for me. It's smaller than what I'm used to in Victoria, but not as bad as I thought I might end up with here. Some of the places I looked at on the internet were like shoe boxes!"

"Square footage is a premium here," I agreed. "I lucked in to this place, and when the owner decided to sell, I bought it. When I moved, I decided to keep it and rent it out. The value keeps going up, so it was a good investment."

She nodded in agreement. "Renting is good for now, until I discover the city more. And figure out my plans." She flashed a grin. "See how long you put up with me."

She made me smile. "I have a feeling that isn't going to be an issue."

Richard's phone rang, and he excused himself. Becca peeked in the cupboards, shutting them with a satisfied nod. She leaned against the counter. "So, Reid, what's his story?"

I bit back a laugh at her attempt to be casual. I played along. "Story?"

"He is, ah, single?"

"Yep."

She traced the countertop, not meeting my gaze. "Seeing anyone special?"

"Becca," I began, "I'm not in the habit of talking about my employees' personal lives, but I will say this. Reid is single, not seeing anyone that I know of, and is a really genuine guy."

I held back the fact that he was more than interested in her.

She flushed. "Sorry, I didn't mean to put you on the spot."

"You didn't." I huffed out a long breath. "We have no policy against relationships in the office, but we do expect our staff to behave appropriately at all times."

"Of course."

"That being said, I think you and Reid have a lot in common and that you'll work well together," I advised. "What you do outside the office is none of my business."

"Okay." She smiled.

I leaned forward with a wink. "Here's a little clue—Reid loves peanut butter cookies. Any kind, any brand. If they have peanut butter, he's all over them."

A huge grin broke out on her face. "Okay, thanks for the tip."

"No problem. I'll have my lawyer send you a lease agreement."

She held out her hand. "Perfect."

AFTER BECCA AND Richard left, I tried to work. It was a useless effort, and eventually, I gave up, instead, studying the boards Richard had left.

Today, Bentley had planned to inform the other two companies they were no longer in the race and we would move forward with The Gavin Group. It was a swift decision, but based on what we had seen and heard, it was right, and there was no use wasting time.

Aiden came in, carrying two cups of coffee. He offered me one and sat in front of my desk. He stretched out his long legs and sipped on the steaming brew. He had his shoulders hunched and a frown marred his usual cheerful expression.

I waited a few minutes, expecting Bentley to stroll in, but he never appeared.

"What's up?"

Aiden scrubbed his face. "Bent asked me to do something for him this morning."

"Okay. From the look on your face, I'd say it's something you don't want to do."

He took a sip and set his cup on the desk.

"Emmy asked him to have me look for her brother, Jack."

"Wow. That's out of left field."

"I know." Aiden looked past me, staring out the window. "She told him with the wedding coming up, she wanted to reach out. Have her brother there with her, or at least give him the chance."

I thought about what I knew of the situation. Jack had left her alone when she was seventeen, informing her she was on her own. He'd decided he had looked after her long enough and it was time for him to live his own life, and he disappeared. She had been longing for contact from him since then. Her upcoming wedding must have triggered that longing.

"You don't agree?"

"Bentley is concerned that if I find him and he refuses, it will break Emmy's heart. I agree with him."

"There is that possibility. He could also do the opposite. At least, either way, Emmy has an answer."

He nodded, not speaking.

"What are you going to do?"

He met my gaze. "I'm torn. Part of me wants to tell her I tried but couldn't locate him. Except, knowing Emmy, she won't give up. Eventually, she'll want to try again. If she finds out I lied, she'll be furious. The other part of me tells me I have to do this and give her closure, even if it hurts her." He hunched closer, his voice low. "I have a bad feeling in my gut about this."

I knew Aiden and his instincts. He was usually right.

"Bent asked you to do it?"

"Yeah. He's torn too, but you know he can't say no to her."

I pondered the situation for a few minutes. "I think you have to try, regardless of your instincts."

His head dropped to his chest. "I knew you'd say that."

I finished my coffee. "It's the right thing."

"I know." He glanced at me with a frown. "You okay, Mad Dog? You look tired."

I barked a laugh. "You're not the first person to say that to me today."

"What's going on?"

I couldn't tell him. I didn't know what was going on, so I certainly had no way of explaining it to him. Besides, with the stress he was feeling about looking for Emmy's brother, I didn't want to add to his worries.

"Nothing. I was up late, that's all."

He grinned. "Does Dee look as tired as you do?"

I shook my head, forcing a smile. "I never kiss and tell. We've had that conversation."

"Right. I'll take that as a yes."

He stood and stretched. "Okay, I'm going to go and put together a package to send to the PIs. See what they find. I guess I'll take it one step at a time."

"It's all you can do."

"I suppose so."

He left, still unhappy.

I hoped his gut was wrong this time, but with Aiden, it rarely was.

I glanced at my phone and picked it up, overwhelmed with the need to call Dee. Her voice always helped steady me, and her calm demeanor would be welcome.

Except, what could I say to her?

A ghost from my past had shown up and I didn't know what to expect? For all I knew, it meant nothing. Jill could simply be messing with my mind. She had done it previously—many times. I could be making something out of nothing.

I tossed the phone onto my desk and rubbed at my face in frustration.

I had my own gut feeling in regard to this. And it wasn't a good one.

⌒

BY TUESDAY, I began to relax. There were no other phone calls, no unexpected visitors, and nothing came in the mail. I convinced myself that Jill had seen me, and just to be a bitch, tried my old number, heard my voice and left me a message.

This morning, I asked Sandy to have my home line disconnected. She frowned in displeasure when I asked her politely not to divulge my cell number if anyone called and asked for it.

"Do you think I fell off the turnip truck yesterday, Maddox? It's standard operating procedure. I would never give that number out, unless I had your permission." She sniffed, indignant and pissed off.

I sent her flowers to apologize, fumbling with all the information they required for me to place the order since usually Sandy handled that task if needed. I didn't think I could ask her to send herself flowers, although she would have been more generous than I was with the arrangement. She did kiss my cheek and pat me on the head as if I were a schoolboy when they arrived. Apparently, she had forgiven me.

On Saturday, I had helped Dee arrange the furniture that I'd sent over. We'd ordered in Chinese, eating it on the sofa while watching a movie. I lost myself in her for a few hours, but once again, left her sleeping in her bed to go to my condo and prowl away the hours, unable to sleep except for a nap on the sofa.

Sunday, I made excuses not to attend brunch. Dee came upstairs later, concerned and not convinced when I told her I was catching up on work due to a deadline.

"Aiden and Bentley didn't say anything about a deadline. They were wondering why you weren't there as well. We were worried you were ill again."

"They don't work with finances. I have different deadlines."

"Maddox, what is going on? Are you rethinking this?" She flipped her finger between her and me. "Us? We can stop this right now if that's what you want."

"No," I snapped. *"We are not stopping anything. You're overreacting. I had work to do, and that's all. Leave it."*

She stood, angry. "Fine. I'll leave you to your work."

She stalked out and I raced after her, catching her before she reached the door. I spun her around, crowding her against the wall.

"You're not leaving."

She pushed on my chest. "Yes, I am."

"Not before I apologize." I bent to kiss her, but she turned her face away and my lips landed on her cheek. I nuzzled the skin, dragging my mouth across her skin to her ear.

"Forgive me, Deirdre." I bit down on her lobe. "Please."

Her hand rose, pushing on my arm, but the gesture was weak.

I slid my hand under her chin, turning her face. "I apologize."

"I was worried," she whispered.

"Good. I like you worried about me." I captured her mouth, kissing her until her legs gave out and she was clinging to me, her hands gripping my biceps. I swept her into my arms, carried her to my bedroom, and apologized for the next few hours. I made sure she knew how deeply I meant it. Several times.

Aiden appeared in my door, snapping me out of my thoughts.

"Hey."

"Tacos later?"

"Sure."

"You want to meet us there? Or are you heading home?"

"Van is bringing me some invoices we need to take care of. I'm gonna wait for him, and I'll head over. Should I call Dee?"

"No, she told Cami she has a meeting after work and she'll meet us there too."

"Okay." I paused, then asked. "Any news on Jack?"

"They found a lead. I'm using Reid for some less conventional searches, and they're following it up on their end."

"Okay. Keep me in the loop if you can."

He left, and I worked until Van arrived. I heard the sounds of his heavy footsteps, the keys jangling from his belt before he walked in. Almost as tall and wide as Aiden, he filled my doorway. He was dressed in denim, his standard uniform, his plaid shirt stretched over his broad shoulders, tight on his arms. I waved him in, and he shook my hand, his grip firm and strong.

"Maddox, thanks for staying." His eyes crinkled at the corners with his smile.

"No problem."

He handed me a file folder, the cover stained with coffee rings, the corners bent. "These invoices have to be paid before the supplies can be delivered."

I glanced through the documents. As usual with Van, everything was in order. PO numbers, invoices, job files. All approved by him and signed off by Bentley.

"I'll take care of the transfers tonight. You'll have your supplies tomorrow."

"I appreciate that."

"Got a gig this week?"

He laughed, running a hand through his hair. "No. I have some coming up, though."

"Send me the info. We'll come, have a couple of beers, and listen." I winked. "Before you get discovered and leave us."

He shook his head. "Nah. It's a hobby. I sowed those wild oats years ago. I'm too old for that shit now."

It was my turn to laugh. At thirty-nine, Van was hardly old. He was a rugged son of a gun, and I knew, a big hit with the women when he played his gigs. He had a headful of dark hair I envied with some grays scattered in, giving him a slightly weathered look they seemed to like. His jaw had a five-o'clock shadow at nine a.m., which got heavier later in the day. He was fast with a smile and flirted shamelessly, but his brown eyes were clear, his attitude forthright, and he was a straight shooter. He was a master carpenter, a Blues man at heart, and he played his guitar the same way he crafted a piece of wood. Silky and smooth. We enjoyed hearing him play.

"You and me both."

He stood with a snort, towering over me. "You're still a young pup, Maddox."

"There's only a few years between us, Van. You're hardly an old man."

His face turned serious. "More than a few, plus I've done a lot of living in those years." His smile returned. "Anyway, I'll let you know about the next gig."

I reached out to shake his hand. "We'll look forward to it."

"Appreciate that. You'll, ah, bring your ladies? I'll reserve you a table."

I tried not to laugh. Obviously, news traveled fast with the office grapevine.

"We'll do that for sure."

He left, and I finished the transfers. I glanced at my watch, but it was still early. I decided I would head to the restaurant, get us a table, and have a beer. I grabbed my coat and headed downstairs. I had walked to work this morning, so I went outside to hail a cab. Before I could raise my arm, a voice greeted me.

"Hello, Maddox. Miss me?"

I turned slowly, meeting Jill's eyes. Cold, void of emotion, icy pools of blue glared at me. I could remember a time I thought her eyes were incredible—the color unique and special. Until the day I realized the icy color reflected her soul.

I drew in a long breath to calm my racing heart. "No, Jill, I haven't missed you at all. I haven't given you a second thought, actually. Excuse me, I have someplace to be."

I began to turn around when she grabbed my arm.

"Not so fast."

I looked at her hand that was fisting my coat, the red nails like talons gripping the fabric. Grimacing with distaste, I pried her hand off my coat, resisting the urge to wipe off the feel of her skin on the fabric.

"Don't touch me."

"That's not what you used to say."

Anger began to replace the anxiety, and I crossed my arms.

"What are you doing here, and more importantly, what the fuck do you want?"

She smirked and tossed her hair. It was darker than I remembered, almost black under the streetlights. She was dressed for an evening on the town, her high heels making her almost my height. Her makeup was heavy, her lips a crimson slash in her face.

I'd found her beautiful once. Now I saw the ugliness she hid from the world.

"I'm working here for the next while. Imagine my surprise when I saw you in a restaurant, laughing and enjoying yourself with all your rich friends. I checked you out, Maddox. You've done well for yourself."

I barked out a laugh. "Your opinion of what I have or have not done means nothing to me. Why don't you crawl back into whatever rathole you came from and leave me alone?"

"I don't think so."

"I beg your pardon?" I snapped, enunciating each word pointedly. "You have no choice in the matter. I have no interest in seeing you again."

She gripped my arm once more. "I think you need to come with me, Maddox. You want to hear what I have to say."

"Nothing you say has any interest to me, Jill."

Her eyes narrowed, and any pretense of politeness disappeared. "I insist."

I shook off her grip, not wanting to touch her again. "Insist all you want. It's not happening."

I turned to hail a cab when she spoke. "It's your decision, of course, but either you come with me for a drink, or tomorrow, I'll be showing up in that fancy office of yours, and I won't be leaving until you see me. I'll cause such a scene, you'll regret it." She paused and huffed. "Is it worth it to avoid a drink with me? Either way, you're going to listen to what I have to say."

I knew Jill and that she wouldn't hesitate to follow through on her threats. The thought of having to explain her sudden reappearance to Bent and Aiden made me reconsider. I hated scenes, and I had witnessed Jill cause many of them years ago. I glanced across the street at one of the local bars. Being a Tuesday, it wasn't busy and we rarely went there, so I doubted anyone would recognize me.

Without acknowledging or looking at her, I strode across the street. Her satisfied laughter grated on my already tight nerves. I headed to the farthest corner, not giving her a choice. She followed, sitting beside me at the high table. I frowned and moved to the stool across from her.

She lifted one eyebrow but remained silent. The waitress appeared, chirpy and friendly, asking for our order. I needed a drink.

"Whiskey, neat," I ordered.

"Dirty martini," Jill said. "Extra olives."

"Would you like to see the appetizer menu?"

"No," I snapped. "We're not staying long."

Jill smirked.

We were silent until the drinks appeared. I tossed back the liquor, feeling the burn as it went down, warming my throat. I hated the smug look on Jill's face, and I decided to cut to the chase. I knew she was enjoying my discomfort, and I was tired of giving her that satisfaction. Plus, I didn't want to be in her company a moment longer than necessary.

"You have five minutes to say whatever it is you want to say. Then I'm leaving. I don't care what you do to get my attention. I don't give much of a fuck."

"So rude."

I leaned forward, gripping the edge of the table. "What do you want, Jill?"

She took a drink of her martini, sliding an olive from the skewer and popping it into her mouth. Even in the muted light, I could see the years hadn't been kind to her. She looked harsh and older than I knew her to be. Her skillful makeup and dyed hair didn't hide that fact.

"I studied voice and drama at university, you remember? I always wanted to be a star."

I rolled my eyes. I didn't care about her life's aspirations.

"I managed to get some roles, small ones, and I've spent the past few years traveling with different companies. Sadly, no matter what I have done, I've never made it much past the ensemble. I had the understudy roles a couple of times, but I never got to play the lead role and get my break."

I snorted. "I can imagine what you've 'done' to get the roles."

She ignored me. "I'm tired of traveling. Of being invisible—one of the swing. I hate struggling to make ends meet and not having a place of my own. I've decided to give up the touring shows and settle down." She slid another olive into her mouth, her smile pure evil. "And I've decided you're going to help me do that."

I gaped at her as if she were insane.

"Why the fuck would I do that?"

She reached into her purse, pulling out a small envelope. She slid it toward me. I stared at it, my stomach clenching with anxiety. Carefully, as if it would bite, I wrapped my hand around it and dragged it toward me.

I lifted the flap and let the contents slide onto the table. Pictures. Six in total. I lifted them, surprised to see my hand wasn't shaking, and gazed at the images.

They weren't a revelation or a shock. I had known before I opened the envelope—known that somehow, she had returned to force me to relive that darkness. The images were my greatest moment of shame, the ones burned into my memory, captured on film. Brought to life with a burning intensity that made me feel ill.

I was motionless. She laughed, the sound jarring me back to the moment.

My head snapped up. "Where did you get these?"

"Oh, Maddox." She shook her head, her eyes glittering with satisfaction. "You used to tell me I never planned things out, I was never prepared. I think I proved you wrong." She tapped the photos. "I checked you out. Quiet, boring Maddox, who planned to be an accountant. How things changed for you."

"I am an accountant."

"No, you're a partner in one of the biggest companies in the city. Such prestige. Glowing articles of the three friends who built their company from the ground up and kept their friendship—squeaky-clean images, real do-gooders, all of you. Wouldn't it be a shame if something happened and that reputation was tarnished? I wonder how long the friendship would last if one of you destroyed everything you all worked so hard to create?"

Ice-cold fury raced through me. It was all I could do not to launch myself across the table and strangle her. Dropping the photos upside down on the table, I curled my hands into fists on my knees and struggled for control.

"What do you want?" I spat out.

She tapped her chin with a dark smile. "I want a house in a place of my choosing. And five hundred grand." She ate another olive. "To start."

She drained her martini and slid off her seat. "Once we agree to that, we'll figure out a yearly fee. I don't want to work anymore, and I want to enjoy life."

I barked a laugh. "I think you have me confused with a billionaire. I'm not rolling in it."

"I think you can afford me."

I called her bluff. "Why would I do that?"

"I may not be a star, Maddox, but I know a lot of reporters. They'd be happy to run the story I tell them about us." She pushed the pictures in my direction. "About you."

"It would be a lie."

She laughed, the sound sending a shudder down my spine. "Not according to the pictures I have."

She reached over and arranged the pictures into a neat pile, sliding them into the envelope. She laid a business card on top, tapping it with her red talon. "I'm staying in a hotel. I move around a lot, so I don't have a place. This is my email and cell number."

She smiled, bright and cold. I flinched when she tapped my cheek.

"I know this is a shock for you. I'll give you some time to think. You have a week to get in touch with me, or I go to the papers and bring your life crashing down around you."

"Why?" I asked. "Why are you doing this, Jill?"

She leaned close, her fake smile gone and the hatred screaming out of her eyes.

"You called me names. Degraded me. Dumped me. All because

I tried to show you what you could be. A real man—not the weak imitation of one you are."

"You were the one who degraded me," I spat out through tight lips.

I started at the feel of her lips dragging across my cheek.

"Not when I tell the story, Maddox." She tapped the envelope. "This time, I call the shots."

She stepped back, smirking. "A week. Since you disconnected your phone, you had better call me, or I'll be at your office."

She turned and walked away.

CHAPTER 10

MADDOX

I HEARD DEE'S quiet knock, but I ignored it. The same way I ignored the texts and calls from Aiden and Bentley. Earlier, I had fired off a fast text saying something had come up and I couldn't join them for tacos. I had no idea what else to say.

After I left the bar and took a cab home, I stumbled upstairs and grabbed the closest bottle of whiskey. I didn't care how expensive it was or the fact that it was meant to be savored. I needed it to stop the barrage of thoughts and memories in my head. I took a hot shower, keeping the bottle in my hand and letting the water wash away the feel of her touch and the smell of her in my nose. I wished I could wash away everything else.

The knock sounded again, but I didn't move. I wasn't sure I could. I had drunk a lot, and I didn't want to see anyone. In front of me were the pictures spread out on the wooden floor like a bad advertising graphic.

Me, my face cold, determined. My pupils so wide, my eyes were black in my face.

Jill on her knees, tied up, tears coursing down her face.

A whip in my hand. Blood dripping from a mark on her shoulder.

My hand bunched in her hair, a snarl on my face as I screamed at her.

My erection, hard and evident behind the jeans riding low on my hips.

The last one, of me driving into her from behind. Welts on her back, her face obscured from the camera, sweat dripping from my skin.

They told a sordid story. One of pain and sex. Jill dominated, me in control.

The pictures lied, because it was the exact opposite.

But that wasn't the story the world would hear—or see.

I bent forward, squinting as I looked at the pictures. I tasted regret. Felt shame. Allowed the anger to emerge. I tightened my grip on the bottle I still clutched even though it was empty.

Blackness edged in, my body giving in to the alcohol and exhaustion.

As I succumbed, I heard another knock.

As I slumped to the sofa, one thought was clear.

Once Jill released the stain on my past, I would never hear that knock again.

⌒

I WOKE, BLINKING and confused, in the dim light of the morning. The skies were overcast and heavy—much like my head. I sat up, tentative and already in agony. I clutched at my head, the pounding intense and unending. My stomach heaved, and I fought down the nausea. My phone was on the floor, discarded and dead. The photos lay there, reminders of what I had to deal with. I glanced at my watch, shocked to see it was past ten. I was late, hungover, and unreachable. I was surprised Aiden wasn't at my door. I knew if he were worried enough, he'd have no qualms about getting Reid to hack in to my passwords to get into my apartment on the fancy system that he created.

I gathered up the pictures and took them to my office, locking them in my safe. Slowly, I made my way to my bedroom and plugged in my phone. I swallowed three Tylenol with some water and stepped in the shower, ignoring my discarded clothes from the previous night. I didn't want to think about her touching the cloth. I would throw them out later.

The hot water felt good on my stiff shoulders, loosening the tight muscles. I dried off and sent a short text to Aiden and Bent, saying I was ill but on my way in. There were several missed calls and texts, but I ignored them. I dressed and took a cab to work, unsure if I should be driving yet. I made it to my desk, managing to get past Sandy who was busy on the phone as I slipped by.

She appeared ten minutes later carrying a mug of coffee. She set it on my desk with a plate of dry toast.

"Thanks," I mumbled. "Not hungry." I cleared my throat, pushing the plate away as my stomach heaved. "I think I have a touch of food poisoning."

"Right. The twenty-six-ounce variety. Eat your toast. You'll feel better."

I didn't reply, and she flounced out.

Aiden came in shortly after, frowning. "Mad Dog, you had me worried. Sandy says you're hungover. What's going on?"

"I'm not hungover. I ate something that didn't agree with me," I lied. "Been up all night."

He studied me. "Right." He clapped his hands, the loud sound making me wince. "The architect has the final mockups of Ridge Towers done. We're seeing them in an hour."

I forced some enthusiasm into my voice. "Great."

"Richard is dying to see them so he can incorporate them into his designs."

"Okay. I'll make sure he gets them."

"He's coming here next week for another client. He'll be in the office on Tuesday." Aiden rubbed his hands along his thighs. "Bent is still wary of sending them on the internet. I keep telling him we're fine, but he insists."

I huffed out a sigh. "It's his company. He calls the shots."

Aiden frowned. "It's our company, and I know that. I hope he can get past what happened and realize it was one man, with one goal—to destroy him. It's not going to happen again. Our systems are secure."

I swung my chair around, staring out the window. "You never know when people are going to try to destroy you, Aiden."

He was quiet for a moment. When he spoke, his voice was serious.

"Maddox, are you all right? Do you need to talk to me about something?"

"No," I responded, not turning around. "Nothing."

I didn't even hear him leave.

Later, I joined in the meeting with the architects. After eating the toast, drinking two mugs of coffee, and taking more Tylenol, I felt better—physically. Mentally, I was still all over the map, but I fell back to my old habit of camouflage. I kept my face expressionless and my voice neutral. I smiled at the right times, offered suggestions and praise. I was enthusiastic about the scale model and the drawings that went with it showing the details. No one knew of the turmoil in my head.

No one would, because I had to figure out a solution—on my own.

Dee accepted my excuses when I texted her of my food poisoning. I told her I hadn't even heard her knocks and apologized for worrying her. She told me she would check on me later. I knew she was waiting for me to extend her an invite, but I placed my phone on the desk without issuing one. I couldn't face her.

The next two days, I met with staff, went over budgets and schedules with them. I attended meetings and offered opinions. I ate lunch with Aiden. Teased Sandy. Spoke with Dee, although I didn't see her. She hesitated at the end of every call, waiting. Waiting for me to tell her that I would see her tonight or make plans for the weekend. I wanted to. I was desperate to spend some time in her soothing company. To sip whiskey with her and talk about the flavor. To hear her low laughter and lose myself in her for hours.

But I was afraid she would see past the mask I was wearing. I was having enough trouble hiding from Aiden and Bentley. They knew something was wrong. They knew me far too well, no matter what I did to hide my turmoil. I didn't want them to know, but not being any closer to a solution, I began to think I had only one option.

And it killed me to think about it.

Thursday afternoon, Bentley strode past my office, his face grave. He didn't stop, although I heard him tell Sandy he was gone the rest of the week and to cancel whatever was on his calendar. I frowned at his unusually brusque tone and departure.

Aiden followed behind him, a folder in his hand. He looked weary and upset. He stood still watching Bentley leave, his shoulders drooping. He glanced into my office, and I lifted my eyebrow in a silent question. He came in, shut the door, and sat in front of me. There was only one thing that could have happened.

"You found Jack?"

He nodded.

"That didn't take long."

He shrugged. "The information wasn't hidden. Simply put, no one had looked until now. With today's technology, things can happen fast."

"He doesn't want to see her?" I guessed, knowing Aiden was right. It would break her tender heart.

"He's dead."

I sat up straighter. "*Shit.*"

"He has been for a long time."

"How?"

"He died in an avalanche during a mountain climb in Alaska. His body was never recovered, but we traced his steps and he was part of the expedition."

"Surely, there are records? Why wasn't Emmy notified?"

He laughed, the sound bitter. "Yeah, bad ones, but we found them. His name was misspelled, but Reid and I pieced it together with the PIs. His passport was on him when he died. He left no next of kin information, and no one was looking for him. We used the pictures Emmy had provided and one of the guides, who survived, positively identified him."

"Shit," I repeated myself.

He shook his head. "Jack died about a year after deserting her. She's been waiting all this time, thinking he'd come back, holding on to the idea she still had a brother."

"She can mourn his loss but know he hadn't ignored her all these years. I think that will help her."

"Bentley is afraid what this will do to her. Her brother was her only family."

"No," I disagreed. "Emmy is strong. She isn't alone anymore. She'll have the closure she needs, and Bentley will be there for her. He'll help her through it. You know how much he loves her. He'll make sure she's all right."

He was silent, his head hung down, his hands clasped between his legs.

"Aiden, I know this is what you feared. And I know you hate to be the one who discovered the truth, but Emmy wanted it. She'll be okay."

He nodded. "Yeah."

"We'll help both of them. We all will. Whatever she needs. That's what friends do."

He stood, running the file between his fingers as he studied me.

"That is what friends do when they are *allowed* to help."

I tensed at his words, knowing he wasn't talking about Emmy anymore.

"We'll let Bentley tell us what she needs," I stated, hoping he would drop it.

"Will you ever tell me what you need, Maddox? Or are you going to keep letting whatever has you so fucking stressed eat you alive?"

"I'm fine."

He shook his head sadly. "Another lie." He walked to the door, his hand on the handle, gripping it hard. "I would lay down my life for Bentley. For you too. Given that I'm willing to do that, the least you could do is talk to me. Trust me."

"I do trust you."

"No. If you did, you wouldn't be killing yourself."

Our eyes locked.

"Sometimes, Aiden, you have to face things alone." My voice sounded unconvincing, even to my ears.

"And sometimes, you don't. Figure it out, Maddox. I'm here when you do."

He left, shutting the door behind him.

⌒

DEE

I SHIFTED THE bags on my shoulder, fumbling to press the elevator button. The doors opened, and I stepped in, groaning in frustration when I realized I had pressed down instead of up. Resigned, I let the doors close, knowing I would have to wait for the elevator to return to the main floor anyway.

I stepped to the back, lowering my heavy bags. Between the groceries and my bulging messenger bag, they were a lot to handle.

The doors opened, and another passenger stepped in as I rummaged for my keys. I glanced up to ask the person to press my floor and froze. Maddox was in front of me, his back turned my way. His shoulders were stooped and his hair in disarray.

Was he ignoring me? I hadn't seen him since Sunday, and it bothered me more than I wanted to admit. He had told me the office was crazy busy, and on top of that, he wasn't feeling well, but it felt more like an excuse than the truth.

I cleared my throat. "Maddox."

He turned his head, and I gasped when his face came into view. His skin was sallow, and he had dark circles under his eyes. His scruff was thicker and he looked thinner.

He hadn't been lying—he was unwell.

His eyes widened as he turned. "Dee, sorry I didn't see you."

I stepped forward, cupping his face. "Maddox, what is it?" I asked, anxious. "What's wrong?"

He flinched at my touch, which horrified me, but before I could withdraw, he covered my hands with his, pushing them onto his skin. He leaned down and pressed his forehead to mine.

"It was the flu. I'm getting better."

"You should have let me come see you."

He shook his head, stepping back. "I didn't want you to get it. I've been laying low." He leaned around me, pressing the button for my floor. When we arrived, he held the door open for me.

I tapped my foot. "You're coming with me."

A glimmer of a smile played on his lips, but he shook his head. "Maybe tomorrow."

I braced myself against the wall. "Fine. I'm coming with you."

He sighed and scrubbed his face. Using his foot, he stopped the doors from closing and grabbed my bags. "Okay, Dee. I'm not great company, but I'll come for a coffee."

"You're staying for dinner. You need to eat."

He followed me, his voice so quiet I almost didn't hear his reply.

"I need you more."

HE DOZED ON the sofa as I made a quick dinner, throwing together a wonton soup with ginger and garlic. He refused whiskey, instead asking for water. I studied him as he'd walked around, finally settling on the sofa. He looked like Maddox, but something was off. His suit, although expensive and tailored, was plain and a dark blue. His shirt was white and his tie a solid gray. When he toed off his shoes, his socks were the same color. There were other things. The knot in his tie was slightly crooked, his top button undone. There was no pocket square and his cuff links were simple silver discs. Even his watch had a solid black band and face. Nothing bold or colorful. Maddox was dressed more conservatively than I had ever seen Bentley dressed—and that was saying something.

He was also paler than I had ever seen him, and even when he smiled, it didn't reach his eyes. They were tormented and anxious. He looked older than his years and exhausted.

Something was very wrong, and despite his words, it wasn't the damn flu.

When dinner was ready, I carried in the steaming bowls and sat beside him, gently tugging on his arm. He woke, instantly tense, relaxing a little when he saw it was me.

"Hey, sorry," he mumbled, accepting the bowl.

"No need to apologize," I assured him, letting him continue to lie to me. "The flu takes a lot out of a person."

He nodded, tasting his soup. "This is great."

"I thought I'd keep it light for you."

"Thank you."

We ate in silence, and I was pleased to see a little color return to his face as he devoured the soup. I realized, whether it was the flu or something else, he hadn't eaten much lately. I was glad I had made extra that he could take home.

He set down the bowl with a smile. "That was delicious."

"More?"

He slouched against the cushion with a sigh, his shoulders looser than they had been when he arrived. "Maybe later."

"Okay."

I took the bowls and returned with more water. Anxious to ease him, I sat on the end of the sofa and placed a cushion on my knee, patting it. "Come here."

He raised one eyebrow suggestively. "Isn't that my line?"

I tugged his hand. "Stop. Come here, Maddox."

He stood and shrugged off his jacket, then loosened his tie. He faltered when he realized his top button was already open, but he tugged the one below it open too. He tossed his glasses on the coffee table and lay down, face up, his head resting on my lap. He sighed as I ran my hand over his head, his body relaxing. I didn't talk, but I smoothed my hand over his brow in a constant pattern. The longer I touched him, the more relaxed he became. His hands loosened, resting easily on his stomach. His shoulders lost their tension, and the tight lines around his eyes disappeared.

Long moments passed, and I wondered if he had fallen asleep. I didn't want to stop or move and disturb him. The intense satisfaction of knowing I was helping him in some way surprised me. Until that moment, I hadn't realized how much I had missed him. His smiles and laughter. His warm voice and bossy attitude. I had been restless and upset, worried and annoyed over his absence, but all of it vanished when he was near. I desperately wanted to know what made him look that way, but I knew he wouldn't tell me until he was ready. I hoped he was confiding in Bentley or Aiden, because whatever he was carrying was too heavy to cope with on his own.

An unexpected feeling hit my chest and I held my breath. I wanted to be that person for him. To share his troubles and ease them the way I was doing right now. I had never wanted to be that person for anyone except my sister, and the feeling was different.

I cared about Maddox. More than I should. But it was there, and although I wasn't sure what to do about it, I knew it wasn't going to change.

His eyes fluttered open, the light blue of his gaze strangely vulnerable. I could see his hidden pain and fear, and I wanted to stop both. Wordlessly, I shifted, lowering my face to his at the same time he reached up, clasping his hand around my neck.

Our lips touched. Tasted. Rubbed lightly, then fitted together seamlessly, and Maddox kissed me.

It was nothing like any kiss we had ever shared.

MADDOX

I FELT THE slight stiffening of her body and heard her sharp intake of air. Opening my eyes, I saw Dee leaning close, her eyes filled with a different emotion from anything I had ever seen her express.

Wonder.

Our gazes locked, and I had to kiss her. To feel her mouth on mine once more. Tasting her, breathing her in, I felt the rest of the world evaporate.

Nothing mattered except this moment and this woman.

We kissed endlessly. Deep and hungry. Light and sweet. Long passes of our tongues and gentle bites of our teeth. Her very oxygen became mine. I needed her to breathe, to survive.

Our mouths never separating, I stood, swinging her into my arms. I knew the way to her bedroom, carrying her in the dark. In her room, I stood her on her feet, undressing her with gentle hands, refusing to break our connection. She pulled on my shirt, tugging on the buttons impatiently. I had no idea which direction my cuff links were tossed or how she managed to get my belt off, and it didn't matter. Skin to skin, we fell to her bed, disturbing the pillows and messing up her pretty lace.

I didn't care.

Dee buried her hands in my hair and wrapped her legs around my waist, holding me tight. My arms were steel cages keeping her trapped to my body. I needed to feel her all over me. To know she was real and to ground me to this moment.

One I was uncertain I would ever get again.

Because as she stroked my head and eased my stress, a stunning moment of clarity hit me. The solution to solve the problem.

But with it came the pain of leaving her, leaving everything behind me that I loved, to protect them from the shame of my past. At this point, it was all I could think to do. Jill would effectively destroy everything I held dear and hurt everyone I cared about. I couldn't allow that to happen.

Dee moaned, and I hitched her leg higher, sinking deep within her warmth. We moved slow and deliberate. I rocked into her body, refusing to break our connection. She moved with me, as if we had done this for a thousand lifetimes, our bodies so in tune with each other, it was effortless.

My orgasm was a gradual build, growing and encompassing my entire being. It was intense, making me finally give up Dee's mouth and bury my face into her neck as I came. My body shook with the strength of my release, and she sobbed my name as I moaned hers.

"Dee . . . my Dee," I groaned.

We stilled, our bodies sated. I tugged her blanket up, tucking it around us, as we lay quiet in the aftermath of our passion.

"You called me Dee. You've never called me Dee when we're together this way."

I pressed a kiss to her head, hearing her unspoken question.
"Why?"

"Why did that feel like goodbye, Maddox?"

"No," I lied, my voice steady. "I was showing you more of me. More of us."

She burrowed close, her arms holding me tight. I held her equally hard, not wanting to give her up, to let our moment pass.

To become only a memory.

Except, I feared it would.

When she was asleep, I slipped out of bed and looked down at her. She made me feel love, to know it could exist for me, and I knew, even if I left, I would always love her. I would miss her for the rest of my life.

Because she was right.

Goodbye seemed inevitable.

CHAPTER 11

MADDOX

I WANDERED AROUND my condo, restless and uptight. The silence in the room was too loud, yet the stress inside me screamed.

Everything had been going too well. I should have known it. From the moment I saw Jill, heard her grating voice, I had felt the impending doom, and there seemed to be no way out.

Except, I had found one.

I could tell Jill what she wanted to hear to lull her into a false sense of security. At the same time, I would dissolve my partnership with BAM, leave the city, and let Bentley and Aiden carry on without me. The pictures would do her no good if she had nothing to take away from me. She would have already taken everything I held dear. I had enough money; I never had to worry about it, but I would lose the family I had created. The only real family I had ever known.

I would be forced to walk away from the only woman I'd ever loved. Would ever love. My chest ached at the thought of leaving her. Or never seeing her smile or hearing her voice. Being with her in those rare, unguarded moments we'd been having. The intimate, close seconds when her guard was down and I could see *more* growing in her eyes. More for me.

The thought of leaving them, and Dee, made me ill. I couldn't sleep. I couldn't eat. All I could do was to think, my logical mind looking for a different solution and coming up empty.

The depth of the scandal could cause Bentley, and his company, irreparable damage. He had worked tirelessly to make BAM what it was today, and I couldn't let my past destroy it. I would have to tell them the truth. Give them permission to distance themselves and the company from me in case Jill tried something stupid.

As for her, she could have her house. But that was all she would get—it would buy me some time. I would be long gone, and make sure she couldn't find me.

I had already spoken privately with a lawyer on the steps I would need to take to sever my business relationship with Bentley and Aiden. To his credit, the lawyer didn't even blink when I told him my reasons and gave me a lot of advice.

Now, I simply had to take the next steps. Those included severing my personal relationships, and that was going to kill me.

I yanked on my hair in frustration, staring out the window, lost in the swirling thoughts in my brain. My phone chimed again. It had been going off all weekend, but again I chose to ignore it. Ignore the texts and emails. The quiet knocks on the door.

I knew Aiden and Bent were checking on me. That Dee was confused and wanted to help. None of them believed my half-assed attempts to deflect them.

I wasn't ready to see them. Face them. Say the words out loud.

Suddenly, the condo was too closed-in. I needed space to walk off those feelings. The bitterness was seeping in, taking hold, and I needed to clear my head. I grabbed a jacket from the closet and headed for the elevator. I walked aimlessly, my mind too occupied to take in my surroundings.

Eventually, I stopped, realizing I had walked past our office building and farther into the downtown core. Glancing at my watch, I was surprised to see I had been walking for over an hour. To my left was the Fairmont Hotel, and I decided to go inside and sit at the bar. Maybe a drink would help.

After tossing back a shot, I accepted another whiskey from the barman, made my way over to a corner table, and sat down facing the window. I nursed my drink, staring blindly at the people walking along the sidewalk, not paying attention to much else. I startled when a voice broke through my thoughts.

"You look like you need a friend."

My head snapped up, and I met the steady gaze of Richard VanRyan.

"Richard," I said, confused. "What are you doing here?"

He indicated the chair opposite me. "May I?"

"Of course."

He sat down, setting his glass on the table. "I know I'm not due in the office until Tuesday, but another client wanted a meeting tomorrow so I flew in early. I came down for a scotch and saw you sitting in the corner." He studied me as he sipped his drink. "Would you rather be alone?"

"No." I waved my hand. "It's fine."

His hazel eyes were shrewd as he pursed his lips. "I'm not sure fine is the right word, Maddox. Pardon my bluntness, but you look like shit."

I had to laugh. "No offense taken. I feel like shit."

"Want to talk about it?"

I shut my eyes. "I wish I could, Richard, but with our relationship being what it is, it would be highly inappropriate."

He chuckled. "My wife, Katy, would tell you I am the king of being inappropriate." He reclined in his chair, relaxed. "I realize we're about to work together, but it's the weekend. I'm not on the clock, and as far as I'm concerned, we're two guys having a drink on a Sunday afternoon. Blowing off steam."

The offer was tempting. I wanted to talk, and given the decision I had come to, I technically wouldn't be talking to a business associate. Lifting my glass, I downed the amber liquid.

"I'm leaving BAM."

His eyes widened, and he lifted his glass, swallowing the contents. He stood, taking our glasses, returning a few minutes later with doubles for us both. He set my whiskey down in front of me, took a sip of his fresh scotch, then pulled his chair closer to the table.

"Talk to me."

I scrubbed my face with my hand as I thought about what I could say. "Something has come up from my past. Something I never expected to surface, but it has." I met his gaze. "The scandal would damage everything Bentley has worked for. The fallout would be enormous. Given the campaign we're about to embark on, let's just say, when this comes out, the entire 'family first, home, you've found it,' thing will blow up in our face."

He pondered my words. "Does this past include some criminal activity?"

"No."

"Did you hurt someone or something?"

"Not in the way you think, no."

"So, it's more . . . personal?" His voice drifted off as he posed the question.

"Yes. Personal, and frankly, mortifying."

"So, what, you're going to give up your career, walk away from your friends, and leave your life, because of something you did in your past? Something you're ashamed of?"

"It would embarrass the company. Stain the entire project. I'm going to advise Bentley to let me leave, then wait a few months before he begins the campaign to make sure I've been out of the picture long enough."

"You haven't spoken to Bentley or Aiden yet?"

"No. I've been giving the entire fucked-up situation a lot of thought."

"What about your pretty lady? Dee? What does she think you should do?"

I lifted my glass, taking a long swallow. "I haven't told her, either."

Richard's brow furrowed, and he sipped his scotch.

"You know, often decisions made on your own are the worst ones of all. We can never look at the problem objectively and tend to see only one side."

I snorted into my glass. "There is only one side to this mess."

"I doubt that."

"No one else can make this decision."

"Agreed. I know I don't know you that well, Maddox, and Bentley and Aiden even less. But I see the strength of your friendship. The respect you have for each other. I think they'd want the chance to have their thoughts on your decision heard. In fact, I'm certain they would insist."

"I can't allow Bentley to risk the reputation of his company."

"Don't you think he should have a say in the matter?"

I sighed, unsure how to respond. "I can't put him in the position to choose between our friendship and his company."

Richard nodded, looking thoughtful. "You're not in a rush to leave and go home, right?"

Thinking of how claustrophobic my condo had felt, I was in no hurry to return. "Nope."

He stood. "Let's go to my suite. I have a bottle of scotch, and we'll have some privacy. I have a story to tell you."

Confused, but intrigued, I followed.

Richard handed me a glass, settling into the chair opposite me in his suite. He pulled his phone from his pocket, scrolling through photos until he stopped at one screen. He smiled at the image, then handed me his phone. I studied the picture of the pretty woman with dark hair and blue eyes. Beside her was a toddler who looked a great deal like her, and she held a baby with eyes I recognized.

"Your family?" I asked.

"Yes. My wife Katy, our eldest daughter, Gracie, and our newest,

Heather." His grin was so wide his eyes crinkled. "Or as Gracie calls her—Hedda. Gracie's lisp slays me every time."

I handed him back the phone, noticing the way his finger traced over the picture and his smile appeared again before he slid his phone into his pocket.

"Before I met my wife, I was an asshole. A total, complete prick—or as many preferred to call me, 'Dick.'" He raised his eyebrows. "I was egotistical, narcissistic, and frankly, a nasty bastard. Anything I wanted, I took. The place I worked was cutthroat, and I fit in well. I didn't care what I had to do or who I had to step on to get what I wanted. I didn't care about anyone or anything. My coworkers, the women I dated, anyone in my life, to be honest. Including my wife, who was my assistant at the time. I was especially cruel to her." He exhaled hard. "In fact, I was so cruel I manipulated her to get what I wanted. I forced her to marry me to make myself look good."

"I don't understand."

"Katy is astonishing. She draws people in with her warmth. I needed that warmth to make me look like a better person to get what I wanted."

"Which was?"

He smirked, lifting one eyebrow. "My job with Graham."

"Holy shit," I muttered. "You two seem so close."

"We are." He sat back, sipping his scotch. "I'm not going to bore you with all the sordid details, but I changed after I married Katy. No one could be immune to her warmth—not even me. *She* changed me, and I fell in love with her for real. Luckily, she returned my feelings. But I couldn't live with the lies I had built. I came clean with Graham and told him the truth. I expected to be fired—thrown out of the company that had helped to change me. But Graham and his wife forgave me and gave me a second chance. After everything I had done. The horrible excuse for a human being I had been, they still believed in me."

He shrugged as if to say, *"Can you believe that?"*

He crossed his legs, swinging his foot. "So I think I understand what you're going through. And I think you need to talk to your partners before you make such a drastic, life-altering decision." He paused. "My scariest moment of truth turned out to be the best decision of my life. I would be lost without my girls. My family is everything to me. Graham and his family are part of that circle. It happened because I was honest and trusted someone I cared about enough to be truthful and allow them to help me. It wasn't easy, but it was worth it."

After a moment of silence, he chuckled dryly. "Tighter than a clam, aren't you?"

"Pardon me?"

"I told you my story, Maddox. A handful of people know the truth about Katy and me and what happened. You could blab that to anyone or use it against me not to hire the firm. But I trust you enough to know you won't. I think you can trust me in return."

I huffed and drained my glass, setting it on the table. "I'm really not comfortable."

"Don't go into details if it's easier. Give me the gist."

"A woman—" I blew out a long breath "—from my past has some photos of me, of us, in a compromising position. They especially portray me in a very bad light. She is threatening to release them unless I pay her. Except, given what I know of her, it's never going to end. She'll want more. I can't risk it."

"Hmm. I assume these pictures are of a sexual nature?"

"Yes."

He tugged on his hair, tapped his chin, and sipped his scotch.

"Was the sex consensual?"

"Yes," I retorted. "Completely. In fact, it was her idea. I went along with it." I shook my head. "I never should have agreed, but I was young, naïve, and stupid. I was high, drunk, and I lost control. I trusted her and I shouldn't have."

"What were you doing, Maddox?"

I heaved a sigh. "I was dominating her. Or trying to. I discovered quickly causing someone pain wasn't my thing. I had no idea what I was doing and it went . . . badly."

"Were you aware of the camera?"

"Fuck no."

"Have you seen the pictures?"

"Yes. She gave me a set. She says she has more, plus backups."

"What does she want?"

"A house and five hundred grand, for starters. Those are her words."

He tapped his chin, deep in thought. "You think if she releases them, it will make a mockery of the image you're trying to create for Ridge Towers?"

"I know it will. How can we push the family aspect when one of the partners is shown brandishing a whip with a tied-up woman? Not exactly the image Bentley was going for. And from the values Graham keeps, he won't want to be associated with us either. Everyone loses unless I walk away."

"But you lose."

I lifted one shoulder. "My mistake, so I need to take the responsibility."

"I disagree."

I had no response.

A smile quirked the corner of his mouth. "We could appeal to a whole other crowd. Change up the campaign."

I tried not to laugh. "It's not funny."

"Not right now. But it will be one day. At least I hope so, for your sake." He leaned forward, resting his arms on his thighs, earnest. "I think there's another solution. Meet with Aiden and Bentley. Trust them and be honest. Give them the options. I think not only will they be on your side, they'll help you fight." He grinned. "You have your resident genius, plus the giant on your side. Don't discount the power of a very influential boss. I can only imagine what ammunition they will come up with to help. This woman is betting you'll hand her the money quietly. If you fight back, she might back down. I'm not a lawyer, but she took the pictures without your consent and is now trying to use them to blackmail you. And she was a willing participant. That doesn't look so good on her either."

That gave me pause.

He grinned. "Let her do her worst. Call her bluff." He shook my shoulder. "Talk to your friends, Maddox. Let them help. Don't try to handle it on your own."

"What about Graham?"

"I'll talk to him if we have to. We'll keep going forward until . . . well, until we have to stop. Which I don't think we will." He drew in a long breath. "And tell your lady. She deserves the truth. I think she'll surprise you too."

"You're full of advice, aren't you?" I chuckled, feeling lighter.

He sipped his scotch. "Well, Katy would tell you I'm still an asshole and express my opinion far too freely, but that's beside the point. I like you, Maddox. I think our two companies will work well together for many years, and I hate to think of you not being part of that adventure."

I stuck out my hand. "Thanks, Richard."

He winked and shook my hand. "Part of the service." He stood. "Now go and talk to them. I'm going to call my wife."

I made my way to the elevator and pulled out my phone, texting Aiden and Bentley.

> Can you come to the office? I need to talk to you. It's important.

Their replies were swift.

> On my way.

> Be there soon.

I pushed the button going down, focusing on Richard's advice. *Trust them.*

I hoped my trust wasn't misplaced.

CHAPTER 12

MADDOX

AIDEN AND BENTLEY arrived together, both looking confused. When they saw my face, their expressions turned to concerned. Immediately, they sat with me at our boardroom table, all in our usual spots. Bentley at the head of the table, Aiden to his right, and me to his left.

I wondered as I looked across the table if today would be the last time we sat that way.

In front of me were two envelopes. Bentley's gaze flicked to them briefly, then he returned his stare to me.

I spoke. "Before we start, how is Emmy?"

Bentley sighed. "Grieving. I hated to be the one to tell her what Aiden discovered, but I think that perhaps it gave her some peace. She's mourning Jack's loss, but she has her answer. She can move on."

"She's strong. She'll be okay."

"Yes, she will. I'll make sure of it."

"I know."

Our eyes met, his worried, mine anxious.

"What's going on, Maddox?"

I ran a hand over my face. "The night we had dinner with The Gavin Group, I saw a woman who looked familiar. It happened so fast I convinced myself I had imagined it." I inhaled and blew out the air. "But I hadn't. It was Jill."

"That girl from university?" Aiden asked.

"Yes."

"Fuck," Bentley swore.

"She showed up on Tuesday night, insisting we talk."

Aiden scowled. "What the fuck did she want? Is she bothering you?"

My hands curled into fists on the boardroom table, my knuckles turning white from the pressure.

"Bothering is one word." I gritted my teeth. "She's blackmailing me."

They looked startled, sharing a glance, then returned their attention to me.

"With what?" Aiden asked calmly.

I slid the larger envelope his way. He opened it, his eyebrows rising as he looked at the pictures, but he said nothing. He passed the photos to Bentley.

The silence screamed in my face.

Bentley passed them to me, and I tossed them on top of the envelope.

Bentley stood and paced. "This happened that spring. When I left university to open BAM, didn't it?"

"Yes. You were busy and rarely home, and Aiden was swamped with finals. It was a short, destructive relationship. You met her one time, and it was brief and not particularly pleasant."

"I didn't like her."

"No, neither of you did, which probably made her even more interesting to me."

He stopped pacing, bracing his arms on the back of a chair. "You changed after you split. You were withdrawn for a long time. But you never talked about it."

I ran a hand through my hair. "I was embarrassed, horrified, and ashamed, Bent. I broke it off and avoided her at all costs. She left at end of term for an acting job, and I thought I would never have to think about it or her again. Until she showed up the other night."

I pushed the other envelope his way. He opened it, scanning the document I had created on our heavy, embossed company letterhead.

Bentley read it and scowled, lifting his eyes to meet mine, then handed the letter to Aiden. He read it slowly, his brow furrowed as he made his way through the short document.

"Explain this, Maddox," Bentley demanded.

I leaned forward. "She wants a house and money—a yearly payout. If I don't give it to her, she is going to put these pictures out there. To the media, on social sites, everywhere. Once they're out there, that's it. BAM will forever be associated with them. The scandal will be huge. You don't want that stain on your company, Bent."

"*Our* company," he said.

I continued as if he hadn't spoken. "If I pay her, shut her up for now, and leave, if it ever comes out, you can distance yourself. Spin it so you can keep your reputation clean and not affect the company. Say you fired me the second this came to your attention. Whatever you need to do."

"And what do you plan on doing? Where will you work?"

I barked out a laugh. "I don't need to work. You know that." I huffed out a long exhale of air. "I haven't given it much thought, but I'll probably move . . . somewhere. Get as far away as possible, so if it hits, the fallout for you will be minimal. I'll find some little company that needs an accountant and take it on. I'll be fine." My voice barely shook as I lied.

"Right. So you want to dissolve our partnership, leave town, and sever our friendship. Over some photos?"

"I think it's for the best."

"What about Dee?"

I shook my head, unable to answer.

Bentley picked up the letter, tearing it into pieces. "Not fucking happening, Mad Dog."

"Bent—"

"No!" he roared. "What the hell are you thinking? That is *not* how this works. How we work! *Jesus,* Maddox! Where is your logic?"

My anger suddenly matched his, and I stood and pounded the table. "I am thinking logically! I'm thinking about you and Aiden, and the company you worked so hard to build up! I know what your reputation means to you, and I *won't* be the one to destroy it all."

Our eyes locked, both of us leaning over the table. I swallowed, but my voice was still raspy. "You mean too much, Bent. This place means too much. I can't do that to you."

Aiden placed himself between us, pushing us apart with his arms. "Okay, guys, let's calm down. Maddox, sit down. Bentley is right. You're not going anywhere, you stupid fucker. We're going to figure this out." He ran a hand through his hair. "Damn it, I need some coffee and a Danish so I can think."

Despite the anger, I felt my lips twitch. "Always with the food."

"I think better on a full stomach."

I dragged a weary hand over my face. "I'm not sure how much we can come up with."

He pulled the photos close and studied them, flipping them over to study the back. "I have some thoughts. This was a while ago."

"Yeah. Last year of university."

He whistled. "She's been holding on a long time."

"Yeah, no shit." I snorted. "She recognized me and checked me out. She saw her financial opportunity and took it."

"You trust me, Mad Dog?"

"With my life."

"Okay." He pulled out his phone. "I'm bringing in some help." He strode out of the boardroom.

Bentley flipped the photos facedown. "No offense, Maddox. But

I don't really want to stare at those."

"I don't blame you."

"So, just for information . . . is this—" he tapped the photos "—is this what you like?"

"No. You know how unsettled I was back then. I was still figuring myself out—my likes and dislikes." I sighed, letting my head fall back. "Jill liked it when I ordered her around, and she suggested we move it to the next level. I wasn't that into it at first, but, ah . . ." My voice trailed off.

"Tell me. Nothing you say is going to shock me now," Bentley said dryly.

I hung my head as I spoke. "I was high and drunk. I lost control of the situation and myself. Things went bad pretty fast."

He was aghast. "Maddox, you were doing drugs?"

I met his shocked gaze. "Yeah, I did, Bent. I was looking for an outlet, trying to find my place. I did a lot of things with her I'm not proud of. She was a destructive force in my life. Brief, but caustic.

"I had no idea she took pictures, and it never happened again—at least not for me. I stopped seeing her after that, and she wasn't very happy about it."

"I remember. She obviously held on to her grudge."

"I guess this is her payback."

He nodded, averting his eyes.

"I'm sorry I wasn't there for you then when you needed a friend. Maybe I could have helped if I'd been around more."

I shook my head. "No. This is on me. Don't start with that. You've always been a good friend."

He huffed out a long breath.

"You are, Bent. You and Aiden. I'm sorry my bad decisions could hurt what you've worked so hard to build up." I paused and sighed. "I'm sorry, Bentley. I really am."

He snapped his head up. "Shut up, Maddox. We've all made mistakes. Granted some of them weren't captured on film, but we still made them."

"They weren't big enough to harm those around us."

He leaned forward, once again angry. "*Bullshit.* May I remind you what happened to Emmy? Because of my ego, she was hurt. Aiden's stubbornness almost cost him Cami. We all do things we regret. But the one constant is that we have been there for each other. And it's not changing now. So forget the fucking apologies and let's figure this out."

I was taken aback by his words. "Okay," I muttered.

"And stop referring to BAM as *my* company. It belongs to all of us. *We* make it what it is. We make the decisions, and we do that together. Stop this arbitrary shit decision-making. Am I clear?"

"Crystal."

He dropped his voice, tapping the table rapidly with his finger. "You know what angers me the most? The way you've handled this. Instead of coming to me, you took it upon yourself to decide to walk away. If you think some stupid photos of you brandishing a whip are going to bring down our company, you're mistaken. Furthermore, if you think I would let these ludicrous pieces of paper end our friendship, then you need to give your head a shake, Maddox Riley. We're family, and I don't walk away from family. I'm angry you didn't trust me enough to know that."

He pushed backed his chair. "I need to go home to Emmy. You figure out how to handle this with Aiden and keep me in the loop. I'll do everything I can to help. Excuse me."

Stunned, I watched him walk out, passing Aiden in the doorway. They spoke for a moment, and he left.

Aiden sat down. "Well, you've pissed him off. That's good. A pissed-off Bentley is a fighter."

"So glad I could be of further use."

He ignored my sarcasm. "I have Reid coming in."

I groaned. "Is that necessary? I'm already embarrassed enough."

"It is." He glanced at the photos again and shook his head. "Who knew you had that kinky shit in you, Mad Dog? You hide it so well under your cool attitude and hip suits. Do you carry a whip in your briefcase for when the mood strikes?"

I rolled my eyes, knowing he was trying to lighten the mood. It was how we handled things when the atmosphere got tense. "Shut up or you'll be the first to find out."

With a chuckle, he pushed the photos toward me. "Who else knows?"

I tugged on my scruff. "Richard VanRyan."

His eyebrows shot up. "What?"

"I ran into him. He could see I was upset, and we started talking. He shared something from his past, and without going into a lot of details, I told him what was happening. He's the one who convinced me to call you and talk instead of walking away."

He stared at me, astonished, then his head fell back as he laughed. "Mad Dog, I'm usually the one fucking something up. But when you do it, you do it well. Sex pictures, an attempted resignation, and a confession to a new business partner." He wiped his eyes. "Bent is gonna be thrilled with that news. You have been busy."

I tried not to smile, but my lips quirked. Only Aiden could summarize the mess into a comedy sketch.

His expression became serious. "Would you have done that, Maddox? Walked away?"

"To protect what we've built and not drag your name and Bentley's into the mud with mine, yes."

He leaned over and gripped my shoulder. "Not happening. You're not going anywhere. You're going to push back and shut her down."

I met his gaze. It was intense and hard.

"Okay," I agreed.

Reid appeared in the doorway, carrying a huge tray. He placed it onto the table with a grin.

"Hey. Got the coffee and Danishes. Now let me have a look at the nudie pics. This should be fun."

I STOOD, HELPLESS, watching Reid and Aiden. We had moved to Reid's office, and the sound of the constant keystrokes and their mumblings were driving me mad.

"Have you been in contact with her?" Aiden asked, glancing up from behind Reid's shoulder.

"No. She gave me a card with her email and cell number."

Reid looked at me. "She doesn't live here, right?"

"No, she's part of a traveling drama troupe. She's in a hotel. She didn't say which one."

"We need to find out."

"All right," I agreed, confused.

Reid tapped the photos. To his credit, he had been nothing but professional, other than the one comment. "These are stills. From a video."

I felt ill.

There was a video?

"Oh fuck," I groaned.

"No, this is good. And she printed them from a cheap printer, probably a small one of her own. Which means she keeps these on her computer and maybe a backup," Reid mused, typing fast. "At least, she would have a backup, if she were smart."

He extended his arm. "Give me her card. You need to let me work. I need her email address. I will be emailing her from your account and setting up a meeting with her. You're going to meet her wherever and whenever I tell you."

"Okay."

He frowned, turned his head, and spoke to Aiden in a low voice. Aiden nodded.

"When you meet her—" Reid crossed his arms "—you'll tell her you know there's a video and demand to see it."

"Why would I want to see it? I don't even want to see *her*."

"I'm sure you don't. But you need to tell her you do."

"And?" I prompted.

Reid smirked. "You don't want to know what happens next. Just know I have your back and this is going to be over—fast. Trust me on that."

"What if she has a backup?"

Reid grinned—wide and evil. "Trust me. I've got it."

Aiden squeezed my shoulder. "You should go home. Have you told Dee?"

"No." That wasn't a conversation I wanted to have.

"You have to, Mad Dog. If this doesn't work and it comes out, it would be better coming from you. You owe her that."

"Damn it, I'm sorry I ever got involved with Jill."

"I'm sorry too. That I wasn't there for you."

I waved him off. "I was an adult, Aiden. I could make my own choices, including taking the drugs. She said and did all the right things. Neither you nor Bent liked her. I should have known."

He shook his head. "Exactly like Bent with that girl he had who caused him such grief. The more we said we disliked her, the more attractive she became."

"I suppose."

"Reid and I are going to figure this out. You need to go talk to Dee."

"Okay."

"Good luck."

I had a feeling I was going to need it.

"Thanks. Both of you."

⌒

I OPENED THE door, offering Dee a tight smile. I had texted her, asking her to come upstairs once I got home. I was nervous, my stomach twisted with anxiety.

"No remote today?" she asked.

"No."

She came in and sat on the sofa. Without asking, I poured us each a generous whiskey and handed her a tumbler. As she lifted it to her mouth, I caught sight of her thumb, and with a curse, I reached for her hand.

She transferred the glass to her left hand and allowed me to hold up the right. "Dee, what have you done?" I was horrified at the mangled flesh on the end of her thumb.

"I've been anxious."

"Because of me," I stated the fact.

"I know something is wrong. Terribly wrong. I was with Emmy and Cami earlier, when you texted Aiden and Bentley. They tore out of the house, and now you've asked to see me."

"I'm sorry."

"Please, can you tell me? Whatever it is, we'll deal with it."

Her words hit me. "We will?"

She shifted closer. "Maddox, I'm your friend. Your lover too, but most importantly, your friend. You can talk to me."

"I'm not sure you'll want to be either once you hear what I have to say."

"Let me be the judge of that."

I swallowed another mouthful of whiskey. "Before I start, how is Emmy? I know Bent says she's trying to come to terms with her brother's death."

"Yes. She's sad and needs to grieve, but she's going to be fine. Cami and I spent the afternoon with her, talking."

"Good."

I stood, walking around the room. "I'm not sure where to start, Dee."

"Pick a spot, and we'll go from there."

I sucked in a deep breath. "Okay. There is someone—a woman—from my past. She's trying to blackmail me."

She was startled but remained calm. "Go on."

"I met her in university. I thought she was beautiful and bright. She seemed to have it all. We were together for a short while." I sighed and groaned. "It was the biggest mistake of my life."

"Why?"

"She hid the real person she was under her charming persona. She had a way of getting me to do things I didn't really want to do. She could manipulate me—something I didn't allow anyone else to do." I rubbed the back of my neck as memories pricked my brain, making me uncomfortable. "I was going through a bad time. Bent was setting up his business and hardly ever around. Aiden was writing finals of two majors. He was either at school or at the library. If he was at home, he was studying or sleeping. I was feeling lost and at a crossroads. For a short time, she made me feel better."

"What happened?"

My shoulders felt tight and my neck ached. I rolled my arms, trying to release the tension. I sat beside her, reaching for her hand. Absently, I kissed her thumb, hating the fact that it was her worry over me that caused the bitten flesh.

"You need to stop doing this to yourself."

"Okay," she whispered.

I kissed it again, then released her hand.

"I've always liked control, Dee. In my life, my work, and as I discovered, with sex. I liked the feeling of being in charge. Jill liked it too. In fact, she more than liked it. She craved it."

"Oh."

"She wanted more. She pushed me constantly. Taunted me to get me angry. She wanted me to be more *physical* with her." I couldn't look at Dee. "She liked to be . . . hurt."

She stiffened.

"She mesmerized me at first, but I found her wearing. She liked to draw attention to herself. She'd cause scenes, be rude to people. We argued about it constantly. She'd yell and try to get me to hit her. Punish her. Things got bad."

"How bad?"

"As I said, I was unhappy. I was drinking too much, and I started doing drugs. Nothing heavy, but I smoked up a lot and tried a few pills."

"Maddox . . ."

I shrugged, daring to glance her way. She looked upset but not disgusted—yet.

"Like I said, young, stupid, and unhappy. A bad combination."

"I think you're stalling."

She was correct. I was stalling.

"We had an argument. I should have left, but I stayed and got drunk. We tried a new drug." I exhaled heavily. "X it's known as, I believe. Ecstasy."

"I'm aware of the name, Maddox." Dee rolled her eyes.

"I didn't know how it would affect me." I swallowed and dropped my head. "It was bad. Really bad. My careless decisions and stupidity even doing drugs led to one of the worst moments of my life."

I pushed off the sofa, pacing.

"And this moment? She is somehow using it against you?"

"Yes. She has pictures, possibly a video of it. What it contains would cause a scandal for the company. It would hurt those I care about the most. So I offered to walk away."

She gasped. "Leave BAM?"

I met her eyes. "Leave everything."

Realization dawned in her eyes. "I think you'd better tell me what's in those pictures."

"Do you really want to know?"

She sat back, crossing her legs, one foot swinging in anger. "Yes."

"I really—"

"Just tell me, Maddox! Enough!"

I swung around, throwing up my hands. "I tied her up! I beat her with a whip, and I fucked her hard. Is that what you want to know, Dee?" I roared. "I used her *exactly* the way she wanted."

"The way she wanted?"

"Yes. She kept egging me on, calling me names, telling me I wasn't a real man, that I didn't have the guts to be one. She taunted me. I hit her. I screamed at her. I fucked her, and I didn't care!"

She stared at me in silence. I waited for her to get up and walk out. Instead, she spoke, her voice quiet. "But you did care."

All of a sudden, I was back in that room, the sounds and sights all around me.

Jill's taunts at my ineffective snaps of the whip were fast and furious. Goading me that I wasn't enough. I would never be enough. The rush of the drugs as they tore through my body, burning me from within. The inability to think coherently, feeling as if my body belonged to someone else. The anger building as I tightened the ropes I bound her with. The crack as the whip hit her back. Her laughter and continued jibes. Striking her over and over again. Then once more with fierceness I didn't know I could feel. Grabbing her hips and fucking her, screaming in her face as she arched her back, wanting more. Feeling nothing until I saw her shoulder. The blood dripped from where the whip had cut into her flesh. Me, stumbling away, horrified at the sight.

I realized I was sitting on the floor in my condo, and Dee's arms were around me. She was rocking me and I was shaking. I hadn't been lost in my head. I had spoken the words out loud.

I had told her. I had told her everything. And she was still there with me.

"Shh, Maddox. I'm here."

I calmed, finally looking up at her.

"What happened?" She spoke gently.

With a heavy sigh, I dropped my head to the wall.

"I untied her and cleaned her up. She was furious."

"Because you hurt her?"

I shook my head. "Because I hadn't. She had a couple of small welts on her back and the only real damage was the cut on her shoulder. It was the sight of the blood that jolted me into reality. I never finished beating or fucking her." I passed a weary hand over my face. "She yelled and started to call me all sorts of names, trying, I think, to get me to return to that anger. But the shock of what I had done, what I had allowed to happen, was too much, and I was able to think. I had a complete moment of clarity, and I knew I could never see her again. She was toxic, and if I stayed with her, she'd make me toxic too. Just like my father."

She gripped my hands. "You're *nothing* like your father."

"I figured that out."

"So you left?"

"Yeah. She came to the house a few days later and tried to get me to change my mind. We had another huge fight, and I told her what I thought of her—the real her. She didn't like it much. She slapped me and left, but she told me I'd pay for it." I barked out a humorless laugh. "I guess she meant it."

"And you never saw her again?"

I rubbed my hip reflexively. "A few days later I got clipped by a car going past me too fast. I jumped back, but the bumper caught me and I went down. I caught a quick glimpse of the driver, and I swore it was her, but I wasn't able to prove it. Her roommate insisted she had been home when it happened, and since I wasn't seriously hurt, I left it."

Dee frowned. "And the other night . . . the car that spooked you. The woman you thought you recognized. That was her?"

I nodded. "Another one of her signature moves."

Dee shook her head. "Crazy bitch."

I felt a smile tug on my lips. Dee rarely swore, and it seemed strange to hear curse words fall from her sweet lips. She stood, brushed off her pants, and met my gaze.

"So these pictures, I assume they make it look worse than it is?"

I rubbed my head. "It was awful regardless, and I'm ashamed of my actions, but yes."

"I want to see them."

"No," I protested, horrified at the thought. "I don't want you to see me that way."

"Give them to me, Maddox."

"No. This isn't up for discussion."

"Either you give them to me, or I walk right now."

"*Why?* Why do you want to see them? Jesus, I don't even want to look at them."

She tapped her foot. "My reasons are my own. Let me see them."

Cursing, I pushed off the floor and got the envelope from my office. Wordlessly, I handed it to her.

She opened the flap and scanned through the pictures. Once, then twice. She shoved them back into the envelope before she spoke.

"You have a plan other than leaving your entire life behind and letting her win?"

"Yes. Aiden and Reid have something." I rubbed the back of my neck. "I don't think it's exactly legal."

She held up the envelope. "And this is?"

"No."

She tapped the envelope on her hand, her expression intense.

"These photos are not the Maddox I know. The man I know you to be. You would never hurt another person, which is why you stopped. Why you were horrified. Why it proves you are nothing like your father. You let yourself be talked into something you didn't want." She tilted her head. "She told you that you had the control, Maddox, but she lied. *She did.* She manipulated you and tried to make you something you're not. Something you never will be."

"She wasn't wrong about me liking control."

Dee reached over and cupped my cheek. "Being in control is different than violence. You control me, *us*, in the bedroom, but you have never treated me with anything besides respect and tenderness. I have never once been afraid."

"And now? Now that you've seen those pictures and know what I've done?"

I searched her eyes. There was something in her gaze I didn't understand. An emotion I couldn't pinpoint.

"These pictures confirmed my initial thoughts. They don't reflect you—the Maddox I know. I wasn't afraid of you before I saw them, and I am not afraid of you now."

"What are you thinking? Talk to me."

She shook her head. "What I'm thinking isn't important."

"It is to me."

She kept talking as if I hadn't said anything. "You need to deal with this and end it."

"I know." Turning my face, I pressed a kiss to her palm. "Can you forgive me?"

She shook her head. "I don't need to forgive you."

"But I need it."

"Then you have it. You can't change your past, Maddox. It's part of you. But what you need to do is forgive yourself. You will never get over it until you do."

My eyes widened at her words.

"You made a huge error in judgment, the same way I did when I trusted someone I shouldn't have. And if you let her, she will keep on hurting you." She leaned up, kissed my cheek, then turned away, pausing at the door.

"Do what you have to do."

"Even if it's wrong?"

Her eyes glittered in the late afternoon light. "I hope Aiden helps you nail her ass to the wall. I want you to burn those pictures, destroy whatever she has, and tell her to go to hell."

I was shocked at the venom in her voice.

"Or you can let her win. Once you decide what you're doing, you can let me know." She pulled open the door. "I hope you fight."

She shut the door behind her, her words echoing in my head.

She wasn't saying everything she wanted to, but she hadn't told me to go to hell.

She hadn't told me to stay away from her or that she found me disgusting.

I hope you fight.

I hoped she meant fight for her.

I picked up my phone, dialing Aiden.

"Hey," he answered.

"Tell me what to do."

His laughter was low. "Excellent."

CHAPTER 13

MADDOX

I DREW IN a deep breath, fighting my nerves. I needed to play the plan exactly the way Aiden had instructed me. I schooled my features and relaxed my shoulders.

I could do it.

Using my account, Reid had sent Jill an email, telling her I wanted to meet with her in private. She responded, saying we could meet in her hotel room on Monday since it was her day off. She said she was looking forward to continuing our talk. Reid sent a response stating I would see her at ten on Monday morning.

Little did she know there was no longer anything for us to discuss.

I stepped out of the elevator on the fourth floor. The scent of a strong disinfectant did nothing to cover the years of dirt ground into the carpet or the subtle smell of mildew that hung in the air. The dull wallpaper had seen better days, and the silk flowers of the arrangement on the fake wood table were dusty. The place was not exactly the Hilton.

I followed the hall to Room 431 and knocked.

Jill answered the door, overdressed and made up for a Monday morning. She looked exultant, sweeping her arm in a grand gesture. "I've been waiting."

I stepped in, hiding my distaste. The room was a disaster. Clothes strewn around, bed unmade, and last night's dinner tray on the floor, an empty bottle of wine laying on its side.

"You took your time. I thought I was going to have to come for another visit, Maddox." She simpered. "You know I hate to be kept waiting."

"I don't know anything about you anymore, Jill. I never really did. But as I told you, I'm a busy man. It takes time to make arrangements."

She grinned, her crimson lips stretched across her teeth at the word "arrangements." A smear of lipstick stuck to her front teeth, as if she had bitten into something and it left behind blood. It was fitting.

"You have a video."

Her eyebrows rose. "Someone is clever."

I tamped down my revulsion. "I want to see it."

"Why?"

"Why not?" I countered.

She regarded me, her arms crossed, red-tipped talons tapping on her forearm. "First things first."

"Which is?"

She moved past me to the chipped desk. Her laptop sat to one side, but she ignored it and picked up a pile of papers.

"These are the houses I'm interested in."

Knowing I had to play the part, I flipped through the pages, amusement mixing with my anger.

"Something funny?"

"There is no way in hell I'm buying you a house worth over a million dollars. Nor will you be living in Toronto." I tossed the pages onto the desk. "You need to leave the province. I'd prefer the country, but I'll settle for a few provinces away from me."

She pouted but didn't look surprised. "What's my budget?"

I played along. "Five hundred thousand and you get two hundred thousand a year. That's it. You can live a nice life in Alberta on that."

She tried to hide her smile but failed. She thought she had won. I needed her to think that way.

I remembered Reid's words.

Get her to open the video.

"Now, let me see the video."

She moved past me, opening her laptop. She pushed some keys, frowning.

"What's the matter?"

"Nothing."

She clicked a couple of more keys, biting on one of her talons as she watched the screen. She muttered something about stupid laptops, leaned down, and pulled an old USB drive from her bag and plugged it in.

"There," she stated, victorious.

She turned the laptop, showing me the screen.

It was as I had described it to Dee. The images were grainy, the video short, but I watched as the entire, sick situation unfolded. Her jibes and taunts. My desperation. My inept use of the whip. I had never used one before that night and certainly never again after this occurred. I had no fucking clue what I was doing, and it was plain to see.

Also obvious was the fact that I was out of my mind. I was sweating and stumbling, barely able to stay on my feet. I was raging and angry, and watching myself, I had to avert my eyes several times. It wasn't long, but it made me sick to my stomach to see myself that way.

Dee was correct—that was *not* me.

The video ended, and Jill stared at me. The lust and need in her eyes were revolting.

I shook my head in abhorrence. "Not in a million years, you crazy bitch."

She uncurled herself from the chair, striking what I imagined she thought was a seductive pose.

"We were good together. We could be again."

"No. You were toxic and I was stupid. We were *never* good."

"Seeing that doesn't turn you on? Not even a little?" she purred.

Turn me on? I was trying not to be ill.

"Not even one little bit. It sickens me. You sicken me."

"Don't make me angry, Maddox." She glanced down, running her finger over the laptop. "I'd hate for this to get into the wrong hands by accident."

"Nothing is getting out, Jill. You have nothing."

"I have everything. Pictures, the video—"

I interrupted her. "The video makes you look worse than me."

She shrugged. "I'll get rid of that and use the pictures."

I felt my phone vibrate in my pocket, and I smiled. "What pictures?" I asked quietly.

Her eyes flew to the screen.

"You couldn't find them when you looked, could you?"

She sputtered. "Wh-what?"

"Your video was gone too, wasn't it? That's why you used your memory stick." I shook my head. "What a shame. I think if you check your cloud account, you'll find it all gone from there too." I tilted my head. "A word of advice, Jill. You need to use different passwords."

Her eyes widened to the point I wanted to laugh, not that any of it was funny.

She grabbed her USB drive, holding it aloft. "I have this!"

"Do you? I would check again."

She sat down, her hands shaking so hard she could barely get the drive into the laptop. She tapped on the keyboard frantically. Her screen glowed blue with the reset screen. That was all that remained. Everything was gone. When her gaze met mine, it was venomous.

I couldn't stop my victorious smile.

I lifted my hands. "Oops."

She launched herself at me, screaming obscenities. I tried to defend myself, lifting my arms to block her, but she managed to scratch my face. Blood ran down my cheek and my eye burned, but

I didn't give her the satisfaction of seeing me flinch. I gripped her arms, holding her back. She glared at me, her icy blue eyes filled with loathing.

I pushed her away, hating her touch.

"It's over, Jill. You're going to finish your current show and leave town. I don't ever want to hear from you again, do you understand?"

"You owe me," she spat.

"I owe you nothing. You're not getting a fucking house or one goddamn penny from me. You leave me alone, do you hear me?"

She raised her hand to strike again, and I grabbed her wrist, narrowing my eyes. "You got one in, that's all you get," I hissed, anger bubbling under my skin, rage taking over.

Triumph spiked in her eyes, bringing me back to my senses.

Releasing her wrist, I stepped back. "Oh no. You don't have that kind of control over me. Never again."

"I have other copies of the pictures!" she shouted in desperation.

I could tell she was lying, grasping at straws.

"Give it up. It's over, Jill. I'm not your ticket to easy street."

With a scream, she lunged and grabbed her laptop, throwing it at me. I sidestepped the object, and watched as it hit the wall, the screen shattering and falling to the floor in pieces. She had one hell of an arm.

"Well, so much for that."

"You bastard!" she seethed.

I laughed, the sound bitter. "Yes, I'm the bastard. You come here wanting to destroy my life, and *I'm* the bastard."

I shook my head. "I almost let you do it too. I almost let you fuck with my head again."

I dug into my pocket and threw some cash on the bed.

"What is that?"

"All you're ever going to get from me. Buy yourself a new laptop and forget this ever happened."

I stepped over her old laptop and paused at the door.

"God knows I plan to forget you."

I heard her muffled screams and curses all the way to the elevator.

For the first time in days, I was able to take a deep breath.

⌒

AIDEN WAS WAITING for me when I entered our office building. He had wanted to drive me earlier, but I insisted on going alone. I took a cab instead, as a precaution, not knowing what would happen while I was at the hotel.

"Are you tracking me?" I asked, swiping at the oozing cut on my face.

"Yes," he replied. "I have all our cell phones tracked. I knew you were on your way back." He eyed me warily. "She got you good."

I nodded as we stepped into the elevator. "She did. Hurts like a bitch."

"It went well. Other than the blood," he stated.

I laughed dryly. "You should know. You were recording it."

"Yeah. We got it all. Insurance. Although, I doubt we'll need it."

The elevator doors opened, and I hurried toward my office, hoping to bypass Sandy. My attempt failed. She looked up, her expression aghast as she stood.

"Maddox Riley. What on earth!"

"Nothing," I assured her. "It's nothing."

"I'll be the judge of that. I'll be in your office in a moment."

I sighed. "Sandy, please. I need to get out of these clothes, and I want a shower." I wanted to get the scent of that hotel room, *her*, out of my nose. Her touch, albeit brief, lingered on my skin like a festering sore, and I wanted it gone. "If you have to look after I'm done, fine. But I need that first." I met her gaze, silently pleading for her to understand.

"You have fifteen minutes. The dry cleaner was here earlier and dropped off a load of shirts and two of your suits. They're in your closet."

"Thank you."

Aiden followed me into my office and settled on the sofa. He stretched his arm across the back.

"I'll be waiting. Be sure to remove the wires before you get in the shower."

"Thanks." I snorted. "I wouldn't have thought of that."

"Yep," he said, inspecting his nails. "It's what I do."

The shower was as hot as I could handle. The water burned as it hit my torn skin, but after a few minutes, the ache faded. I soaped up twice and finally stepped out, feeling more in control and less tense. I studied my face in the mirror with a wince. She had come really close to my eye with those talons of hers. The two superficial slashes in my skin would heal, but they still stung. In my dressing area, I dried off and tugged on a fresh shirt. Too exhausted to bother, I pulled on a pair of dress pants, forgoing a tie or jacket. I had no plans to see anyone today.

Except, my office was full when I pulled open the door. Aiden, Bentley, and Reid were all waiting. Sandy stood by my desk, her arms crossed and her foot tapping.

"Jesus," I muttered.

"Sit down," she ordered.

Knowing it was useless to argue, I complied. She grabbed my chin, turned my face to the light, and studied it.

"Maddox Riley, I expect this of Aiden or even Reid. But not you."

I winced as she dabbed at the scratches with antiseptic. I felt as if I were eight, being reprimanded for playground antics.

"Sorry," I mumbled. "I didn't plan on it."

"You're lucky she missed your eye!"

I lifted my eyebrow. "How do you know it was a *she*?"

"Oh, I told her the whole story," Reid piped up. "She wanted the hotel address so she could rip a strip off the bimbo, but I said no."

The back of my neck prickled with embarrassment, my mortification now complete. "Well, at least you held back that piece of information."

Sandy tsked. "I made him tell me. I swear the three of you are trying to put me in my grave. Kidnappings, stalkers, and blackmailers.

The trouble you keep getting into! Seriously, all of you need to stop that madness." She smeared some ointment on my skin a little too aggressively, making me grimace. "Now you look like you've been in a street brawl. Messing up your good looks." She made a strange noise in the back of her throat. "Can we try to stick to making money and building things? Is that too much to ask, boys?"

I met her eyes, my annoyance evaporating. Only concern met my gaze. She had always been a rock for all of us. I wrapped my hand around her wrist, squeezing it.

"Yeah, we can do that, Sandy."

She patted my cheek in one of her motherly gestures. They were rare but expressed her feelings. She leaned closer. "Nothing has changed, Maddox. We all make mistakes. You should be grateful for good friends."

"I am," I assured her. "And for you."

"I would think so."

We exchanged a smile. Her face softened for a moment, then she straightened up.

"Okay. I'll let you get on with things."

"Thank you."

She nodded, knowing I was thanking her for more than a dab of antiseptic cream or her help. Her assurances meant more than I could ever express. She meant more to me than she knew.

"All right. No more shenanigans. I'm ordering lunch, and we're going over your schedules for the week. Richard is here tomorrow, so you need to be on your best behavior and not acting like a bunch of brawling hoodlums. I have to order in some bagels for him. He loves those."

She swept out of the office, and I laughed.

"Well, we know who her favorite is now. And it's not one of us."

"Brawling hoodlum," Bentley mused. "Never been accused of that one until now. Thanks, Mad Dog."

"Glad to be of service."

"I don't know why she said she expected that sort of behavior from me." Aiden pouted. "I thought I was her favorite."

"No way, man." Reid smirked. "I am."

"I can fire you, you know," Aiden warned him.

Reid leaned back, folding his arms behind his head. His new shirt was almost wrinkle-free, but still casual. "I don't think so." He grinned. "My ass is perfectly safe. Maddox and Bent are on my side."

I regarded him, serious. "I owe you, Reid. I don't pretend to understand or know all of what you did, but I'm eternally grateful."

He hunched forward, resting his arms on his knees. "I helped a friend," he replied. "What I did doesn't matter. What *she* did was wrong. I shut her down. Simple. I can explain it if you want, but I think it's best left alone."

"No, I'm good with being in the dark." I hesitated. "Should I have taken her laptop? It was in pieces on the floor, but to have been sure she couldn't get something off it?"

Reid shook his head. "Nah. It was scrubbed. I checked every angle. She had only ever copied the video to her USB drive once and made those stills she showed you. She never even printed herself a copy of them. They're gone."

My relief was so profound I sagged in my chair.

"Thank you," I stated sincerely.

"Anytime."

"For fuck sake, I hope not," Bentley interjected. "I can't take much more."

Internally, I agreed with him.

Reid stood, scratching his stomach. "I'll let you get on with the dull side of this place. I'm going back to my programs." He paused in the doorway with a grin. "I'd love some pizza for lunch, if you were, you know, *offering.*"

"Tell Sandy it's on me."

He winked, lifting his shoulder. "I thought so."

He left with a wave, and I heard him calling to Sandy. I had no doubt a tremendous amount of pizza would arrive shortly. I didn't care either. He could have anything he wanted.

He now owned Bentley and me.

Totally.

Even more surprising was I was all right with that. I trusted the kid, because I knew why he did it.

He trusted *me*.

Bentley cleared his throat. "You okay, Mad Dog?"

"I will be. I hope there are no repercussions."

"If there are, we'll deal with them. The way we do everything. As a team. As long as we're clear on something."

"Which is?" I asked, already knowing his answer, yet somehow needing to hear the words.

"That you're done with this shit about leaving."

"Yes. If you still want me here."

"I never wanted you to leave."

"I didn't think I had a choice, Bent. In hindsight, I wasn't thinking clearly. I was reacting—and I panicked."

He stood, tugging on his sleeves. "I understand why you felt the way you did. I appreciate the fact that your first instinct was to protect me and our company. But you missed one key point. It is *our* company. The three of us. BAM. Without you, we're just . . ." He shrugged, at a loss for words.

"Sheep," Aiden said.

"Sheep?"

"Yeah." He smirked. "BA—like sheep, you know? BAA-BAA." His eyes twinkled. "Not anywhere near as cool as BAM."

Bentley's lips quirked. I felt a chuckle building in my chest. Aiden began a loud braying noise, scrunching up his face as he imitated a bunch of wooly animals.

I gave in and began to laugh. Bentley followed, with Aiden laughing at himself the loudest. We all needed it after the past days of tension and worry.

When the amusement settled, I wiped my eyes, careful of the tender spot on the left side of my face. I huffed out a long exhale and stood, rounding the desk. I extended my hand to Bentley.

"Seriously, Bent. I apologize for all the shit. I appreciate everything. Your—" my voice faltered and I cleared my throat "—your friendship would have been a terrible thing to lose."

He came forward, shaking my hand, then shocked me by yanking me hard and pulling me in for a hug. "Not happening, Maddox."

Before I could react, Aiden jumped up, wrapping us both in his thick arms.

"Group hug!"

I knew they expected me to push them off. But for one instant, I basked in the moment, letting it wash away the negative emotion of the day. I stretched my arms.

"You're crushing me, Tree Trunk."

Aiden stepped back, flexing. "I was being gentle."

"Whatever."

I sat, flipping him off. Bentley watched us, amusement written on his face. He walked toward the door as I grabbed my laptop, flipping open the lid.

"Okay. Let's get some work done. Oh, and Maddox?"

I looked up. "Yeah?"

Before he could speak, Aiden started to laugh and pushed past him, disappearing down the hall.

"He told you I spilled my guts to VanRyan." I groaned. "Can't he keep his mouth shut about anything?"

"I'm not upset. I spoke with Richard, and he told me he basically forced you to talk." He paused, his hand drumming on the door. "It's sometimes easier to talk to a stranger. I'm grateful he convinced you to talk to us before you did something stupid. And so we are clear, what you were planning was stupid."

"I know that now."

"Okay then. The subject is closed."

"Okay," I agreed.

He met my eyes, nodded, and shut the door behind him, leaving me with my thoughts.

CHAPTER 14

MADDOX

I COULDN'T GET hold of Dee. I texted her, tried to call, and even knocked on her door. She didn't answer and I didn't hear any sounds of her moving inside, so I left it alone.

Worry wriggled at my mind all night, and I was tense and unable to sleep.

I tried again the next morning and finally got a reply.

Sorry. Worked late. I will see you tonight. Tacos? We'll talk after.

I sighed in relief. Tacos were normal for Tuesday. Tacos were *us*. I replied.

Yes.

I set down my phone and went about my day, feeling more settled.

Richard was his usual larger-than-life self. He was all over the mock-ups, blown away by the concept model, and he spent a long time talking to Liv, who was helping design the show model. As she discussed the elements, pointing out the different aspects of the designs and choices, I watched his concept come to life. He asked Reid a hundred questions, often shaking his head in response to the technical jargon Reid responded with. Richard made notes, sketched, and jotted down ideas. He used his hands as he visualized something. His voice rose, and he paced as he threw out captions and additions to the campaign, planning the various stages as we grew closer to completion of the project.

During the morning break, he sat beside me, took a bite of bagel, and washed it down with more coffee.

He ate a lot of bagels, charming Sandy into extra cream cheese. I noticed mine didn't get the extra helping. Aiden noticed it too and complained.

Sandy ignored Aiden, other than a cuff to the back of the head. I laughed at his shocked expression.

"This is going to be off the charts," Richard exclaimed. "The more I see of your plans, the more excited I am. You'll sell out before you break ground on the first building. We're going to hit hard and loud. We'll have them lining up for the second one."

"Then what?" Bentley queried.

Richard grinned, swallowing the last of his cream-cheese-laden bagel. "You build more and I'll sell them."

Aiden grinned. "I like that idea."

"I know," Richard shot back. "We're a great team."

He was correct. We were.

⌒

LATER THAT NIGHT, I reclined in my chair, sipping a beer. The cold liquid soothed the burn of the jalapenos that had been liberally scattered on the nachos and the mounds of hot salsa I had used on my tacos.

Richard relaxed beside me, wiping his mouth. He lifted his beer to his lips. "Great place."

I was surprised when Richard asked to accompany us to dinner. He didn't seem like a taco kind of guy, but we assured him he was welcome, and he seemed to enjoy himself. He certainly gave Aiden a run for his money with the number of tacos he ate.

"You eat a lot," I goaded him. "Almost as much as Aiden, which is impressive."

He grinned. "Carbs. My weakness. I try to watch it, but I can't resist bagels, and I love Mexican. Katy isn't a fan, so when I can get some, I grab it. Besides—" he paused, taking a sip "—it gives me a chance to hang with your crew." He lifted an eyebrow. "You have great friends. You're a lucky man."

I knew what he was saying. "I do. And thanks to you, I'm still part of the crew."

"Nah. You would have figured it out. I just gave you a push." He picked at the label on his bottle. "So you got it, ah, sorted?"

"In a manner of speaking. I think the problem has been dealt with."

He tapped his eye. "I assume she wasn't overly impressed. She got you bad."

"Ah, no. She was pretty pissed. Not that I cared, to be honest."

He smirked. "I imagine not. Your genius was a big help, I assume?"

"He was."

"You still seem tense."

I glanced across the table at Dee. She was listening to something Aiden was saying, a smile playing on her lips that didn't reach her eyes. She looked like Dee, but I felt her reserve toward me. Her eyes had widened when she saw my face, but she simply asked in a low voice if I was all right. I had assured her I was fine and it looked worse than it felt. She had sat beside me during dinner, but her attention had been elsewhere, and she had been quieter than usual. The truth was, so had I.

I wanted her alone so we could talk, but before I could suggest leaving early, she had moved to sit next to Cami. The distance between us felt like three miles rather than three chairs away.

He followed my gaze. "Your lady not happy?" he asked, turning in his chair to give us a little privacy.

"I haven't seen her alone since things, ah, came to an end, so to speak, so I'm unsure," I confessed. "She seems a little off."

"Well, if it's any consolation, every time I look over, she's watching you," Richard assured me. "I'm sure she's waiting until you're alone. Maybe she needs some reassurance. As I have discovered, women often do." He smiled indulgently with a wink. "I enjoy reassuring my Katy. It does us both good."

"You are spending too much time with Reid. You're oversharing, Richard." I shook my head in amusement. "I really don't need to hear that."

He laughed, slapping me on the shoulder. "Your resident genius does suffer from TMI overload. I find him amusing and highly entertaining.

"I'm going to bring my wife with me one of these trips, once Heather is a little older. I can't get Katy to leave her when she's still so young." He lowered his voice, showing a slightly softer side to his personality. "I can barely stand to leave them myself."

"We're happy to do this via video," I offered. "Bentley would be fine with it now. We know Becca arrives soon, and I think we have it all under control."

"I appreciate that. I already spoke with Bentley, and he said the same thing. I wanted to come see the models myself and speak to our other client. Now, I think I have things going, I'll be using video more, but I'll still come out on occasion. Katy would enjoy a trip here. She likes visiting Toronto, although she prefers the quiet of home."

"We'd all love to meet her. We're looking forward to working with you."

He drained his beer and stood. He extended his hand. "Me too, Maddox. Me too."

⌒

RICHARD LEFT, SHAKING hands and promising to be in touch

soon. I stood not long after he departed and said my goodbyes.

"It's been a long couple of days. I'm heading out." I hesitated a moment, then held out my hand. "Are you ready, Dee?"

For a brief second, I thought she was going to refuse, but she kissed Cami's cheek, said her goodbyes, and gathered her purse and jacket. She slid her hand into mine and we walked in silence to the car. I opened her door and waited until her seat belt clicked into place, then climbed into the driver's seat. I sighed as I started the car, feeling the exhaustion creeping in.

"Tired?" Dee asked.

"Yeah, I am."

"I could drive."

"No, it's fine." I pulled out of the parking lot, heading toward the condo. "I didn't know you could drive."

"We can't afford a car . . ." Her voice trailed off, and she cleared her throat. "I mean *I* can't afford a car, but I do drive."

I looked over, noticing the way she had her head turned, looking out the window.

"You can borrow my car anytime, Dee."

"Thanks, I'll keep that in mind."

"You're really missing Cami, aren't you?"

"Yes. It's hard to adjust to only thinking about myself. Cooking for two, shopping, what we would save money for . . . I have to remember it's just me now." She gentled her voice. "I'll get used to it."

I wanted to tell her she didn't have to get used to being alone, that she had me, but I knew it wasn't the moment to push it.

Traffic was light and the trip home swift. In the elevator, I pushed my floor.

"Come for a drink?"

She offered me a tight smile. "I thought you were tired. Perhaps another night would be better."

I *was* tired. Tired of her politeness and the distance I felt between us.

In two steps, I had her pushed against the wall, crowding her with my body.

"I don't think so, Deirdre."

She stared at me, the expression in her eyes catching me off guard.

Worry, resignation, hurt, and anger. All swirled in her hypnotic gaze.

"Dee," I whispered. "Talk to me."

She traced down the scratches on my cheek. "Your face. She did that to your face."

"It's fine. I promise. It will heal in no time, and we can forget it."

"Can we?"

"Yes," I insisted, cupping her face and pressing my mouth to hers.

She stiffened, and I was about to pull away when it happened. She flung her arms around my shoulders, pulling me closer. Her mouth opened to me, and we both groaned. We shared hard, long caresses—kisses filled with need and passion. Want and desire. I threaded my hands through her hair, angling her face, deepening the kiss, drowning in her taste. She whimpered, the sound so filled with longing, I thought I would explode. I moaned as she slid her hands up my neck, caressing my skin. I pressed closer, wanting to disappear into her. Needing her as I had never needed before. I dropped my face to her neck.

"With me, Deirdre. Come home with me."

"Yes," she groaned in my ear.

The elevator doors opened, and we stumbled out, still close. I held her tight all the way to the door, fumbling with my keys as she nuzzled into my neck in a very un-Dee-like manner.

Inside, impatient and desperate, I covered her mouth with mine, wanting her taste again. I lifted her and carried her to my room. I pushed off her suit jacket, yanking at the row of round buttons, desperate to feel the silk of her skin under my hands. Small pearls hit the hardwood of my bedroom floor, scattering and bouncing, the tiny pinging sounds echoing in the room.

"I liked that blouse!" Dee gasped.

"I'll buy you a hundred more," I growled, shoving the material off her body. "If you like the damn skirt, lose it before I help you."

She fisted my shirt, tearing it open. My buttons joined hers on the floor, although the noise was dull as the flat discs hit the wood.

She smirked. "I can't afford one of your shirts, sorry. You'll have to take it out in trade."

I grinned, tossing my glasses to the dresser. "Oh, is that how you want to play tonight, baby?"

Her skirt was gone with a flick of my hand and a tug of a zipper. She fumbled with my belt, and my pants followed fast along with the rest of her clothes, and soon we were naked. I didn't even stop long enough to admire her pretty lingerie. I shredded it too quickly. I grunted in pleasure as her hand wrapped around my cock.

"You're always hard," she murmured. "So hard and big and so warm."

She was good for my ego.

"Only for you, Deirdre."

I tossed her on the bed, laughing as she bounced. I crawled up the mattress, hovering over her, sliding between her open thighs, nestled against her warmth. Our eyes met in the dim light—green meeting blue, yearning and alive—the anger gone, dissipating in the darkness.

"I need you right now. Tell me I can have you."

"Yes."

One thrust of my hips and I was inside her. Wet heat surrounded me, welcoming my cock into her body. Her head fell back, my name falling from her lips. I wrapped my arms around her shoulders, lifting her as I sat back on my heels. She moaned as I slid deeper, and I hissed at the sensation. Our mouths fused as we rocked, our movements a choreographed dance our bodies knew well.

Everything from the past few days disappeared. She always made the world disappear. All that existed in the moment was her touch. How she felt sliding on my cock. The way her breasts pressed to my chest, her nipples hard pebbles on my skin. Her mouth melded to me, her velvet tongue twisting with mine.

She was all that mattered.

She was here. I didn't have to leave her. The enormity of it, the relief, washed over me. I tightened my arms, feeling my orgasm approaching, desperate to feel hers.

"I need you, baby. I always fucking need you."

She whimpered, burying her face into my neck.

"Maddox . . . oh God!"

"Give it to me, Deirdre. I want to feel you." I bit down lightly on her neck. "Come for me, baby. Come with me."

She cried out, her arms gripping me tightly, her voice shaking. I couldn't speak, the only sound leaving my throat a long, deep groan.

We stilled, and carefully, I laid her down, straightening her legs and rubbing them. Separating myself from her was difficult, so I stayed close, grabbing the blanket and drawing it over us. I settled beside her, wrapping her in my arms. We were quiet, letting our bodies settle. I kissed her head, nuzzling into her hair, inhaling the scent of fresh citrus and sun.

"You smell like summer."

She hummed.

I ran my fingers over her shoulder, enjoying the feel of her silky skin. Her fingers traced lazy circles on my chest. I liked how her touch made me feel.

"You were angry with me earlier, Dee."

She stilled her movements then tilted her head, meeting my gaze. "Yes," she answered honestly.

"Tell me why. Talk to me."

She shifted, sitting against the headboard. She tugged up the blanket, tucking it under her arms. I moved myself beside her and turned to face her. She remained silent, her fingers bunching the blanket in a restless, repetitive motion.

I was surprised at her hesitance. Dee always spoke her mind with me. "Tell me why you were angry."

Her eyes flashed to me. "I still am."

"Okay. Because of Jill? What she did? What I did?"

"I hate what happened, but I told you before, I'm not angry over your past."

"You're upset over what I did to stop it?"

"No."

"Then explain, because I can't fix it if I don't understand."

"You can't fix it, Maddox. You don't see it!"

"See what?"

"You were going to leave—walk away from your life!" Her voice caught. "From everything—including me."

I grabbed her hand closest to me. "I didn't want to."

"But you would have."

I studied her. "The thought of me leaving made you angry?" I offered her a slight smile. "Bentley and Aiden certainly told me off for my stupidity."

She pulled her hand away, crossing her arms. "It's just—" She stopped speaking.

Instantly, I knew. My thoughtless reaction had brought out some deep-seated pain she hid. But I needed her to tell me.

"Say it, Deirdre," I murmured. "It's going to fester, so let it out."

"Everyone leaves," she whispered. "My dad walked away without a thought, my mom didn't love me enough to fight, the one person I cared for used me, and . . ."

"And?" I prompted

"And I found out you were going to go too. Just walk out of my life and leave me behind. Like everyone else." Her head bowed. "Even Cami."

I knew what she felt wasn't about Cami, but I also knew she was struggling.

"I didn't want to leave, Dee. The thought of doing so was killing me."

She lifted her head. I was shocked to see the tears flowing down her cheeks.

"But you would have."

I slid my hand up her neck, wiping away the tears. "No, baby, I don't think I could have. It was a knee-jerk reaction caused by panic. The thought of not seeing you, not being with you, was tearing me up inside. Just thinking about it wrecked me. When I told Bent and Aiden what happened and they laid into me, I was relieved. All I could think about was they would help and I could stay."

"And next time?"

"There won't be a next time. I promise."

"I-I'm afraid to trust you."

"And that's on me. But don't shut me out, and don't walk away. Give me another chance." I pushed up on my knees and straddled her, gazing down into her face.

"Baby, I know your parents were shit. What that asshole did was unforgivable. But I'm not any of them. I'm here. I'm not going to leave you. Give me a chance to prove it."

"You-you make me want things I don't think I can have, Maddox."

My heartbeat picked up. I wanted to wrap her in my arms, tell her I loved her and she could have anything she wanted. Show her everything she needed was right there with me. But I knew if I pushed it, she would run. Still, her words alone gave me hope. She was feeling more for me than she was ready to admit.

Yet.

But I could be patient.

I inhaled deep. "You do the same for me, Dee. Why don't we take it as it comes, okay? You stop being angry, and I'll stop being an unthinking asshole, and we'll just be us."

"Us?"

"Yeah." I lowered down and kissed her gently. "Us. We'll figure it out."

"Okay."

I kissed her again, smiling against her mouth.

"Was that our first fight? Because I think make-up sex is in order."

"Of course you do."

But she kissed me back.

CHAPTER 15

MADDOX

I WAS ANXIOUS for the next couple of days, but I finally started to relax. Aiden had one of his security guys, Joe, follow Jill, and he reported she went to the theater every day, hung with the cast, and spent a lot of time at the bar in her hotel. She flirted with many men, picked up a few, but was always alone the next evening. Nothing seemed out of place. Joe had seen her toss a bag into a dumpster the day after our confrontation, and he grabbed it. It was her laptop, broken and useless. He removed the USB and hard drive and tossed the laptop back into the dumpster. Reid destroyed the drives, showing me the fragments left in the aftermath. Somehow, it made me feel better knowing they were gone.

Aiden lifted an eyebrow at me. "So?"

"Sorry, I was elsewhere. What did you say?"

"I asked if you wanted Joe to keep following her—or actually, Simon, since I need to switch them up now."

"Why the switch?"

"She noticed Joe last night and came on to him at the bar. He, ah, doesn't really want to have to pretend an interest. He says she's not the type of cougar he likes." He made a pawing action. "She's got claws, and he thinks she'll use them."

Reflexively, I brushed the corner of my eye. It was healing but still ached. "Yeah, I don't blame him. Don't worry about having Simon take it on. I think we're good. Jill was always reactive. I think if she had Plan B, she would have done something by now."

"Okay. I checked, and the show she is in ends soon and goes to the States, so she'll be gone."

"I'll feel better once she is," I admitted. "You were right, though. I pushed back, and she walked away."

He leaned forward. "I'm sorry, what? I didn't quite hear you. I was what?"

I lobbed a pen at him, which he caught deftly. "Get out of my office, Aiden. I have work to do."

He stood, pocketing the pen. "You still said it."

"No proof of that."

His laughter echoed down the hall.

"You of all people should know better than to say that."

I had to smile.

Fucker was right again.

———

DAYS PASSED AND life resumed. I relaxed and stopped looking over my shoulder. Jill's show was over, and she had departed. I didn't hear from her again, and I was grateful to put it all behind me.

The office was busy, and plans were full steam ahead for Ridge Towers. Richard and Becca were in constant contact with us, and we all looked forward to the final reveal of their campaign. Richard and I kept in contact personally, our relationship evolving into a real friendship. He reminded me of Bentley, his private persona different from that which he presented to the world in general. He was loyal and supportive, and I enjoyed our varied conversations. His wit made me laugh, and his passion for his work and family was infectious.

Reid was especially excited about Becca's arrival in the office. He'd never seemed so invested in any other equipment as he was for her usage. Nor could I recall the outfitting of one office requiring so many phone calls to check on details, as he made to her. It was going to be interesting when she arrived.

The best thing that had happened since the turmoil with Jill was the subtle shift in my relationship with Dee. There was no doubt we had grown closer. We were similar in so many ways, including the fact that we liked order and we both preferred routines. Ours had come easily. Tuesdays were tacos and often bowling or some silly activity with our friends. Thursdays became family dinner night with Aiden and Cami. Dee seemed more at ease with them as a couple and the change in her role in Cami's life, and the evenings were fun. Sundays were brunch with Emmy and Bentley. Aiden and Cami were often there too, the six of us a lively group around the table. The past couple of Sundays, we guys had spent the afternoon watching sports in the media room, while the girls worked on wedding plans.

Dee and I arrived and left together, often sitting with our fingers intertwined. I enjoyed being able to drop a kiss on her cheek or forehead, and she always accepted the hand I offered when we were ready to go. She was relaxed and seemed content. It was rare I ever had to pull her thumb away from her mouth anymore, letting the tender skin finally heal.

I found myself looking for ways to make her smile. To show me the one smile she had that was only for me. The right side of her lips would curl up slightly higher than the left, creating a tiny dimple by her lopsided mouth that made me want to kiss it. So I would. Her eyes shone every time I did, which made me look for another reason to get her to smile.

But it wasn't only the times with our friends when she was different.

When we were alone, she was more open . . . softer. Wanting to be close. Seeking my affection. And for the first time in my life, I wanted to give it. I found that any chance I could get to touch her, I took it.

"Taste this," she requested, lifting a spoon.

I wrapped my arms around her waist, sampling the sauce.

"Good?" she queried. "I wondered if it needed something."

"It's great." I dropped my lips to her neck. "Almost as tasty as you are."

Her laughter was always my reward.

It was rare a day passed when we didn't see each other. Texts happened several times while we were at work, and my favorite moment of the day was when she walked in my door.

I smiled at her, dropping a long kiss to her mouth when she entered the condo. It was late and I knew she was tired, but I was glad she had come up to see me.

I offered her a sip of my whiskey, and she let me hold the glass to her lips as she tilted her head back. I watched her swallow, the movement of her throat muscles oddly arousing. I held up the glass, the slight imprint of her lipstick visible. I turned the glass, lifting it to my mouth directly where her lips had been. Keeping our gazes locked, I drained the glass. "Now that was incredible," I spoke quietly. "Dee-enhanced flavor."

She gave me that smile, then stepped back a few feet.

"I bought you something today."

"Oh?" I asked, bemused, looking for a bag. "What was that, my Dee?"

Her eyes never left mine as she reached to her hip, tugging at the bow resting on the side. In one fluid movement, she shrugged off the silky dress she wore and stood in front of me.

Red satin, black lace, and ribbons met my eyes. Her breasts overflowed the demi-cup corset. Her waist looked tiny, held in by the rigid structure of the design. Black stockings, red high heels, and lace garters encased her legs. And she was bare.

My cock lengthened, desire pumping through my blood fast. Blindly, I set the glass on the ledge beside me. I closed the distance between us, circling around her, running my finger over her bare back and shoulders. A delicate shiver ran down her spine, her chest moving fast with her rapid breaths.

I leaned down to her ear. "Do I get to unwrap my present, Deirdre? Or do you want to be fucked like this?" I kissed her neck lightly, swirling my tongue on her skin.

"Yes."

"Greedy girl tonight, aren't you?" My laughter was low and earned me another shiver.

"Maddox," she whispered. "Please."

"Hmm . . . Unwrap you now . . . or after?"

"Whatever you want."

I snaked my arm around her waist, pulling her close.

"Both."

She stayed again that night. In fact, she stayed a lot of nights. Some of the best ones were when we were quiet, reading or working, but in the same room. She would sometimes stroke my head while we talked about mundane topics or plans. She fell asleep several times, and I scooped her up, carrying her to my bed.

She never left without a kiss.

I never wanted her to leave at all.

And I was ready to tell her. I hoped she was ready to hear it.

Aiden came in, interrupting my thoughts. He flung himself into the chair, munching on a huge sandwich.

I glanced at my watch.

"Bit late for you for lunch isn't it?"

He shook his head, swallowing. "I had lunch. I needed a snack, so Sandy got me a sandwich to tide me over."

I snorted. "Some snack."

"I worked up an appetite. I was out with Van earlier, looking at Bentley's newest project. He wants to put a small workout room in the basement, so I went to give him some advice. Gonna be great when he's done."

"That will be an added feature."

"Yeah. There's a built-in sunroom in the rear of the house with a hot tub in it Van's going to remodel. It'll add another level to the place."

"Great. Bentley's found some terrific properties lately."

He wiped his mouth, crushing the napkin and tossing it into the wastebasket. He lifted his arms. "All net!"

He slouched in the chair as I chuckled.

"He has some great projects on the go. I talked to Van about the cottage too. We're going to go up this weekend and have a look at the property."

"Awesome." I picked up a folder. "Have you seen these leads for other pieces of real estate?"

He took the folder, shaking his head. "Anything good?"

"I like the one on page two. Great potential for investment."

He opened the file and began studying it in his unique, methodical way. I knew not to rush him, so I opened my copy, rereading the particulars.

Aiden and I looked at the door as Bentley hurried into my office.

"What are you two doing tonight?"

We shared a glance, both of us knowing we now had plans.

I relaxed in my chair, twirling my pen. "What's up?"

"Emmy had the sniffles this morning and when I spoke to her just now, it's a full-blown cold. She can barely swallow, and her taste buds are nonexistent."

"And?"

"Tonight is cake testing. She can't taste anything, so she can't go. I don't want to go alone, so I'm using you two as backups."

Aiden grinned and clapped his hands together loudly. "Cake? I'm in."

"The consultant is going to work with us on our tuxedo choices while we're there as well. Save us another trip. The girls are coming after for a dress fitting."

"We all own tuxes. Why do we need new ones?" I asked.

Bentley ran his hand through his hair. "I don't know. I've never been married, or been involved in all these decisions. Something about special occasion and custom fabric—really, I have no idea. I'm simply doing what I'm told to do."

"You said this was going to be small."

"It is small, but I want her to have everything she wants. This woman, Jen, is simply taking the little stuff off her plate. I have to admit, since the girls met with Jen, Emmy has been more relaxed. She tells Jen what she wants, and Jen handles it all." He smirked. "I pay the bills. It works out well for all of us."

"Okay, what time?"

"Seven. She works from her loft. Emmy's message says the cakes will be waiting, we'll do the tux thing, and after, I can go back to being blissfully ignorant of the entire procedure. My other job is to show up and say I do."

We all laughed, because it was true.

"Okay. I'll drive us over," Aiden offered.

"Great. I'll let Emmy know, and she can contact Jen. I'll get the address."

"Okay. Tell her I hope she feels better."

He frowned. "She looked bad this morning and I was worried. If she gets worse, I'll take her to the clinic."

"I'm sure she'll be fine," I assured him. "Lots of colds going around. Maybe take her some soup later."

"That's a good idea. In fact, I'll call Andrew and ask him to go get her some now. And ginger ale. She likes ginger ale when she isn't feeling well."

I hid my grin. Bentley always fussed over Emmy. I didn't bother to tell him his houseman, Andrew, was probably ahead of him. He was very fond of Emmy too, and I knew he would look after her well.

Bentley left, and I grinned at Aiden. "I'm surprised you didn't demand dinner first."

He chuckled. "Nah, the sandwich was a good snack. We can grab dinner after we're done. I want room for cake. Lots of cake. I hope there's chocolate."

"You are such a girl."

He rolled his eyes. "Like you weren't thinking that too."

"I was hoping for carrot cake, actually."

His eyes lit up. "Maybe we can request it."

I picked up the file I'd been reading when Bentley came in. "We'll see, I guess."

⌒

AFTER ARRIVING AT the right building, Bentley pressed the intercom button, and the door opened. We took the elevator to the top floor as Emmy had instructed, entering a vast room. The three of us stood in the middle of what I could only describe as a cyclone. Everywhere we looked, there was color. Bolts of fabric, dresses scattered, shoes lying on top of tables. Wedding dresses hung from the ceiling, lacy trains moving in the air. A huge boardroom table held multiple laptops and monitors plus stacks of invitation and gift samples. Garment bags draped over the chairs. Racks of suits and tuxedos lined the walls. Another table was set up with arrangements and candles, more color swatches piled high. Wedding cakes, fake ones I presumed, were arranged on a shelf. There was so much to take in; I had to shut my eyes. It was overwhelming.

"Holy shit, what is this place?" Aiden hissed.

"Hell," I muttered. "This is hell. Bent, I thought we were going somewhere to eat cake, then a tailor shop?"

"I have no idea," Bentley replied, confused.

"Ah, the three musketeers!" A voice greeted us.

Like a single unit, we spun, to face . . . *Jen?*

He was tall and thin, wearing a kimono with vibrant colored parrots on it, black pants, and flip-flops. He had his bright white hair buzzed, and it matched his short goatee and mustache. Gold glinted in his ears and at his neck. He clapped in delight. "Oh, you are all stunning!"

We exchanged puzzled glances, Bentley looking especially shocked.

Jen came forward, his hand outstretched. "Now, let me guess. You must be Bentley. Your Emmy described you to a T." He winked. "Of course, I may have cheated and checked you out on the internet.

But your pictures don't do you justice! So imposing!"

Bentley blinked and reached out his hand. "Bentley Ridge. How do you do, ah, *Jen?*"

"Jensen Bailey. But I prefer Jen. Aren't you utterly delicious!"

Aiden chuckled, and Jen swung in his direction. "Now you, Tree Trunk, have to be Aiden. Take me to the gun show, my good man."

With a grin, Aiden flexed, and Jen clapped his hands in glee. "Oh, I know the exact tux for you. Tom Ford always gives extra room in the shoulders and forearms. We'll have you comfortable and dashing!"

He turned to me. "And you are exactly as your Dee described. Maddox, the silver fox. Look at you with those bedroom eyes and slim build. I bet you're all muscles under that shirt, aren't you?"

I heard two words in that sentence. *Your Dee.*

I wanted her to be mine.

Aiden began to laugh. "Mad-dox, the silver-fox! That's awesome!"

"Shut it, Tree Trunk." I hissed.

"Both of you shut it," Bentley demanded. "I'm sorry, I, *we*, had expected a woman. Emmy never mentioned your gender."

Jen shook his head, settling his hand on his hip. "Of course she wouldn't. It matters not to her if I am a man or woman—simply that I do my job and make her life easier. Does it bother you?"

"No."

His gaze swung to Aiden and me.

"Boys, do we have a problem?"

"No," Aiden and I spoke in unison.

"Excellent." He turned to Bentley. "Your Emmy is a force unto herself, and I'm thrilled to be assisting her. No matter how simple a wedding is, the devil is in the details. I know you want the day to be perfect for her—am I right, or am I right?"

"Absolutely. Whatever she wants, she gets."

"Then we're on the same page. With me in charge, all your guests will see is a perfect day. All you will see is a happy bride."

Bentley nodded, seemingly at a loss for words.

Jen pointed to a table I hadn't noticed in the chaos. It was set with plates and cups, and lined with boxes all with a bakery logo emblazoned on the side. "You go sit over there. I'll go and get a knife, some utensils and we'll start with the cake tasting. I hope you boys are prepared for heaven!"

He disappeared around the corner, and the three of us sat, dumbfounded. Aiden broke the silence. "Emmy never mentioned *Jen* was a guy?"

Bentley shook his head. "Not that I recall. All I remember is her telling me she met a friend of Cami's who was a wonder with wedding details and decided to use them for help." He shook his head. "We've both been so busy lately, she might have, and I missed it."

Aiden chuckled. "I like him. He's gonna be fun."

"He's been very helpful. Taken a lot off her plate. He narrows everything down to a couple of choices, and she picks what she likes best," Bentley mused.

"Have you been any help at all?"

Bentley chuckled and shook his head. "No. Other than asking her to marry me and giving her carte blanche with the bank account. I only want to make her my wife. I'd happily do it at the registrar's office and have tacos for dinner after we were done. But she wants something more, so I'm giving it to her."

Jen came around the corner. "Spoken like a true man in denial. Good thing she has me." He sat in front of us, smiling. "Weddings, no matter how small, need attention. I handle all that and let her have the day she is dreaming of. You look after the rest of her life. Deal?"

Bentley relaxed and grinned. "Deal."

Aiden clapped his hands. "Enough of what Emmy wants. I want cake."

Jen grinned, reaching for a box. "And cake you will have."

CHAPTER 16

MADDOX

AIDEN GROANED, LICKING the icing off his fork. "The banana chocolate cake. And the fudge one."

I shook my head. "No, the carrot. And that salted caramel thing."

"Torte," Jen informed me. "It's a torte."

"I liked the vanilla with the buttercream frosting," Bentley said. "And the red velvet."

"That spiced raisin one was pretty awesome too," Aiden pointed out.

Jen laughed. "So far the cake none of you have mentioned is the coconut."

We all grimaced. None of us liked coconut, although I admitted it looked nice. It tasted like shit.

"I think I need a few more bites, you know, before we decide." Aiden grinned.

"Which kind?" Jen asked, lifting the knife.

"Um, all of them. Just to be sure."

Jen's laughter was loud and highly entertaining, as we tasted the cakes. He shared horror stories of bridezillas and fainting grooms. Disappearing bridesmaids and fathers' speeches that had run the gamut from oversharing to threatening. All of the stories made us laugh.

I rolled my eyes. "You've already tried them all twice, Aiden!"

"Hey!" he protested. "I'm doing this for Bentley. I take my role as best man seriously."

I snorted, then held out my plate. "As second-in-command, I think I need more carrot cake."

Jen sliced a generous piece and slid it onto my plate. He held up a piece of vanilla and Bentley accepted it with a grin.

"I'm not sure how to decide," Bentley admitted. "I don't think Emmy wants a seven-layered cake."

"Maybe we should draw straws," Aiden offered.

"Or vote," I mused.

Jen shook his head. "We could go a different route and have a cake table."

"What is that?"

"Instead of one cake, have them all. We can have servers there, and guests can pick one piece or a taste of each, the way you have tonight."

Aiden grinned. "That's my vote!"

Bentley pursed his lips, then looked at Jen. "Do you think Emmy would like that? There won't be a cake to cut, and I think that was something she wanted."

"We can do both. We'll do the white one with the buttercream icing you liked as the wedding cake. Emmy already chose a simple three-tiered design. That will be the centerpiece. You cut that one, have pictures, and the guests still get to choose. It's a very pleasing option." He smiled. "Terribly extravagant, but pleasing. I think Emmy would love it."

"Done." Bentley nodded.

"Woo-hoo," Aiden crowed, finishing his cake and setting his plate on the table. "So, ah, what happens to the rest of these cakes? You don't throw them out or something awful, do you?"

Jen chuckled. "No. They go home with Bentley."

"Oh."

Jen stood. "Of course, I could always put a few slices into another box." He winked. "That happens on occasion."

I cleared my throat, and Jen patted my shoulder. "Or two boxes."

Aiden beamed. "Jen, don't take this the wrong way, but I think I love you."

Jen waved his hand. "Happens all the time."

I had to laugh. I bet it did.

⌒

"DO YOU LIFT small children on a daily basis?" Jen murmured, measuring Aiden's arms. He double-checked the tape measure with a shake of his head.

Aiden grinned. "Only on Thursdays. Otherwise, I use Cami." He mimicked an imitation of Cami on his hips riding him, making Jen guffaw and slap his arm. I held back my chuckle at his lewd gesture.

When Jen tried to measure Aiden's chest, he stared over the top of his half-moon glasses in amazement. "I have four inches of tape measure left over. You're built like a brick shithouse. Solid."

Aiden's head fell back, his chest shaking with laughter. "Bentley would tell you I'm full of shit too."

"Uh-huh," Bentley muttered, tapping away on his phone. "He is."

Jen patted Aiden's arm. "Ignore him."

"I usually do."

Jen finished with Aiden, describing the cut he was having made for him, then I was next.

"Now, you, Mr. Silver Fox." Jen winked. "Gucci. Their suits are wonderful on lean frames." He wrote down measurements and notes, efficient and professional.

"What color?" I asked, as he measured my arm length.

"A dark charcoal gray. All of you. Emmy felt black was too harsh."

"What about the girls?" I queried.

Jen smiled. "A rich blue. Bentley's favorite, I believe." He reached for a jacket. "Slip this on. It's the wrong color, but you'll see what I mean about the cut."

I studied my reflection. "Nice, but it needs something."

"No," Bentley objected. "Classic tuxes."

I shook my head, catching Jen's eye with a subtle wink. "No, it's bland."

Aiden hunched forward, his hands resting on his knees. "I like mine plain, but I know you prefer to jazz things up, Mad Dog. What did you have in mind?"

"A vest."

Jen nodded. "Always an option. Bentley's will have one."

"It will?" Bentley asked.

"Oh yes. Emmy wants you in the full package. Tails, vest, a top hat if I can talk you into it."

"I don't fucking think so. I am *not* wearing a top hat."

Jen shrugged. "Your choice. But you're wearing tails. And a vest."

"We'll see about that."

I hid my smile. "Well, if Bent gets a vest, I want one." My gaze fell on a wild fabric sample, and I grabbed it, holding it to my chest. "Like this."

Bentley's eyes almost burst out of his head at the bright swirls of teal and green. A vein pulsed in his forehead like a volcano about to erupt. "Like hell."

"Yep," I egged him on. "I need it to pop."

"I am going to pop you if you don't shut up. No fucking swirly vest. And if you think you're wearing one of your clown-loving pairs of socks, you can think again, Maddox Riley. Black socks. Gray tux. No swirls. It's my fucking wedding."

"Groomzilla, I presume?" I managed to get out before I started to laugh. Aiden leaned back, his guffaws loud, and even Jen couldn't stop his amusement.

"Your face, Bent." I snorted. "You should see your face."

He glared at first, but then stopped when he thought about it. "Holy shit, I said that, didn't I? *My wedding*. Like those shows." He wiped a hand over his face. "A few hours in here and I turn into a damn girl." He joined in our laughter.

Jen wiped his eyes. "Oh, you three." He pulled a fabric swatch from the pile. "Emmy already knew you would want a vest, Maddox. She chose this—it will go with the ties and pocket squares, which match the girls' dresses."

I took the fabric from his hand, studying the print. The silver and deep, rich blue brocade was subtle but striking. "I like this."

"I thought you might. I am having it made for you to go with the suit."

I looked over to Bentley. "Will this bother you?"

He shook his head. "No, I'm over my tantrum. But I don't want a patterned one," he insisted.

I slipped off the jacket and sat down, still grinning.

Jen waved Bentley over. "You each get a different tux, catered to what suits you best. The same with the girls. Same color, different dress. Emmy wants everyone happy."

Bentley was patient as Jen measured him, but he frowned often.

"Tails?" he repeated. "I was hoping for a simple, classic tux."

Jen walked to a rack, pulling off another jacket—that one longer. He stood behind Bentley. "Arms up," he instructed.

The jacket slid across Bentley's shoulders. It fell mid-thigh, the cut sophisticated and suited to his broad shoulders. He stared at his reflection.

"You will have a vest as well, but the same fabric as the tux, unlike Maddox. It's an old-fashioned look, but very stylish again. The cut flatters you."

"It looks good, Bent," I offered.

"It does suit you," Aiden said.

Bentley tugged on the sleeves, still silent.

"Emmy thought you would like it. She wanted you to wear it,

but if you prefer a more modern cut, I'll tell her," Jen stated.

"I like it," Bentley said. "I didn't think I would, but I do. I'm surprised."

"I think your Emmy knows you rather well."

A smile lit Bentley's face, softening his serious expression. "Yes, she does. Okay, Jen. Tails, it is. But no hat."

Jen grinned, helping Bentley off with the jacket. "That was my big wish," he admitted. "I do love a man in a top hat."

"Sorry. Not happening."

"That's fine. But so you know? The socks are blue, Bentley. There is no point in arguing over it either. You're going to lose."

"Fine," he huffed. "Blue socks."

Jen nodded. "Blue socks."

I hid my smile. The old minx knew exactly what he was doing.

⌒

THE GIRLS ARRIVED, chatting as they came in. My gaze found Dee's, and she smiled, her dimple appearing like a small dip in her skin then smoothing out. Like a magnet, I was drawn to her side, and I immediately wrapped an arm around her waist. I pressed a kiss to her cheek, my greeting low so only she could hear.

"Hello, my Dee. You're a sight for sore eyes."

Her gaze was warm and her body loose in my embrace. The first time I had called her "my Dee," she had been startled, but she was used to it now. Neither of us was big on endearments, but I thought she liked the slightly possessive feel of my name for her. I knew she loved it when I called her Deirdre in private, but that brought a whole other reaction from her.

"Did you pick out a cake?"

I led her into the room with a laugh. "Oh, we over-picked."

Jen embraced her and Cami, filling them in on the idea. Cami grinned from her spot on Aiden's lap, stating she was sure Emmy would like the idea.

"She does," Bentley spoke up. "I texted her to make sure."

Jen stood back, smiling widely. "What a lovely wedding party you all will make. Now, girls, time for a fitting. Do you want the dresses a secret until the day?"

Cami stood. "Aiden has already seen the sketches, but yes, I think I would like the final dress a surprise for the day of the wedding."

I looked at Cami, amazed. "I didn't know you designed the dresses. You never said anything."

She smiled, looking shy. "Yes, I did. Emmy's too."

Aiden draped his arm around her shoulders, tucking her into his side. He dropped a kiss to her forehead and grinned proudly. "They're spectacular."

"Hush," she admonished him.

I inclined my head. "Given how talented you are, Cami, I'm sure he's telling the truth."

Bentley nodded. "I have no doubt. Emmy said you made her dream dress. I can hardly wait to see her in it."

Cami looked down, her cheeks flushed.

Dee laughed. "Stop embarrassing my sister."

"All right." Jen clapped his hands. "You know where they are. Go slip into them and I will be along."

"How long will you be?" I asked.

"Half an hour or so." Dee looked hesitant. "You don't have to wait."

I shook my head. "Yeah, I do. Go do your thing. We'll be here when you're ready."

She squeezed my hand, a delighted smile on her face. "Okay."

⌒

THE AIR WAS cool but pleasant when we left Jen's place. I helped load the trunk with the extra boxes, including mine, and turned to Dee.

"It's a great night. Fancy walking home?"

"I'd like that."

We waved off Aiden, Cami, and Bent, and watched as they drove away. I held out my hand, entwining my fingers with Dee's, and we headed home.

I told her how shocked we'd been to discover Jen was a man and me recounting my reaction to the chaos that surrounded him, made her laugh.

"He is eccentric and uninhibited, but he is so good at keeping others organized. His business is booming."

"How did Cami meet him?"

"In one of her classes. I think he was a guest lecturer. They started talking and formed a friendship. He often asks for her advice on fashion. He is very sought after, but for Cami, he agreed to help Emmy."

"I like him. He's a riot." By the time I relayed the entire vest story, she was almost weeping with laughter.

"Oh, I wish I'd seen that."

"It was the funniest thing." I sighed. "It felt good to laugh."

She reached across, hugging my arm. "I know. It's good to be back to normal, yes?"

I dropped a kiss to her head. "Yes." I stopped at the corner. "Through the park or the street?"

"It's late."

I chuckled. "The park is well lit." I tugged her into my arms and kissed her. "I promise you'll be perfectly safe."

"Park, then."

I steered her across the street, asking about her day. We took our time strolling through the small park. There were several other couples out walking and a few joggers getting their last run in for the day, and even a pretzel cart still open and doing business.

I looked at Dee. "Pretzel?"

"Oh yes."

"Mustard or cheese sauce?"

"Um, cheese sauce, of course."

I kissed the end of her nose. "Of course. Grab a bench and I'll bring it over."

I waited behind the short line, glancing at Dee, and my heart swelled. The streetlight caught the color of her hair, turning it into a fiery glow around her face. She was elegant and lovely sitting on the bench, her legs crossed, foot swinging.

The thought of those legs wrapped around me later made my cock twitch, and I shook my head to clear it. I heard her low laughter, and I knew she was thinking the same thing. She was so perfect for me. I had the feeling she was beginning to see that.

I winked at her, got our pretzel and the small cup of cheese sauce, and joined her on the bench. A slight wind stirred her hair, and she shivered a little. I looked around and stood, holding out my hand.

"There's another bench around the corner out of the breeze. We can sit there."

She followed, and we settled on the wooden planks. "Better?"

"Yes."

It was a little dimmer and more secluded, yet we could still see other people. We ate the warm pretzel, watching as the park grew emptier, sharing bits of our day. The pretzel cart shut down, his day done. He wheeled his cart in the other direction, and the area became deserted.

"I think we scared everyone away," she mused, wiping her mouth. "That was so good. I can't remember the last time I had one."

"I know. Probably the last baseball game I went to with Bent and Aiden."

"You have a little cheese sauce by your lip," she pointed out.

I wiped at the corner. "Okay?"

"No, it's still there."

I wiped with my finger and looked at it. It was clean. "Did I miss it again?"

She turned, lifting her hands. I lowered my face so she could get the smear, but she surprised me when, instead, she cupped my face, pressing her lips to the side of my mouth.

"Oh, my bad," she breathed out. "It was a shadow." She brushed her mouth over mine again. "My mistake."

I smiled against her lips. "I think, Deirdre, you simply wanted a kiss."

"And if I did?"

"All you have to do is ask."

She shifted closer. "All you have to do is take, Maddox." She ran her tongue over my bottom lip.

With a low growl, I jerked her toward me, crushing her to my chest and sliding my tongue into her mouth.

She tasted of salt, pretzel, and Dee. It was intoxicating. I fisted her hair in my hands, tilting her head and kissing her harder. She clutched at my jacket, her hands wrinkling the lapels, yanking on the fabric, and I didn't care.

I wanted her closer.

I slid my arm around her, holding her tight. She wrapped her arms around my neck, playing with the hair at my nape. Her breath filled my mouth. Her scent filled my head. I groaned low in my throat. She whimpered her reply. Our tongues touched, danced, fought for control. I retreated; she advanced. I pushed back; she relented. It continued until we were breathless, needy, and gasping for air. Lost to the moment.

To each other.

I buried my face in her neck.

Emotion I never thought I would experience burst from my heart. Words I never thought I would express to another person fell from my lips.

"I love you."

Dee stiffened, drawing back, her face shocked.

"Don't . . ."

I silenced her with my mouth.

"I love you," I repeated.

She shook her head. "No."

I cupped her face, holding her head still. "I love you."

"You can't," she whispered, fear filling her eyes.

"I can and I do. I love you, Deirdre Wilson. With every fiber of my being, I love you."

She clutched my wrists, prying my hands from her face. She stood, jerky and uncoordinated.

"We need to go home now."

I gaped at her. "That's all you have to say?"

"What do you want me to say?"

A ripple went through my chest, and I stood, staring down at her. "I want you to tell me what you're feeling."

Her thumb went to her mouth, her teeth moving so fast I knew she would bring blood. I snatched it away, holding her hand within mine. "What are you thinking, Dee?"

"That you're caught up in this wedding craze. You don't mean it. Let's go home and forget what you said."

I stepped back as if she had slapped me. "Forget it? Caught up? I'm not caught up in anything except the fact that I love you. I've loved you for weeks and I was waiting for you to feel it too. Waiting for the right time."

"You don't love me."

Anger and rejection made my voice sharp. "Don't tell me how I feel."

"Maddox, let's go home. It's late, I'm tired, and you'll regret this in the morning."

"The one thing I'll regret is your reaction. I tell you I love you—something I have never said to another person—and you tell me I don't?"

"It's not part of our arrangement!" she insisted, her voice rising in pitch.

I stepped closer, holding her hand against my chest. "*Fuck* the arrangement, Dee. Forget all that shit. This is you and me. Now. Us. I love you."

She shook her head. "No."

"So, what? All this has just been fun? The dinners and laughter? The closeness? You're telling me that was all fake? All part of the arrangement?"

"No, Maddox!"

"Then what are you saying?"

Our eyes locked, her gaze tormented. Mine pleaded with her, bleeding love and need.

"I care about you, Maddox. I've always cared."

"But . . ."

"I don't love you. I can never love you."

I stepped back, pain lancing through my chest.

She didn't love me.

She could never love me.

I stared at her, my spine rigid, my neck tight.

How did I misjudge the situation so badly?

I lifted my hand, shocked to feel wetness on my face.

Reality hit me—cold, bitter, and excruciating.

Once again, someone had denied me love, and I was letting that person see my weakness.

I dashed away the traitorous dampness and cleared my throat.

"Well, that changes everything, I suppose."

"It doesn't have to."

I barked out a laugh. "Yes, Dee, it does."

"We can forget what happened, what you said. Go back to how it was twenty minutes ago."

I shook my head. "I can't stop loving you, Dee."

A tear ran down her face. "And I can't start loving you, Maddox."

I felt the fissure in my heart, the one that had begun to mend and heal the last few weeks, burst apart. My voice turned cold and distant.

"Then I suppose it's done."

Without a word, she turned and ran. And I let her.

She ran from me. The love I offered. The life I wanted to share with her.

I sat down heavily, my legs no longer able to support me. I had no idea how much time passed before I stood. Forcing my feet to walk, one slow step at a time, I made my way toward my condo building. My mind was blank, my brain working overtime to stop her words from breaking through.

"I don't love you. I can never love you."

At the edge of the park, I lifted my head and looked across the street. The lights in my penthouse that automatically came on at dusk burned high above the street. Like a martyr, I counted down ten floors, finding Dee's windows. They were dark.

With a heavy sigh, I knew I didn't want to go to my place quite yet. I walked down the street to the coffee shop and sat at the old counter, sipping the bitter brew. The lump I felt in my throat made it difficult to swallow, but I kept going, losing track of time, drinking cup after cup.

Dee's words played on repeat in my head. Every time I heard them, it was as if a fresh wound opened. I felt exhausted, my shoulders hunched over, too weary to hold myself straight.

She had witnessed my pain, the agony her denial had drilled into me, yet she still left.

I couldn't wrap my brain around the woman who walked away and the woman I had fallen in love with.

Resigned, I wondered if I ever would.

"Hun, are you all right?"

Blinking, I looked into the concerned gaze of the waitress and cleared my throat.

"Yes, thanks. I'm fine." I lifted my cup, ignoring the slight tremble to my hand. "I'd like a refill if it isn't too much trouble"—I glanced at her nametag—"Valerie."

She tilted her head, studying me. Her brown eyes were kind, the laugh lines around them countless. But she shook her head. "I think, young man, what you need to do is to go home, or call a friend."

"I just need more coffee."

"Sweetie, you've had six cups. You've been sitting there for hours, staring into space. Is there someone I can call for you or something?"

I glanced at my watch, shocked to see she was right. Embarrassed, I stood, tossed a fifty on the counter, and shook my head.

"Sorry, lost track of time. Have a good night." I hurried away before she could speak again.

Outside, I drew in a deep lungful of air, knowing I had to return to the condo.

The area was quiet, the street almost deserted as I began to cross to the other side. I dug my hand into my pocket for my keys, moving on autopilot. My eyes were unfocused, my head elsewhere, when a yell startled me. I looked up, my response too sluggish to stop what was about to occur.

In slow motion, it happened. A car bore down on me, the headlights blinding. My body froze, waiting for the certain impact of metal against bone. A sudden thrust behind me forced my body to jerk to the side, and briefly, it felt as if I was flying. Then pain exploded in my head, my body screaming from the sudden impact.

Burning, tearing agony ripped through me. There were screams, tires squealing, and running feet. Voices that spoke, but I couldn't make out the words or if it was me they were directed toward.

Darkness flickered, gradually engulfing me. I fought it—needing something—needing someone.

"Dee," I breathed out, reaching, searching aimlessly with my hand. "Please."

But I was alone.

I welcomed the black.

CHAPTER 17

DEE

I RAN. BLINDLY, without thought. I ran to escape.

Maddox's words echoed in my head.

I can't stop loving you, Dee.

Then I suppose it's done.

The devastation on his face. The pain in his eyes. The wetness on his skin. The abrupt, cold tone of his voice.

I had done that.

To him.

To me.

To us.

I barely made it to my apartment before I fell apart. I slid down the wall, tears streaming down my face unheeded as I sobbed.

For the anguish I caused him.

My cowardice.

My inability to give him the one thing he asked for.

My love.

I crumpled to the carpet, letting my pain wash over me.

I wept until I had no tears left and my head ached. Pushing myself off the floor, I left my purse and jacket where they lay. Stumbling down the hall, I didn't bother to turn on any lights.

The dim bulbs in the night-lights were all I could stand.

I washed my face and brushed my teeth. Tugged off my clothes and threw on a nightshirt. Left my discarded clothing on the floor.

My bed was cold, my body colder. I drew up the comforter, rolled over, and buried my face into the pillow. Instantly, Maddox's scent hit me, citrus and fresh ocean air washed over me, making my heart clench.

He stayed the night often lately, another one of our rules smashed.

Without my even realizing it, he had broken them all, one by one. And I allowed it. Slowly, surely, he had become entrenched in my life, until I had forgotten what it was like without him. He was part of my days and my nights.

Texts, calls, dinners. Conversations, advice, support, comfort.

I began to crave his smile, his laughter, his warmth. His body.

Sex with Maddox was unlike anything I had ever experienced before—or would again. He commanded my body, my mind, and my release, driving me to levels of pleasure I didn't know existed. He did it all with the greatest of care, the sexiest of smirks, and the most indulgent of touches.

I pushed up on my arms, leaning against the headboard when it hit me.

He would never be in my bed again.

He had obliterated the final, absolute rule, and this time, I had refused him.

The tears began again and I gathered his pillow close, weeping into the fabric, until sleep took me.

A SHORT TIME later, I woke with my eyes feeling like sandpaper and my throat dry and aching. I slid from the bed, padding down the hall to the kitchen. After getting a bottle of water from the fridge, I squinted at the clock. It was four in the morning, but I knew I was done with sleeping. The night had been filled with dreams—images of Maddox. His pain-filled eyes. His arguing. Worse, his pleading.

Every time I shut my eyes, I saw him. His bereft expression. The shock of his tears.

I set down the bottle, and sat at the table as a fresh wave of hurt drifted through me. My reflection stared at me in the darkness as I looked out the window. I ran a hand through my tangled hair, pulling on the twisted strands. My eyes were swollen, my face pale. My mother came to mind, and I realized I resembled her in that moment. Physically, Cami resembled her more, even though for a time, she been worried she also inherited her instability. But Cami was wrong.

I was the one who had.

I ran my finger over the wooden tabletop, letting my thoughts and fears come to the forefront of my brain.

Remembering.

After the affair ended with my former co-worker Todd, I went through a difficult time. It wasn't until it was over that I had realized how deep I'd been entrenched with him. I had based all my decisions on him. Everything I did was with him in mind. Like my mother's incessant behavior, I was fixated on him. I needed him for my identity. I pushed my work aside to make sure he shone. I ignored my friends to spend time with him. When it was over, despite the horrible things I found out and the terrible way he treated me, I was lost without him. I became depressed and anxious. I couldn't sleep, eat, or concentrate.

And like the secret I kept of the affair, I hid the aftermath. Cami had no idea. The people at work had no idea. I struggled and slid deeper, until I finally went for counseling. It took a year of sorting through issues and facing reality before I felt like myself again. Antidepressants, sessions, talking, and tears. When it was over, I swore

I would never again place myself in that position. I would never allow love to make me so weak. I would never again become like my mother.

And Todd had been a blip on my radar compared to the storm Maddox had become in my life. Engulfing, raging, obliterating everything in its path like a catastrophic Category 5 hurricane.

That was how he made me feel.

If I succumbed to him and it blew up in our faces, I would never recover.

So I couldn't allow it.

Shaking my head, I headed to the shower, my actions on autopilot. I stood in front of my closet, unsure what to wear, not caring in the least, when I heard the sound of the alarm system engaging and the door to the apartment opening.

For a moment, I froze. Surely Maddox wouldn't simply show up, not after the way we left things last night?

I heard Cami's voice calling my name. I sagged with both relief and disappointment.

She appeared in my doorway, disheveled, her eyes red and swollen.

"Cami!" Hurrying over, I grabbed her by the shoulders. "What is it? What's wrong?"

"You have to come, Dee. We have to go to the hospital."

Frantic, I ran my hands over her. "Are you hurt? Where's Aiden?"

She shook her head, more tears running down her face.

"He's in the car, waiting. It's Maddox, Dee." She shivered. "He-He's been in an accident. You have to come."

⌒

THE ER WAS busy, the waiting room crowded. Bentley was easy to spot. He paced in the corner, his hands shoved into his pockets. I still had no idea what was going on.

Aiden had been on the phone the whole time we drove to the hospital, his one-sided conversation quiet, his voice intense. He dropped us off and went to park the car, reappearing so quickly, I knew he had run the whole way.

Bentley saw us and stopped his pacing for a moment to give us a hug. His forehead was creased with worry, his eyes anxious.

"Any word?" Aiden asked.

"No. The doctors are still with him. They know I'm here, and they'll be out to update us when they can."

"How did you know?" I asked.

"I'm listed as his emergency contact. Aiden and I both, actually. We also have power of attorney for medical issues for each other." He frowned. "Something I've always hoped would only ever be a formality."

I glanced around. "Emmy?" I asked.

He shook his head. "Too sick. I promised I would keep her updated."

"I called Sandy. She'll be here shortly," Aiden said.

Bentley nodded absently.

"Where was the accident?" I asked. "Was he on his way to work? Did someone run a red light?"

Bentley frowned and glanced at Aiden. Bentley took my hand, tugging me to a chair. "He was struck after coming out of the coffee shop, Dee."

My brain wasn't computing. "But the coffee shop is in your building," I stated.

"The coffee shop down the street from the condo."

I gaped at him.

He bent close, his voice almost a whisper. "Why was he at the coffee shop at three a.m.?"

My chin quivered. "We had an argument in the park. I went home. I thought-I thought he followed."

His eyes widened in understanding, and he patted my shoulder. "This isn't your fault."

"The guy who witnessed it said it was as if the car was headed right for Maddox," Aiden explained. "Fucking hit-and-run."

Ice filled my veins. "What did you say?"

"Some guy getting out of his car saw the whole thing. He yelled and grabbed Maddox's coat. The driver kept going. His friend in the car got a partial plate."

I shot out of my chair, my fists clenched. "It was her!"

Bentley stood. "Who?"

"That crazy bitch, Jill!"

He shook his head. "She left town, Dee."

"No," I insisted. "She's done it before." I grabbed Bentley's jacket. "She did this to him already!"

He wrapped his hands around my arms. "Okay, calm down. What do you mean?"

"In university. Maddox told me she clipped him with her car, but she denied it. Her roommate vouched for her, but he was certain. He let it go, because he had no proof. The first night she saw him here at the restaurant, she pulled so close to the car, he was pinned against the driver's door. He was spooked when he got in the car." I looked at Aiden, sobbing. "It was her, Aiden. She did this to him."

"The witness said he thought it was a woman," Aiden muttered.

Bentley pulled me into his arms, hugging me hard. "Okay, Dee. It's okay." He looked at Aiden. "Go."

Aiden pulled out his phone. "Yep. On it."

Bentley sat me down beside Cami, kneeling in front of me. She grabbed my hand and held it tight.

"We're gonna get to the bottom of it." Bentley assured me.

I could only nod. He tugged his hand through his hair. "He never told me any of that."

"I don't think he wanted to talk about it." I wiped my cheeks.

A doctor came into the room, heading our way. Bentley sprang to his feet.

The doctor looked grim. My tears began again.

"He needs surgery. There are cracked ribs, contusions and deep cuts, and a serious head injury. We also suspect internal bleeding we need to find and stop. His brain is swelling, and we need to relieve the pressure."

I covered my mouth, trying not to scream.

"I'm not going to lie, he's in bad shape. The faster we get in, the better his chances."

My stomach lurched, and I grabbed Cami.

"We need you to sign some papers, Mr. Ridge."

"He is B negative," Bentley stated. "I know that's rare."

"We're checking with the blood bank."

I stood. "No. I'm B negative as well. I want to make a direct blood donation for Maddox."

Cami stood. "You hate needles," she whispered, grabbing my arm. "Let them check."

I drew in a deep breath. "No. Not for Maddox. I'm doing this for him."

The doctor nodded. "That will save us a lot of time. Come with me, and we'll get you started."

I followed him blindly, praying.

⁓

THE MACHINE SPUN steadily, the red blood leaving my body. Blood I hoped would help Maddox. The staff had been great, rushing through the paperwork, getting the procedure started. I couldn't explain it to Cami, or to anyone.

I had to be the one to do it. I wanted my blood inside Maddox, healing him, giving him strength. I owed him that much at least.

I squeezed the ball, letting my eyes shut. A few minutes later, I heard the curtain slide open and felt someone sit beside me. I opened my eyes to meet Bentley's calm gaze.

"He's headed to surgery soon." He nodded in the direction of the bag filling with my blood. "This will help."

"Good."

"Aiden spoke with the police. They're going to investigate. The partial plate and the witness helped."

"Aiden said the witness pulled Maddox out of the way?"

Bentley nodded, scrubbing his face. "He said Maddox didn't seem to notice the car headed straight for him. He yanked Maddox by the coat, so the car sideswiped him instead of a direct hit. It was hard enough, though. Maddox flew." Bentley sighed. "He landed in a pile of garbage, but hit his head on the concrete. This guy's actions saved his life."

I couldn't respond. Because of my cruel rejection, Maddox had been on the street. Because of my words, he hadn't paid attention. Because of me, he was injured and fighting for his life. I covered my face and sobbed.

Bentley shook me gently. "Stop it, Dee. Maddox needs you strong. He's going to have a fight ahead of him."

I shook my head, unable to look him in the eye. "He won't want me there."

Frowning, he tilted up my chin with his finger. "What are you talking about? You had a fight. All couples have fights. When he wakes up, you'll make amends."

I couldn't see him through my thick tears. "He told me he loved me. I told me no."

"What do you mean?"

"I-I told him I d-didn't love him."

There was a beat of silence. "Did you mean it?"

"I don't know."

"Your actions aren't those of someone who doesn't care, Dee."

I wiped my eyes. "I do care. But I don't think I'm capable of the kind of love Maddox wants from me."

He studied me. "I think you're wrong."

"Why would you say that?"

He smiled, pulling a tissue from the box and wiping my cheeks. "I know you, Dee. I've seen the way you care for all of us. How you took care of Emmy after she was kidnapped. Your love for your sister. I've watched the way Maddox has come to life because of you. The way you've changed."

"How?"

He shrugged. "You're more open. You smile and laugh. God, Maddox laughs. In the office, he's relaxed, more involved. He talks about the future, whereas before, I could barely get him to plan for next month. He's . . . happy, Dee. You make him happy. Unless I'm mistaken, he does the same for you."

My hands twisted on the blanket. "He does. But . . ."

He frowned. "Whatever is holding you back, you need to figure it out. But don't give up a chance like this. Work it out with Maddox."

"What if . . ."

He shook his head, looking angry. "Don't even think that." He stood, tugging down his sleeves. "Maddox is going to get through the surgery and recover. We're all going to be there for him. No matter what."

He turned and walked out, his shoulders straight.

I stared after him, his words sinking in.

Was he right? Could I love Maddox? Could I be happy with him? One thing I knew, I couldn't be happy without him.

I sobbed as reality settled over me.

My last words to Maddox were that I cared, but I couldn't love him.

I was wrong.

What if I never got the chance to tell him?

CAMI SAT BESIDE me, her head on my shoulder. I stared down into the cup of coffee I clutched in my hand, the contents long gone cold.

Aiden and Bentley paced. We were in another waiting room on a different floor in the hospital. It was quieter and empty.

Sandy sat in the corner, silent and clearly upset, but her hands busy as she knitted steadily.

A movement caught my eye, and I looked up. Emmy was in the doorway. She was wan and pale, a mask covering her mouth. My gaze flew to Bentley. He crossed the room in fast steps, sweeping her into his arms, lifting her right off the floor. He moved to the corner, sitting down, still holding her. Their voices were hushed, but it was obvious he was glad she was there.

Aiden came over, sitting down heavily beside Cami. She shifted, letting him wrap his massive arm around her shoulder. She sighed, nestling into him. He laid his head on hers, his eyes shutting as he exhaled.

I met Sandy's gaze, filled with worry and sympathy. She gestured to the seat next to her, and I moved over, letting the couples have their moment.

They needed it.

Sandy patted my hand. "Maddox will be fine. He's the strongest of them all."

I nodded as she picked up her knitting once again, her needles flying as she worked. "He finally found his place in this world. It's only right he has the chance to enjoy it."

I couldn't respond.

The surgeon walked in, and we were all on our feet in an instant.

He held up his hand. "He made it through. We had to remove his spleen, and we got the bleeding under control."

"His head injury?" Aiden asked.

"We've put him in a medically induced coma to give him the best chance to recover."

I grabbed Sandy's hand. "For how long?"

"Five days. His body needs a chance to rest and heal. This is the best thing to help with the brain swelling."

"Is there, ah, any permanent damage?" Bentley asked, a frown on his face.

"We won't know that until he wakes up. He's young and strong. He's not out of the woods yet, but he made it over a huge hurdle, and we have every reason to believe he will keep improving." He wiped his brow. "He'll be in recovery for a while, then moved to his room."

"I've arranged a private one," Bentley said.

"Yes, I've been informed you want the best for Mr. Riley."

"Can we see him?"

"Our, ah, regulations state visitors must be family, but I understand an exception has been made in this case."

Bentley crossed his arms. "Yes. And we *are* his family."

The surgeon tilted his head in acknowledgment. "It will be a while until he's in his room. Two people at a time and for short periods—he needs his rest."

"All right."

"The staff will let you know when you can go in."

Bentley and Aiden shook his hand, and he left. I sat down, my legs shaking too much to stand.

"We'll take turns," Aiden stated. "One of us can be with him all the time."

The words were out before I could think.

"I'm not leaving. Until he comes with me, I'm not leaving this hospital. The rest of you can take turns."

No one blinked or argued.

Bentley looked at me and nodded.

"Understood."

CHAPTER 18

DEE

I HAD TO clutch the bedrail when the doctor finally allowed us to see Maddox. I held on so hard the metal shook under my grip, making a clanging noise.

Bentley and Aiden had been the first to go in. Bentley came out, letting Sandy take her turn, then Cami. Bentley had sent Emmy home after convincing a doctor to look at her. Prescription in hand, he escorted her downstairs, waiting until Frank arrived to take her home.

Then he came into the room with me. Seeing my reaction, he slipped an arm around my shoulders. "The machines are there to help him, Dee."

I merely nodded, my throat too thick to speak.

"He's asleep and not in any pain. They're monitoring him closely." He blew out a shaky breath. The slight quiver of his voice let me know he wasn't as calm as he tried to appear. "They said we should talk to him."

"Can-can I touch him?"

"Yes."

I took in a big breath. Then another, trying to calm myself. I approached the side of the bed and slid my hand into Maddox's. I was surprised to feel the warmth of his skin. I sat down on the chair and studied him.

A thick bandage encased his head, obscuring most of his hair. The side of his face was bruised, and the rest of his skin shockingly pale. They had him attached to various machines that pumped and beeped. I broke each one down in my mind so they weren't so frightening to look at. They helped him to breathe and to monitor his vitals. His IV kept him hydrated and his pain under control. I watched the steady rise and fall of his chest and matched my breathing to it. He was so still, and he looked vulnerable with the plain cotton blanket draped over him. I touched it and frowned. It was rough and worn. Serviceable, but not what Maddox liked.

"We need to bring the blanket from the top of my sofa here. He likes that one. It's soft. Maybe the smell would comfort him."

Bentley stood behind me. "Okay. If you insist on staying here with him, you'll need some things brought over. You write a list. Cami and Aiden will go and get them so you're comfortable."

"I don't care about me right now."

He squeezed my shoulders. "Well, I do. I need to make sure you're okay so that you can look after my friend. He needs you strong, Dee."

"Will they let me stay?"

"Yes, I've made the arrangements."

I glanced around the room. Despite the machines and the usual hospital scent, it didn't look like a normal room. There was a small sofa and two large chairs. The walls were painted a muted color with cheerful pictures hung on them. A door stood ajar, showing a private bath.

"Are you paying for all this?" I asked, knowing the room had to be costing a fortune.

"Yes. He will be well cared for until he can go home. When he

3

wakes up, I want him calm. He needs the privacy."

"You're a good friend, Bentley."

He shrugged and glanced away. After a moment, he cleared his throat. "They're keeping him out for about five days. You can't sit here the whole time, so we'll figure out a schedule."

"I've already booked the next few weeks off work," I murmured, unable to take my eyes off Maddox.

"You can do that?"

"I have a lot of vacation time accumulated. I explained that it was a personal matter. If Cami brings my laptop, I can work a little here. My boss was very understanding."

I stroked Maddox's palm and long fingers. I lifted his hand to my cheek, holding it to my skin. I whispered a silent prayer for him, his friends, and the strength I would need to get through the next week and whatever occurred once Maddox woke.

Bentley brushed a kiss on my head. "I'm going to give you some privacy. When you're ready, come get me, and we'll figure everything out."

"Okay."

The door shut behind him, and the only sounds were the machines. I held Maddox's hand, staring at him, fighting the guilt. I knew it was a useless emotion. It wasn't going to help Maddox, yet I still felt it.

"I'm so sorry," I whispered. "I'm sorry my words put you in the path of that car, Maddox. I'll regret that the rest of my life. But I need you to fight right now. Fight to get better and come back. Aiden and Bentley need you." I stifled a sob. "I need you. I need you to open your eyes, tell me you're pissed with me, and call me Deirdre. I'll take it."

There was no movement, not that I expected it. Still, I spoke. "You rest and find your strength. I'll be right here while you do, and I'll be here when you wake." I swallowed the painful lump in my throat. "I promise."

I held his hand to my face and I cried.

⌒

THE NEXT FEW days developed into a routine that I found I relied on. Bentley arrived every morning, Sandy midday, and Aiden late afternoon. Reid came for a couple of hours daily, though his times varied. Cami spent the evenings with me, and now that Emmy was feeling better, she came as well. The hospital staff was very good at ignoring the fact that often there were more than two people in Maddox's room at a time. We were quiet, and I was certain Bentley had made a large enough contribution, nothing was said.

I got to know the nurses and doctors by name. The care and professionalism they showed helped keep me calm.

I made sure to give each person some alone time with Maddox, taking the opportunity to shower, go for a walk, speak to the office, or some other task to stay busy. When it was Maddox and me, I would talk to him about everything. I discussed whatever I was working on for the office, what the nurses were gossiping about, or some silly show I had turned on in the middle of the night—anything so if he could somehow hear, he knew he wasn't alone. As news of Maddox's accident came out, his room began to fill with flowers. The scents were rich and lovely, helping cover the antiseptic smell of the hospital. Every arrangement that arrived, I took a picture of and described it in great detail to Maddox. I read him the notes and tucked them all away in order to send thank you cards once he was well enough.

I touched him constantly. I rubbed lotion into his skin, put Chapstick on his dry lips, and gently stretched his muscles. Aiden had demonstrated some helpful exercises, patiently showing me the right way to move Maddox's legs and arms so that when he woke, his body wouldn't be as atrophied.

The swelling in his brain was going down, and the doctors were pleased. I was counting down the hours until they withdrew the drugs that kept him asleep. They cautioned us it might take him some time to wake fully, and we still didn't know what to expect when he did.

I was intensely anxious. But fewer drugs meant he was on the road to recovery. Whatever happened after he awoke, we could deal with.

He had to wake up, though.

There was a quiet knock at the door, and I was shocked when I glanced up to see Richard VanRyan poke his head into the room. I was sitting beside Maddox, holding his hand, and had been reading out loud. I shut the book and stood, surprised to see him.

"Richard?"

"May I come in?"

"Of course."

He entered, pulling a small suitcase. "Getting in here is harder than Fort Knox," he said. "I had to get Bentley on the phone."

"There've been reporters lurking around."

"I understand."

He stood at the end of the bed, his hands wrapped around the bar. "How is he?"

I ran my fingers over Maddox's face. The bruises were beginning to fade, but were still prominent.

"He is going to be fine."

"Of course he will be."

"They are considering bringing him out of the coma since the swelling has reduced so much. Allow him to wake on his own."

"That's good news."

"It is," I agreed. "Why are you here, Richard?"

He sighed. "I don't know if you know this, Dee, but I spoke with Maddox when all that shit was going down. We got pretty tight. I've been very concerned about what happened after I heard the news, so Katy told me to come and see for myself. I was driving her crazy with worrying."

I joined him at the end of the bed and patted his hand. "That is incredibly kind. Maddox told me about what you did. I know you talked some sense into him."

"I think he would have come to the same conclusion on his own. I helped get him there a little faster is all." He lowered his voice.

"They got her?"

"Yes. They grabbed her before she boarded a flight later that morning. She had been here for a while watching Maddox. Planning this. She thought no one would find out. Her plan had been to hit him, drive away, and no one be the wiser."

"I think she needs to stick to acting, because she's a shit criminal, as well as a shit human."

His words made me smile.

"The only place she'll be acting is in a prisoner drama club. She's facing charges of attempted murder. They have an eyewitness, her signature on the rental car paperwork, and the dent she put in the car when she hit Maddox. Plus, she was so out of it, she sang like a bird, then claimed coercion. She is crazy." I curled my hands in anger. "I hope she rots in prison."

"I think she sealed the deal."

I nodded in agreement.

"How are you holding up?"

"I'm fine."

He chuckled and gave me a fast, one-armed hug. "I learned early on in my relationship with Katy that 'I'm fine' means the complete opposite."

"I'm holding up then."

"Better, but I still think you're sugarcoating it. Are you sleeping?"

"Not much."

"Not eating either, I would say."

"I'm doing the best I can."

He sighed. "Okay, I get it. You want me to mind my own business. I'll let you push me away for now. Why don't you go for a walk and get some fresh air? It's a nice day, and you need the break. I'll sit with him."

I glanced out the window. The sun was out for a change, and I hadn't been outside during the day since this happened.

"He'll be fine, Dee. I'll show him pictures of my wife and kids until he's so bored he wakes up and tells me to shut my mouth."

Again, he made me smile.

"Okay. A short one."

"Nope. I don't want to see you here for a couple of hours. Take a walk, get some food. It will do you good." He pointed to Maddox. "He's going to need you more than ever when he wakes up. So you need to look after yourself." He sat down beside Maddox. "Now go."

I grabbed my purse and sweater, looking over my shoulder. Richard was leaning close to Maddox, talking.

"Dude, you landed in garbage and still managed to hit your head? I am going to hold that over your snooty ass when you come around. You in a pile of garbage—something I never thought I'd see."

I had to shake my head. Aiden and Bentley had been doing the same thing. Teasing him relentlessly. I knew it was how they kept their spirits up and the complexity of their relationship intact. They laughed, teased, and kept it light.

It was how they dealt because they couldn't handle it otherwise.

It showed me how much Richard VanRyan cared.

I slipped away, knowing Maddox was in good hands.

───

AFTER PICKING AT a sandwich, I wandered outside and sat on a bench in the sun, enjoying the fresh air. I let the sounds fade away, concentrating on my breathing.

In, out, in, out. Slow and deep—the same way I did when I sat by Maddox.

"Dee?"

I glanced up, startled at the sound of my name, blank for a moment until recognition set in.

"Lori!"

I stood and hugged my old therapist. She stepped back, holding my arms.

"How are you?"

Before I could respond, she frowned. "Why are you at the hospital? Are you okay? Is Cami?"

My chin quivered, but I hastened to assure her we were both fine.

"What are you doing here?" I asked. "This isn't where you used to work."

"I do a couple of days a week here, plus my office hours, now."

"Oh."

She studied me. "Are you sure you're okay, Dee?"

Something in her voice broke me, and I covered my face with my hands, trying to hide my tears.

"Okay," she soothed. "Come with me."

"No, really, I'm fine."

She tugged my hand. "What did I always tell you during our sessions, Dee? No bullshit. Let's go."

I didn't argue.

⌒

ONCE WE WERE in her office, we sat down in familiar fashion. She was in a straight-backed chair, with tall arms, where she preferred to balance her notebook. I sat in a large, deep armchair that surrounded me, the plushness putting me at ease so our timed session flowed.

But today, there was no notebook and no clock—simply two women talking.

"Tell me," she urged.

That was all it took. I broke and told her everything. How Emmy met Bentley, Cami married Aiden, my feelings of loss. Maddox. My confusion. My guilt. The fear that I did love him but couldn't risk the same behavior as my mother and lose myself. I talked for over forty minutes, and not once did she interrupt me or say anything. She handed me tissues and otherwise listened. When I finally stopped talking, she bent forward, crossed her legs, and leaned on her elbows, staring at me.

"Holy shit."

For some reason, I started to laugh at her declaration.

She shook her head. "How has your head not exploded, Dee?"

I wiped my eyes and shrugged my shoulders.

She leaned back and huffed out a huge breath of air. "Okay, I only have a little while left before I have to go, so I'm going to put this in a nutshell for you."

"All right."

"First, you never should have stopped therapy."

"But I was off the antidepressants and doing so well!"

"You were on the road, Dee, but the journey wasn't complete. I told you then you weren't ready, but you didn't listen." She narrowed her eyes. "You never told anyone you were in therapy. You hid it as if it were something shameful. Without support, we can never truly heal."

I gnawed at my thumb, her words soaking into my befuddled brain. She was right. I had been ashamed I needed therapy. To admit it meant I was like my mother.

"Still abusing your thumb, I see." She tapped my hand. "And no, you are not like your mother, and I'm going to tell you why."

I pulled my thumb out of my mouth, feeling guilty. I hadn't even realized I had muttered my thoughts out loud.

"Dee, you were barely in your twenties when you went through the ordeal with Todd. It forced you to grow up fast, but emotionally, you weren't ready for that sort of relationship. For a normal, well-adjusted adult, it was a train wreck. For someone with no experience, of course it devastated you. You learned from it, but unfortunately the lessons you held on to from it were the wrong ones."

"I don't understand."

"You have avoided love, intimacy for all these years. Used sex as a release without becoming involved. You cut yourself off because of the fear you would become like your mother." She shook her head and held my gaze. "You are nothing like her, Dee. Your mother was ill. The trauma you went through caused a reaction. Simply put—depression. A condition many people suffer from to varying degrees. Some have a bout or two, and that is it. Some suffer from it constantly, the darkness always present in their lives. You have lived in fear of it all this time." She pumped her leg in agitation. "I should have refused to let you stop coming to see me."

A glimmer of a smile touched my lips. "I don't think you can do that."

"No, but I wish I had pushed it more. You need therapy." She paused and gave me a pointed look. "And you need to stop being a chickenshit and admit your feelings for this man."

My eyes widened at her bluntness.

She shrugged. "I'm not your therapist right now. I'm just a friend listening." She leaned forward. "Do you know how precious a gift of love is? You told me how Maddox didn't believe in it either, yet he was brave enough to admit he felt it. Reached out to you. Said the words."

"I know."

"Tell me right now, without thinking, do you love him?"

"Yes."

"Then when he wakes, tell him."

"What if he's changed his mind?" I asked, voicing the fear inside.

"From what you've told me, I don't think that will happen. But if it does, then you'll know you tried. The world won't end, Dee. You'll get out of bed the next day, a little sad and a little weary, but you'll carry on." She smiled and reached for my hand. "You will not fall apart again."

"What if I become my mother with him? Losing myself and becoming only what I think he needs? Putting him above everything else?"

"I don't think he would allow that to happen. He loves you the way you are Dee, not what he wants you to be. And you aren't built that way either. You are far stronger than your mother, and you need to see that."

"How can you be so sure?"

"Because you're not the same girl you were all those years ago. You've grown and changed. You're a woman. A responsible, caring, slightly off-kilter woman who loves a man and needs to stop denying it."

"Off-kilter?"

She raised her eyebrows.

I laughed. "Okay, off-kilter works."

"I'm glad to see you smile."

I sighed. "I don't think I've ever cried this much my entire life. It's not normal for me."

She tilted her head. "Maybe it's time you did cry, Dee. You don't have to be strong all the time anymore. Sometimes crying is your body's way of ridding itself of the stress inside. It is saying 'enough.'"

Again, she made sense.

She glanced at her watch. "Life is meant to be lived, Dee. We have one shot at it. Laugh, cry, love. Don't hide in the shadows—take a page from Cami's book. Grab it and live."

All the air left my lungs as I thought about her words.

She stood, reaching in her purse. She handed me a card. "Please call me. Come see me and let me help you work through it all in your head."

I stood and hugged her. "I will. I promise."

"Good. Now I have to go. I'm meeting my husband and daughter."

"You're married! Oh, how wonderful, Lori. I didn't know."

"It is." She winked. "I highly recommend it." She tapped the card. "Call me."

I followed her down the hall, stopping in the cafeteria to get coffee. I got one for Richard, then hurried back to the room, realizing I had been gone for almost two hours.

I rushed through the door. Richard glanced up. "Oh, here she is. I'll stop talking now. I'm sure you prefer her voice to mine."

He stood with a smile. "Everything's fine, Dee." He studied my face, gratefully accepting the coffee I handed him. "You look like you've been crying. Are you okay?"

I looked at Maddox, lying still in the bed, waiting to wake so he could begin to live again. I was ready to join him.

"Yes," I assured him. "Yes, I'll be fine."

As soon as Maddox woke up, I would be perfect.

CHAPTER 19

DEE

THE NEXT DAY, they stopped the medication that kept Maddox in a coma. Dr. Sampson was very careful as he explained to us that there was a good chance Maddox would still be unconscious for a while and not to panic. The tests showed brain activity, but it was up to Maddox when he woke. Dr. Sampson told us what we saw on TV was not factual.

"He won't awaken in an instant and be fully functioning. It takes time, and his body is still recovering."

We waited for two full days before we saw any change in him. It was subtle. His fingers would twitch. A few times, his eyes flickered open, only to stare blankly and fall shut again. His body would spasm, and on occasion, a guttural sound escaped his mouth. They assured us it was all normal, the pain medication still in effect, and they were positive signs.

I found them frightening, yet with each one, I prayed he was coming back to us. I was never alone now. Someone was always with me. Richard had only stayed for a couple of days, but he was there constantly. After he left, Aiden or Bentley was there, neither one wanting to leave in case he woke. They took turns, leaving briefly to catch up on things at the office, and returning. They dozed in one of the big chairs, always alert. Cami and Emmy sat with me, making sure I ate and showered. The bathroom was the farthest they could get me away from Maddox.

It was late one night while Aiden dozed and I sat with Cami that I told her everything. The affair, the fallout, the deep depression I had sunk into, and the therapy I had sought. I also told her the truth about what happened between Maddox and me. Her eyes filled with tears when I stopped talking.

"Why didn't you tell me about the affair and what you were going through?"

"You were young, Cami. I was trying to look after you. I could barely understand it myself, never mind talk about it with you."

"And Maddox?"

I looked toward the bed. The light in the corner cast a shadow over Maddox's handsome face. He was still, his chest rising and falling with his breathing. Without the noises of the machines, I could hear his steady rhythm and took comfort in it.

The words still frightened me, but I said them. "I love him."

She grasped my hand. "I know."

"I need him to wake up so I can tell him."

She shifted closer. "He will." She hugged me tightly. "I'm sorry you went through all that alone. And I'm sorry you felt you couldn't talk to me." She wiped her eyes. "I struggle at times with all the changes too."

"You do?"

"A couple of weeks ago, I told Aiden how much I missed you. I missed seeing you every day and being able to walk down the hall and talk to you. He wanted to go and buy a big house and have you come live with us. He said he couldn't stand for me to be unhappy."

I peered over her shoulder at Aiden. He was awake, watching us silently. It didn't upset me that he had heard our conversation, especially since I knew Cami would tell him anyway. "That is sweet, but I don't think that's a good idea. I think it's normal we both have to adjust." I threw a wink his way. "You don't need an old woman in your space. You're newlyweds. I'm fine on my own."

Aiden met my eyes and patted his chest. I knew what he was saying, and I loved him for it. He was there and always would be.

Cami sighed. "Maybe you won't be on your own soon."

"First, Maddox needs to awaken and forgive me. Then we'll see what the future holds."

I glanced at the clock and stood. "Aiden should take you home. You have school tomorrow and it's late."

"Always worried about me."

I dropped a kiss on her head. "That is never going to change."

She smiled at me. "Good."

IT HAPPENED WHEN I least expected it. Bentley was at the end of Maddox's bed, texting on his phone. I was rubbing some cream into Maddox's skin, while Aiden worked his other arm in a slow, steady circle.

"He's slid down a little, Aiden. Can you lift him a bit while I adjust his pillows?"

"Yep." He bent down, carefully sliding his arms under Maddox. I shifted and plumped the pillows, and Aiden settled him back on the bed.

Maddox's eyes were open and staring.

Aiden froze, still holding him. "Mad Dog?"

My breath caught. Bentley looked up, his phone forgotten. He leaned on the bed, his voice anxious. "Mad? Buddy?"

Maddox blinked, his gaze flying around the room. His hand clenched, and I slid my fingers between his, squeezing it.

"Maddox?" I whispered, the sound of my voice causing him to turn his head in my direction. I lifted his hand to my chest, cradling it close.

He blinked again, swallowed, looked at Aiden, and spoke. His voice was low, raspy, and it sounded painful.

"What the hell are you doing in my room, Aiden? And why are you holding me?"

Aiden's face broke into a wide grin. "Giving you your biggest fantasy, Mad Dog."

Bentley made an odd noise in the back of his throat. Maddox's gaze flew to him. "Bent?"

"I'm here, Maddox."

Maddox's heart monitor began to climb, his breathing increasing. I leaned over, cupping his face. "It's okay, Maddox. Calm down. Everything is fine."

"I-I don't understand . . ." He began to panic. "Where am I?" He frowned. "Why are you here?" He directed his question at me.

My heart ached at his words. Aiden pressed the button for the nurse. I stroked his head, trying not to react. "Everything is okay," I soothed. "I promise."

His heart rate monitor continued to rise. Beads of sweat covered his brow.

The door opened, and Dr. Sampson strode in, followed by a nurse. "Clear the room." His voice left no space to argue.

Bentley tugged me away. The doctor took my place, leaning over Maddox. "Welcome back, Mr. Riley."

The last thing I saw was Maddox's eyes staring at me as the door shut.

In the hall, I looked at Bentley. He squeezed my shoulder. "He's awake. He knew us. This is all good."

"He wasn't happy to see me."

He shook his head. "He was confused. I would be if I woke up and saw Aiden standing over me, in a strange place."

"Hey," Aiden interjected.

Bentley ignored him.

"They'll help him settle. He'll be fine."

I glanced at the closed door, desperate to be on the other side of it. Panic seized me, and I began breathing fast.

Aiden wrapped his arm around my shoulder, pushing me into a chair. He tilted my head down. "Relax, Dee. Breathe, okay. Just breathe."

I struggled to get in the air. Gradually, the pressure in my chest eased and much-needed oxygen filled my lungs. Slowly I raised my head, meeting two sets of worried eyes.

"I'm okay."

"Good. Maddox is going to be fine. We'll figure it out, okay?"

Aiden sat next to me, letting me lean against his arm. "Bent is right. One step at a time."

I shut my eyes. "Okay."

THEY ALLOWED US to return after what seemed like an eternity. Maddox was awake, the bed slightly elevated. His nose cannulas were gone, the indent from the tubes still lingering on his skin. He had the blanket I had brought from my apartment draped over him. I noticed the way he had his hand wrapped around the edge, as if he were afraid to let go.

I let Bentley and Aiden approach him, standing at the bottom of the bed.

"Hey," he muttered.

They both smiled. "Mad Dog," Aiden said, patting his leg. "Good to see you."

Maddox sighed. "Good to be back."

Bentley sat in the chair. "Do you need anything?"

Maddox's eyes flickered to me briefly, then he shook his head. "The ice chips are stellar."

Aiden chuckled. "That's why we chose this hospital. Stellar ice."

"Are you hungry?" I asked.

Maddox hesitated, then spoke. "No. I'm not sure what I feel. I still don't really understand everything that has happened."

"Give it a little time, Maddox," Bentley urged. "You just woke up."

Maddox nodded, then grimaced.

I moved without thought, pushing past Aiden. I cupped Maddox's face. "Do you need pain meds?"

He stilled at my touch. "The nurse is bringing me some."

"Okay. What can I get you?"

"Um, more ice?"

I grabbed the cup, sliding a cube into his mouth. He shut his eyes. "Good."

I reached into my pocket and found the Chapstick. I ran it over his lips, freezing when his eyes flew open.

"So they don't crack," I explained.

He closed his eyes again. "I know this sounds weird since, apparently, I've been out for over a week, but I'm tired."

"Understandable." Bentley stood. "We'll go get something to eat and let you rest."

"Thanks," Maddox mumbled.

"Dee, you coming?"

I shook my head. "No."

Maddox spoke, his voice low. "I would rather you did."

My heart shifted, breaking a little at his words. "All right, then."

I stepped back, retrieved my purse, and let Aiden guide me out of the room.

It felt as if I were leaving a piece of me behind.

⌒

"IT WAS JILL, wasn't it?"

Maddox's voice startled me. Since he had woken, he had barely addressed me. He had accepted hugs and kisses from Sandy, Emmy, and Cami when they came in the room; spoken quietly with Aiden and Bentley; accepted a fist bump from Reid. Even spoke to Richard on the phone.

But to me, he remained silent and distant. If I asked him a question, his answer was short and to the point. I was at a loss about what to do, but I knew I had to let him make the first move.

I glanced over from my spot in the chair beside his bed. He hadn't told me to leave when the others departed for the night. He hadn't asked me to stay either. When I picked up his book that had been on his nightstand, I asked him if he would like me to read it to him.

His terse, "Fine," was the reply I received. In the hours that we had been alone, he'd only spoken that one word until now.

I closed the book slowly and drew in a breath.

"Yes, it was Jill."

His fingers played with the blanket. "Where is she?"

"In jail."

"Good," he grunted. "That's all I want to know."

"Okay."

Again, there was silence.

"Why do I have this blanket?"

"I knew you liked it. It was softer than the hospital ones, and I thought you would prefer it."

He made another noise. Shifted a little. He pushed at his glasses. They were new—as close as I could get to the other frames I knew he liked. "Did you have these replaced?"

"Yes. I know they need adjusting, but that has to wait until you can get around. Your optician was very helpful getting a replacement pair."

"Yeah, they're fine."

"Would you like something? Some ginger ale or a juice? A sandwich?"

"I'd prefer a whiskey."

I had to chuckle. I could use one myself. "I don't think that's a choice."

"Figured. Maybe a ginger ale."

"Okay, I'll go get you one."

"Are you leaving?"

I paused at the door. "No."

He repeated his question from earlier. "Why are you here?"

"Because you are."

Our eyes met in the diffused light. His were unreadable, the emotions once again hidden in the depths of blue. Then he sighed and spoke. "I'm angry with you."

My heart ached again, but I nodded because I understood. "I know. I deserve your anger, but I'm not leaving."

"What if I tell you to go?"

"Then I guess I'll be in the waiting room. I'm not leaving this hospital until you come home, no matter how often you send me away."

"Still stubborn."

I shrugged.

"I didn't send you away earlier to make you feel bad. You looked exhausted, and I wanted you to eat," he said quietly. "I knew if you went with Bent and Aiden, they would make sure you did."

"Oh." I cleared my throat. "Anything besides that ginger ale?" He hadn't eaten much earlier, barely picking at the light dinner they brought him.

"No thanks."

I knew his throat was sore from the tubes. He swallowed a lot and had been sucking on lozenges. Suddenly, I remembered the box I had seen in the freezer of the small kitchen the nurses allowed us to use.

"How about a popsicle?"

"A popsicle?"

"It would help your throat."

He contemplated it, then nodded. "Orange."

"Okay, one orange popsicle."

I leaned against the wall once I was out of his room. It would take time. My head knew that, even while my heart wished for something different. I wanted him to tell me he still loved me, but sadly, I knew he wasn't ready to say it.

I wasn't sure he even felt it anymore.

I dashed away a stray tear. He had once shown me great patience. I had to do the same for him.

In the meantime, he wanted a popsicle. That much I could do for him.

⌒

THE NEXT DAY, they removed all the medical equipment. Maddox passed the cognitive tests, and although his short-term memory wasn't as sharp as it had been before the accident, Dr. Sampson was confident it would return. Maddox was surprisingly unsteady on his feet, and his ribs hurt a great deal. He relaxed a bit when the doctor explained how much bruising there had been from the accident, plus the surgery.

"It's to be expected, Maddox. You need time to heal completely." Dr. Sampson snapped his chart closed. "I want to keep you another day or two, just to be safe. And you'll need some help when you get home. You shouldn't be alone."

"He won't be," I said, resolute. "I'll be there."

Dr. Sampson grinned. "Your guardian angel."

Maddox simply stared at me. I looked away, hating the expressive look in his eyes. Uncertainty, doubt, and pain. That was all I could see.

"Can I have a shower?"

Dr. Sampson nodded. "I'll get a nurse to assist you."

"No. Dee," Maddox insisted.

My heart rate increased. He wanted me to help him? Dr. Sampson glanced at me, and I nodded. "Of course."

A nurse helped me get Maddox to the walk-in shower. The simple act of getting there exhausted him. He sat down heavily on the shower bench, hung his head, and dropped his shoulders. I left on my underwear, working efficiently so he didn't get cold. He was silent as the warm water rained down his body, lifting his head as I stood behind him so I could shampoo his hair.

"I heard you," he said, his eyes shut.

"What?"

"When I was coming out of the coma, I heard your voice. I felt you touching me."

"Oh."

He frowned as I rinsed away the soap. "I knew when it was someone else touching me. I didn't like it."

"I did everything they would allow me to do."

"I know."

I lathered up my hands, massaging the suds into his skin.

He was silent for a moment. "I heard you cry."

"I'm sorry. Sometimes I got overwhelmed."

His eyes opened, and he focused on me. "You said you loved me. I heard you say that."

I swallowed, frozen in his fierce glance. "I did."

"Because you thought I was dying? You felt guilty?"

"No, because I realized how stupid I was being."

"What are you talking about?"

I inhaled and told him the same thing I had told Cami. He didn't interrupt me. He let me talk and wash him, standing to rinse off, holding the wall for support.

"Lori made me see what a coward I was being." I finished and shut off the water. I wrapped a towel around his waist and helped him sit down again. I toweled-dried his hair briskly. "I know you're angry with me, Maddox. I'm angry with myself and trying to come to terms with the guilt."

"Why are you guilty?"

I lifted his face, stroking his scruff with my fingers. "Because I hurt you. Because my words put you on that street and she got the chance to get her revenge. Because of me, you're here."

He wrapped his hand around my wrist. "Is that why you're looking after me, Dee? Because you feel responsible?"

"No."

"Tell me why."

A tremor went through me. "Because . . . I love you, Maddox

Riley. There is no place else I can be."

Our eyes locked. I refused to look away, needing him to see the truth behind my words.

"I'm tired of denying it. I love you, and even if you don't love me anymore, I want you to know it."

He broke our gaze and sighed. "I need to go to bed."

Disappointment tore through me; the subtle rejection stung. I helped him to his feet and into a set of loose pants and a T-shirt Aiden had brought then settled him into his bed.

"Do you need anything?"

"I'd like a popsicle."

"Okay."

He spoke as I headed for the door. "She was going to come after me no matter what, Dee. The one thing I'm grateful for is she didn't hurt you."

I looked at him.

His gaze focused on me. "I would go through it again, and worse, if it meant you were safe."

He shut his eyes.

HE WATCHED ME all day. I felt his gaze even when others were in the room. When I left to have coffee with Cami and Emmy, so he could have some private time with Aiden and Bentley, he looked anxious.

Unable to help myself, I crossed the room and ran my hand over his head. "I'll bring you a popsicle."

He tugged me close. "Just you. Promise you'll come back."

I felt the well of tears but fought them back. "Yes."

He lay back, satisfied. "Okay."

Later, when we were alone once more, I sat beside his bed in one of the large chairs, my legs curled under me. The room was dim since bright lights still gave him a headache. The silence between us tonight was different. Lighter. I was surprised when he stretched out his hand in invitation, letting me curl mine inside it. He drew circles on my skin.

"Your thumb is a mess."

"I know."

"You need to stop that."

"I'm not sure it's ever going to happen. I've done it all my life."

He harrumphed, then he carefully shifted, lying on his side.

"Bentley told me."

"Told you what?"

"That it was you who alerted the police about Jill."

Sighing, I tucked my legs closer. I hated even hearing her name. "Yes."

He stared at our hands, his voice becoming softer. "And about the blood donation. You saved my life."

"No, the surgeon did. I just gave him one of the tools he needed."

"I'm sure the blood bank would have worked."

"I didn't want to wait. Besides, I wanted to give it to you. Be the one to help."

"I like knowing I have some of you inside me." His lips curled at the corner. "Usually, it's the other way around."

I felt the familiar heat only he could cause bubble under my skin at his provocative words. I looked down at his fingers caressing my hand and shut my eyes, as unbidden, a memory stirred.

I pushed open the closet door, shivering a bit in the morning air. I reached for a blouse, when Maddox stepped behind me. His hard chest pressed to my back, his damp skin warm. His long fingers trailed over my arm, wrapping around my hand.

"I like that blouse," he murmured close to my ear. "But I really prefer it on the floor."

"Maddox," I whispered. "Stop it. I have to get ready for work."

"You look so . . . tempting." He ran his finger over the lace strap on my shoulder. "So pretty in pink."

His finger drifted lower. "Where are your sexy little panties, Deirdre? Are you planning on going bare today?"

My answer came out more breathless than I expected. "No, I have to get them. I was chilly, and I thought I'd put on my blouse first."

Maddox chuckled low, throaty, and sexy. Just the sound made my thighs clench. I didn't understand how he could do that. He'd already taken me in the shower.

How could I need him again?

"I can warm you up, Deirdre." Reaching over, he slid the door closed, wrapping me in his arms, lowering us both to the floor. Before I could react, he hooked his legs around mine, pulling them apart. I looked away from our reflection in the full-length mirror.

Maddox dropped his head to my neck, turning his face to my ear, his breath washing over my skin. He nudged my face forward.

"Look how pretty you are."

I could only stare at the reflection of his hands. He ran them down my arms, then over my chest. I gasped when he tugged down the cups of my bra, pushing out my breasts. They squeezed together, his hands enveloping and stroking the soft mounds. He rubbed his thumbs over my hard nipples, making me squirm.

He swirled his tongue on my neck, then dropped his hands to my thighs, running his fingers up and down in light, teasing strokes. I gasped when he cupped me, his touch possessive.

"Watch me," he murmured, once again nudging my head toward the mirror.

I couldn't look away. I was mesmerized by the movements of his hands. His long, strong fingers. The way his forearms flexed as he worked me.

He opened me, exposing me fully to the mirror. He ran his finger over my clit, making me whimper. Slow, unhurried brushes of his thumb, fingers, knuckles. I never knew what was next.

"Look at you," he whispered, his voice low and tight in my ear. "Everything you hide, Deirdre, all the things that make you, you. Here only for me."

He began small, tight circles, rubbing my clit. Pleasure racked my body as I pushed back against him. His cock was hard and trapped between us. I felt the slide of it, the heat, and wetness of his excitement on my skin.

"Your girlie room filled with pillows and lace." He bit down lightly on the juncture of my neck. *"The sexy, racy lingerie under your businesslike clothes."* He slid a finger inside me, his thumb pressing on my bundle of nerves.

I cried out his name, my hips moving, his cock pressing harder on my back.

"And this." He pressed his fingers deeper, his thumb harder. *"This pretty, sweet pussy. Like a flower. It blossoms for me, doesn't it?"*

"Yes," I panted.

His ministrations picked up, his breathing growing harsh. *"Just for me."*

"Oh God, yes."

"You're going to come on my hand, Deirdre. When I tell you to. Aren't you?"

I could only whimper.

"I'm going to come all over your back. You're going to wear me on your skin all day. Think of me when your blouse sticks and remember how hard you came for me."

I shook, undulated on his hand, cried out his name. Gasped for air. He stroked me harder, one hand splayed across my stomach, gripping me tightly to him.

He grunted and his body jerked. *"Come. Now, Deirdre. Come for me."*

I exploded, crying out and gripping his legs. Wetness covered my back as he clutched me close, his face buried in my neck.

I collapsed against him.

After a moment, he pressed his mouth to my ear.

"Look at yourself, Deirdre. Look how beautiful you are for me."

My eyes fluttered open. My hair was disheveled, my breasts spilled out of my bra, my nipples red. My skin was glowing and pink. My eyes were hooded, my lips upturned at the corners. Maddox's hand still cupped me, and I was splayed open. I was sated, sleepy, and relaxed. I looked . . . sexy?

I met his eyes in the mirror.

"You are so incredible," he murmured. *"I'll think about you all day like this."* He laughed softly. *"I'll be goddamn hard all day too."*

A giggle escaped, and he kissed my neck.

"I have to go get ready for work."

"No. I told you. Me on your skin. Inside you. I want to be all over you all day."

I had to shut my eyes at his words. I wasn't sure I should find them so sexy.

"Maddox," I breathed out.

His mouth covered mine. I knew I would do as he asked.

Simply because he asked.

He gasped, and my eyes flew open. Our gazes locked. My hand gripped his, my breathing shallow.

"What are you thinking about?" he demanded.

I shook my head. I couldn't tell him.

"Deirdre . . ."

A shiver ran through me at the single word.

"That day, in front of the closet. The way you touched me."

His eyes drifted closed, and a smile curled his lips. "That was a good day."

"Y-yes."

He drew my hand to his mouth, kissed the palm, then pressed it to his face. "There will be more."

"Will there?" I hated the need I could hear in my voice, the unspoken question.

"If you want there to be."

"Do you love me?" I asked.

"I told you I did."

"That was before you were hurt. Before I rejected you."

He shrugged. "I said it. I meant it. The question now is: Do *you* love *me*? Did you mean what you said in the shower, or was that your remorse talking? I need to know once and for all."

"It isn't remorse. It's how I feel."

"Then say it."

"I'm scared you won't say it back," I whispered.

"Bullshit," he shot back. "You gave your blood to me. You've been here every fucking day. Bentley told me you refused to leave. You fought everyone. You've seen me at my worst, and you're still here."

He tugged my hand gently. "Stop being a coward, Deirdre. Look me in the eyes and say the words. We'll go from there. Take the chance."

I looked into his eyes. For the first time since he woke up, I saw the fierce determination I associated with Maddox. The fighter.

The man I loved.

I let out a long breath. "I love you, Maddox. I love you so much it terrifies me."

"Do you want a life with me?" he asked.

"Yes," I confirmed.

He reached out, and I leaned forward so he could cup my cheek. "Was that so scary?"

This time, the word was soft. "Yes."

He pulled on me, and I unfurled my knees to hunch over him. Gently, he tugged me down to his face, brushing his mouth over mine.

"I love you, Deirdre Wilson. And if you try to run this time, I'm going to be so pissed that I'll chase you. I'm never letting you go again. Do you understand me?"

"Yes," I sobbed.

"You could make it a lot easier on me if you would get on this fucking bed."

Cautiously, I lay beside him, resting my head on his pillow.

"This is where you belong." He brushed the tears off my face. "Now, stop crying. I want to kiss you."

I sniffled and he smiled.

His arm tightened on my waist. "I wish we were alone."

"We are."

"A nurse could walk in here any minute. I doubt they'd approve of what I want to do to you right now."

"You just had surgery and woke from a coma. You won't be doing *that* for a while," I reminded him.

He smiled and winked. "I still have hands." He lowered his face to my ear. "And a tongue."

My eyes widened.

He captured my mouth and kissed me. It was slow and sweet.

Long, sensuous passes of his tongue. Whispered words of adoration against my lips. Promises of the future.

I felt his forgiveness, his desire.

And his love.

In return, I gave him mine.

⌒

"AHEM."

I woke, still beside Maddox. He slept, his head on my chest, holding me close, my blanket draped over us. Aiden smirked, clearly amused. Cami smiled widely, holding a tray of coffee.

"We thought you could use a little pick-me-up this morning, but I see you've got that covered," Aiden said. "I'm not sure this is in keeping with hospital policy though."

Two nurses had already informed me of that. Yet, neither made me move. Instead, they grinned knowingly and left after checking on Maddox. He barely stirred when they recorded his vitals, then settled and slept again until the next time they appeared.

"You know, this is the second time you've shown up in my room uninvited," Maddox mumbled. "Go away, Aiden."

"I don't think you want that to happen."

"Why is that?"

"Because Dr. Sampson decided to spring you today."

My breath caught. "Really?"

"Yes. He came in here to tell you, but, ah, you were otherwise engaged. He told us and said we could share the good news. He's preparing the discharge papers."

Maddox groaned. "Good. I can go home and get back to my life."

I shook my head as I slid from the bed, ignoring his pout.

"Just because you're getting out of here means nothing. You still need time to recover."

"I'll take it slow."

I laughed. "You certainly will. You aren't going back to work.

You've been hit by a car, had surgery, and been in a coma. You'll be sleeping, resting, reading, and doing what I tell you."

"Is that a fact?"

I crossed my arms. "Yes, it is."

Maddox smiled. "Okay, then. Just wanted to be sure."

Aiden chuckled. "And here we go."

CHAPTER 20

MADDOX

IT WASN'T MUCH of a surprise to anyone to discover how bad of a patient I was when it came to recovery. I lasted about ten days—the exact amount of time Dee stayed home from work with me. After that, I drove her, and everyone else, crazy.

They took turns checking on me. Aiden and Bent would drop by and bring me up to speed on work. I was allowed limited computer time, and I used it to stay on top of my department and Ridge Towers. I snuck in some extra hours until Reid figured it out. He loaded something on to my computer that cut me off after my allotted time. I ordered another laptop, but Dee found it and gave me supreme shit.

"You're recovering! What are you doing?"

"I'm bored. I can't sit around all day. My God, have you seen the shit they have on TV? Speaking of which, if I can watch TV, why can't I work? I'm staring at a screen either way," I argued.

She threw up her hands and walked away. I found it sexy when she was in bossy mode, but I refused to let her know that piece of information.

I called Dr. Sampson and pointed out my argument. He agreed that as long as I continued to recover at home, I could work a little more. I tried not to be smug when Reid disabled the restricting program on my computer.

I failed.

I walked on my treadmill—slowly—building my strength. Aiden showed me some exercises and worked with me.

Sandy came by every couple of days. I let her fuss and tell me what to do. She was going to do it no matter what I said, so it was easier.

Richard called frequently, helping me pass the time as he entertained me with stories of his kids, discussed the marketing, and teased me endlessly about anything he could think of—including the garbage pile incident. He sent packages, often containing childish drawings, as well as thoughtful gifts. Oscar the Grouch, sitting in his garbage can, made Dee laugh hard, and earned a place of honor on the shelves in my den. Every phone call, video chat, and package that arrived made us closer and solidified our friendship.

Finally, after three weeks, the doctor cleared me to return to the office, part time. It felt good to be back at my desk, even if I was exhausted after a few hours. Dee was waiting when Frank dropped me off, and I was lying down before she had to ask.

She curled up beside me.

"I guess I can go home now."

My eyes flew open. "No!"

"But you're getting better."

"I still need you."

"I'll check on you every night. We can have dinner together."

I discovered I loved to cook with her. Our style in the kitchen was similar, and we worked well together. It had become our thing: to decide on menus, list the ingredients we needed, then cook our meal together.

"I still get dizzy in the shower. And really tired." To prove my point, I lay my head on her chest, burrowing close. "I need you to hold me up."

She ran her fingers through my hair and kissed the scar on my crown. The hair was finally growing over the jagged reminder. "Ah, Maddox," she crooned. "You are so full of bullshit."

I grinned against her skin. "Okay, fine. I just want you here."

Her fingers stilled. "What are you saying?"

I tilted my head up to meet her eyes. "Move in with me. Be here every night. When I get home from the office and wake up in the morning."

I saw the wariness in her gaze, and I tightened my grip around her waist.

"Isn't that a little fast?" She stalled.

"Maybe, but I don't care. It feels right." I studied her face. "Don't you like being here?"

"Yes."

"There is plenty of room for your things. You love the kitchen."

"Yes," she agreed thoughtfully.

I nudged her chin with mine. "You love *me.*"

"Yes." This time she said it with a sweet smile.

"Then why not?"

She paused, lifting her hand. I grabbed it before her thumb went between her lips.

"It's not going to happen, Dee. You aren't going to lose yourself being with me. I wouldn't allow it. You make me stronger, and I'll do the same for you. I love you just the way you are." I kissed her thumb. "Defective chewed thumbs and all."

She smiled. "Okay."

Disbelief widened my eyes. "Yeah?"

"Yes."

I kissed her leisurely and deep. As usual, when I was close to her, my cock lengthened, pushing against her hip. She whimpered, pressing herself closer. As long as I moved carefully, sex wasn't an issue now. It was when I moved without thinking that things went haywire.

I had discovered easy, slow lovemaking with Dee was as satisfying as when I fucked her hard. I still talked dirty, and I liked to be in control. Dee liked it as well. I knew, once my body fully healed, we would return to our more vigorous antics. But until then, I simply wanted to be close to her.

Our clothes ended up on the floor. I kissed her soft skin, loving how it felt against my coarser body. Long moments passed with our mouths and bodies showing our love, speaking a language too intimate to voice out loud. I moved with easygoing strokes, buried deep inside her. She whispered my name, gripped my shoulders, and held me close. I lost myself, finding pleasure only she could give me. Cradled by her body, I was home.

Finally, home.

⌒

WEEKS LATER, I glanced at my watch, late on a Friday afternoon. Life had returned to normal. The office was busy, Dee moved in, and all was great.

I shifted in my chair, ran a hand over my chest, and winced. I'd had a tattoo done over my heart and it was still tender. My first—and my last. I'd gotten the idea one night, and I'd talked to Aiden about it. Once I was ready, he took me to his guy and I got inked. It was something I never planned to do—but then again, I'd never planned to fall in love either. Dee was the force behind both deviations.

Dee had wept when I showed it to her.

My Dee it read in cursive ink set into an infinity symbol. It was private, personal, and only a few people would ever see it. The same few people who ever saw the real me.

Dee's appreciation had been rather demonstrative once the tattoo began to heal. She liked to use her tongue and trace the ink. I liked it as well.

Bentley walked in, tugging on his sleeves. I grinned at the tight expression on his face.

"You ready?"

"I can't believe I let myself get talked into this."

"It's tradition not to see the bride the night before the wedding. You're going out to dinner, then taking her to the hotel. I'm dropping off Dee and Cami to join her." I leaned back. "You're not the only one giving up your woman for the night, you know."

He snorted and sat down. *Your woman.* Listen to you."

Aiden strolled in, a cookie in each hand. "Holy shit, have you guys tasted Becca's cookies? They rock!"

Becca had arrived two weeks ago and was busy settling in. Reid was overly fixated on her office setup, deeming it needed tweaking almost daily. It was amusing to watch.

Aiden flung himself on the sofa. "I've had six today. I might not fit into my tux tomorrow."

"Six. Try a dozen. Every time I've seen you today, you've had a cookie in your hand. And one in your mouth." I grinned. "I hope Jen brings reinforcement buttons."

Aiden flipped me off and turned to Bentley. "You ready for tomorrow?"

"I think so. You have the ring, right?"

"For the hundredth time, yes." Aiden patted his pocket. "It's right here."

"Okay. Just checking."

Bentley glanced my way, and I lifted my hands. "I have all the paperwork, Bent. We've got your back."

He sighed. "Fine."

"What time are you coming over?"

"I'll be there in the morning."

Bentley had decided he wanted to spend his last night as a bachelor alone. Knowing Bent the way I did, I wasn't surprised. He would want the time to reflect since that was the way he worked. The wedding wasn't until early evening, so we would have most of the day together, hanging out.

"Great. We'll work out, then go to breakfast. I've booked us a court at eleven. Richard and Katy arrive tonight, and he is joining us for some one-on-one tomorrow, then we'll head to the hotel, relax with a few drinks, and get you married."

Bentley nodded.

Aiden wiped his mouth, licking the crumbs off his fingers. "The girls are spending the day getting pretty." He chuckled. "I don't think they need it, but whatever."

"It's their bonding time. Jen says since neither of us wanted a traditional bachelor or bachelorette party, it was a good substitute. They're getting facials, massages, pedicures. Girlie stuff. Katy is joining them while Richard is with us. He wants to spoil her a little while she's here. The girls are excited to meet her."

I laughed. "I prefer beer, pizza, and basketball."

"I dunno," Aiden mused. "Cami likes it when I get a pedicure. She says she likes it when my feet are soft. I have talented toes, you know."

Bentley and I groaned.

"Go get more cookies. It's better when your mouth is full."

Bentley stood, still looking nervous. "Okay, I'll see you guys in the morning."

He left, and I glanced at Aiden. "What are you doing tonight?"

He grinned. "Spending it with you. Dee told Cami you'd probably pout and feel sorry for yourself if you were alone."

"Whatever," I mumbled. Dee knew me well. I hated being without her now.

Aiden chuckled then stood. "I get it, Mad Dog. Believe me, I get it. So we'll keep each other company."

"Fine. Bring beer. Lots of it."

"On it."

～

I GLANCED AT Aiden across the table the next morning. The nervous, anxious Bentley was gone. In his place was distracted, all-over-the-place, smiling Bentley. He ordered breakfast, asked for a scotch, then proceeded to chat.

Bentley didn't chat. Or drink scotch in the morning.

He talked about dinner, his house, Emmy, Ridge Towers, the lakefront, local news. He never shut up. And he checked his phone constantly, typing with the strangest smile on his face.

Something big was up. Bigger than the wedding.

"How much caffeine have you had, Bent?"

"A few cups. I didn't sleep much last night."

"Did you give Emmy your wedding gift?"

"What? Oh yeah. She loved the earrings."

I looked at Aiden, lifting my eyebrow. The earrings had taken three visits to Darlene, a dozen calls, and four revisions to get them perfect. And all he had to say was she loved them?

"What's going on, Bent?"

"What? I'm getting married today."

"And?"

He huffed a sigh, reaching into his pocket. He hunched forward, lowering his voice. "I don't think I'm supposed to say anything."

I exchanged another glance with Aiden. "Okay."

"But I have to."

I nodded.

"Emmy gave me a present too."

"I think that's customary."

He pulled his hand out of his pocket and opened his fist. "Look."

I stared at a mound of yellow fluff. "Did that used to be a baby chick? Did you kill it in your pocket?"

He glared at me. "No. Look!" He held out an object to me and handed one to Aiden. I took it from him, mystified. Then I saw it.

"Holy fuck."

Aiden let out a curse of his own.

I met Bentley's gaze. His eyes filled with joy. There was no other word to describe it.

"I'm gonna be a dad."

"But . . . I thought . . ."

He chuckled. "You know what I learned last night? When a person is on antibiotics, it cuts down the effectiveness of birth control. When you had your accident, Emmy was sick." He shrugged, his ears turning a dull red. "She, ah, got better. You got better. We celebrated."

"You must have been surprised."

"She's been nervous the last couple of days. About telling me." He took the tiny baby bootie from my hand, rubbing the soft wool between his fingers. "She was so scared, she was shaking. But . . ." He swallowed, the emotion and wonder evident in his voice when he continued. "This is the best wedding gift in the world." He looked at us, tears in his eyes. "I get Emmy, and I'm going to be a daddy. I get them forever. It's so much more than I ever thought, ever hoped to have." He looked down at the ball of fuzz. "I'm the luckiest man on the planet."

I sat back, letting the news soak in, waiting for the shock.

Except, I wasn't shocked.

I started to laugh. Aiden was married. Bentley was getting married and going to be a father. I was living with a woman I was so in love with I couldn't be without her for a night.

All because of a worn rucksack and cup of coffee. Three girls who stepped into our lives and made them complete. Made *us* complete.

I stood, surprising us all when I dragged Bentley to his feet and embraced him. Aiden jumped up, and the three of us hugged it out in the middle of a busy restaurant. Even more surprising, I didn't care.

"Way to go, Bentley. Way to go."

⌒

"LADIES AND GENTLEMEN, I give you Mr. and Mrs. Bentley Ridge!"

Bentley stood, offering his hand to Emmy. She laughed as he tugged her onto the dance floor, twirling her into his arms. They swayed, her tucked into his chest. The smile on his face said it all.

My friend was happy and in love. Joy radiated from him.

The wedding had been picture-perfect. Every detail handled expertly by Jen, who stood on the sidelines, dabbing his eyes as he watched their first dance.

Emmy was a vision of beauty in the dress Cami designed for her. Bentley gasped in awe when he saw her, elegant in cream lace. Dee and Cami were gorgeous as well. Although, personally, I thought Dee was the loveliest of them all. She had flushed when I informed her of my decision when I had her alone.

As weddings went, it was small but befitted Bentley and Emmy. Friends, staff, and close business colleagues attended. We finally met the infamous Katy. Richard's love and pride as he introduced her to us was blatant. The natural warmth he described her having was transparent. She drew you in with her infectious smile and vivid blue eyes. She often chided him for his remarks, and he would kiss her cheek or hair, laughing with her. They were a great couple.

Graham and his wife, Laura, stayed in BC to look after Richard and Katy's children. It was the only way Katy agreed to come to the wedding, and even then, she checked in on them often.

Richard teased her about it, but I noticed him on his phone several times over the course of the day. His girls brought the tough, cocky businessman to his knees, and the love he carried for them was evident. I watched him with his wife, his adoration clear on his face. He looked at her the way Bent did Emmy. Aiden at Cami.

The way I looked at Dee.

We joined the happy couple on the dance floor, and I pressed Dee close. "You look so beautiful. Did I mention that?"

"Not in the last ten minutes."

"Do forgive me. You are mesmerizingly beautiful."

She smiled at me. "Thank you. You look very handsome."

"Jen knows his tuxes."

Dee laughed and snuggled closer.

I felt the stirring of my heart, the contentment that enveloped me when Dee was with me. All she had to do was appear, and my soul eased. I wanted her nearby all the time.

As we danced, a thought crept into my mind, and I began to talk.

"I always thought marriage was a farce. Something I was never interested in. It seemed unnecessary. Antiquated, almost."

She looked at me, quizzical. "And now?"

"It's a promise, isn't it? One made out in the open for all to hear. A promise between two people who love each other. The promise of being together. Loving each other, supporting each other, no matter what. Being that person the other can depend on." I drew in a deep breath. "A written, spoken vow of love. It's quite beautiful, actually."

"You've become a romantic, Maddox Duncan Riley," she teased.

I loved it when she teased me. Called me by my full name. Took over my life. Looked at me as if I hung the moon. I loved everything about her. Even the way she bit her thumb. I never wanted to have a day in my life without her by my side.

I stopped dancing and pulled her into the corner.

"You made me one, Deirdre Anne Wilson. You've changed every stupid idea I ever had about love."

Her eyes widened. "Wh-what are you saying?"

I indicated the room. "I want that."

"I don't understand. You want to dance?"

"No. I want all of it. I want to marry you. Share our first dance as husband and wife. Let the world know you're mine, and I belong to you."

She stared, her mouth open in shock.

"We're already living together, isn't that enough?"

"Maybe once, it would have been. But I want it all. I want that written, stated vow of love with you."

I slid my hands over her arms, cupping her face. "I want this. With you. Please tell me I can have it."

Her eyes were like saucers. I pulled her against me, feeling the tension in her body.

"Don't run, baby. It's just us. It's just a word. Say it."

I waited, patient.

A slow smile spread across her face. Mine grew as I watched.

"Say it again," she whispered.

"Be brave with me, Deirdre. I promise I won't let you down."

A tear fell down her cheek. I kissed it away, my mouth lingering on her skin.

"Give me your vow and take mine."

She melted into me.

"Yes."

EPILOGUE

MADDOX~TWO YEARS LATER

MY PHONE CHIMED with a reminder of my three o'clock meeting. Not that I needed reminding. Every Friday, same time, no matter what else was happening.

It was the most important meeting I had every week.

I shed my suit jacket and unbuttoned my vest, hanging them over the back of my chair. I kept on my shirt but removed the cuff links and loosened the sleeves.

I headed down the hall, my smile already wide, knowing what was waiting for me behind the closed door at the end of the corridor.

I passed the office that now belonged to Emmy, waving at her as I went by. She chuckled and returned my salute, a smile playing on her lips. Across the hall was where Dee worked, though she wasn't in the office today. We had convinced her to join the company. She worked with Bill, our lawyer, as his paralegal; she was excellent at research and a real asset to our company.

I opened the door and stepped inside. What had once been two large offices was now a nursery/playroom, filled with bright colors, soft edges, and endless activities to engage small minds. It was often chaotic and loud, which at one time in my life would have made me run, but now, I lived for every crazy moment.

Bentley was already there, playing on the floor with his daughter, Addison. She was tiny, with an explosion of golden curls. She looked like Emmy, except she had inherited Bentley's bright blue eyes. Always happy and laughing, she was enchanting.

And she had her father wrapped around her little finger.

She looked up, drooling and babbling as she lurched to her feet. Bentley was right behind her, holding her upright as she toddled toward me. I leaned down, scooping her into my arms and blowing raspberries on her tummy, laughing as she squealed.

"How's Uncle Mad's girl today?" I tossed her in the air, catching her as she giggled in delight. "Are you having fun with Daddy?"

"Wearing Daddy out is what she's doing," Bentley grumbled. But he smiled so wide, I knew he was full of bullshit. He was in a good mood today, better than usual, his demeanor almost euphoric.

He held out his arms, and I surrendered Addi to him. She cooed at him, patting his face with her little hands. He tweaked her nose, and she grabbed his finger, shoving it in her mouth.

"Teething again?" I asked, stroking the pink circles on her cheeks.

"Yes. Emmy rubbed some of that stuff on her gums, so it helped."

My favorite noise came from the corner, and I grinned. "Excuse me."

I crossed the room, smiling at Maggie, the woman who looked after the nursery.

"He's all ready for you. I think he's been waiting."

I peered over the edge of the crib at my son. His chubby face was wreathed in smiles as he kicked his feet and flapped his arms for me to lift him.

"Hey, buddy." I sighed as he nestled into my neck, his tiny hands gripping me. "How's my boy?" I kissed his head. He pushed closer, and I stroked his back, enjoying his warmth. My boy was a snuggler.

I thought I knew what love felt like when I married Dee.

Nothing prepared me for the love I felt for my son, Brayden.

Dee and I married in a quiet ceremony not long after Emmy and Bentley were wed. We flew everyone to the Bahamas and exchanged vows under the hot, bright sun. We were surrounded by our closest friends, including Reid, Sandy, Jen, Becca, Richard, and his family. I hired a private plane so we were comfortable, and we all enjoyed the weekend. We kept it simple, because that was how we were. Dee didn't even want an engagement ring, so Darlene created a stunning eternity band, the circle of exquisite diamonds as endless as my devotion. I loved the weight of the heavy platinum band Dee gave me on my finger, a constant reminder of our vows.

We returned to Toronto, and less than a year later, Dee was pregnant. Even though we had talked about it, and she stopped getting the shot, it was still a shock when it happened.

Dee handed me a tall box. Mystified, I opened it, staring at the contents, a thousand emotions running through me.

My broken lamp, the one precious item I had been able to keep hidden all those years, lay within the box. I lifted it with shaking hands. The truck was fixed, the paint fresh. It was attached to a base, a new streetlight beside it. The shade was blue with more trucks on it.

Tears filled my eyes as I trailed my fingers over the repaired memory that was once again clear in my mind. My mother's touch, her sweet smile, and the sound of her voice as she read to me. Dee had given all that back to me with a gift so personal, it helped to heal a part of me I hadn't realized was still broken.

It was mended. Restored with love.

The way Dee restored my heart.

She knew the story of the lamp. How much the broken pieces meant to me. She had already made a collage of the few pictures I had managed to save, and the framed memento sat on my desk, next to a picture of us on our wedding day.

"How?" I managed to ask through my tears, no longer ashamed to

show my feelings.

Dee cupped my face, stroking away the tears. Her expression was tender, her voice filled with love. "I had it fixed. I thought you would like it for our baby's room."

My gaze flew from her face to her stomach, over to the lamp, and returned to her face.

"Our-our baby?"

She pressed a stick into my hand. "We did it, Maddox. You're going to be a daddy."

As I looked at the two blue lines, the enormity of her words hit me. I panicked, wondering how I would handle all of it. Babies came with no instructions. They didn't follow schedules or make sense most of the time. I worried about being a good father since I had no example to follow.

Would I fail?

Then I remembered Richard and the love he had for his girls. The way he was with them. I thought of the change in Bentley. I listened to the comforting words from Dee.

"You will be an amazing father, Maddox. You will give our child love, structure, and security. That is all they need. You have so much love to give them." Her eyes were soft. "I know because you give it to me every day."

Her words centered me, and I calmed. I pulled her into my arms and thanked her with deep kisses for the gifts she'd given me. My memory, my child. My incredible life.

All because of her.

I immersed myself in her pregnancy. Doctor's appointments, ultrasounds. Classes. I read books, watched videos, talked to her stomach every day. Built the crib myself. Well, Bent and Aiden helped, and we yelled a lot, but we did it. When I found out the baby was a boy and I would have a son, I couldn't contain my joy.

Watching him be born was one of the greatest moments in my life.

We named him after the two people who meant more to me than I would ever be able to express. My best friends, my brothers.

Bentley Ridge and Aiden. Brayden.

A small foot kicking my chest startled me and brought me back to the present. I carried Brayden over and sat down beside Bentley. Immediately, Addi started babbling away, patting Brayden's cheek. She loved him, and he watched her with big green eyes and a toothless grin. I settled him on my knee, holding my wrist close. He started pulling at my shirtsleeves—one of his favorite games.

The door opened, and Aiden came in, cradling his infant daughter. She was a tiny baby, and looked even more so in his massive embrace.

"Sorry, the dumpling needed a change." He waved his hand in front of his face. "For something this little and cute, she can make me gag."

"Takes after her father." I chuckled.

Aiden sat down, gently settling Ava into his lap. Addi clapped her hands, and with Bent's help, leaned over and kissed Ava's forehead.

"Good girl, Addi," he crooned. "Baby Ava is so little, isn't she? We have to be careful with her."

She giggled, stuffing a teething ring into her mouth.

Aiden lowered his face, crooning to Ava. "Hey, baby girl."

She watched him, her eyes huge in her face. Her feet moved, kicking at the blanket.

"How's Cami?"

He looked up with a grin. "Great. Jen is keeping her busy with new designs he needs. The business is thriving."

Cami was the only one of our wives who didn't work for BAM. She did work from home with her design business. Taking advantage of the light, we had Van build her a mezzanine floor over Aiden's workout area, and she happily designed her masterpieces there. She also leased space in the same building as Jen for the creation of her garments, employing talented seamstresses. She had returned to work recently after giving birth to Ava. She loved having the baby with her, but was comforted knowing when she was otherwise occupied, Ava was safely here under the care of Maggie and close to Aiden.

That brought me to the point of today's meeting.

"So, Aiden, what did you find out?"

He lifted Ava to his shoulder, his hand fully encompassing her delicate frame.

"There are some good daycare places out there. And some truly bad ones. I think our plan of expanding the nursery onto another floor and hiring more staff would work." He cleared his throat. "I really don't want my dumpling being cared for by strangers, even when she's older."

"Well, eventually, we have to let them go to school."

"Not yet."

Brayden grunted and yanked on my shirt. Bentley leaned over, offering him a small giraffe, squeaking it. Brayden nabbed it, his baby hand still uncoordinated. It hit him in the face, making him frown. He looked so much like Dee when he did that, I had to laugh. I held it for him, squeaking it as he gurgled in delight.

"I think we need to expand." Bentley grinned. "We can hire more caregivers, offer it to the staff as a perk, and, ah . . ." His voice trailed off, his ears turning red.

Instantly, I knew. The euphoric mood had a reason.

"Emmy's pregnant again?"

He beamed. "Yep. I'm going to need the nursery for a long time."

I ran my hand over Brayden's peach-fuzz hair, smirking. "Me, too."

Aiden gaped at me. "Brayden's only six months old!"

"What can I say? My boys are determined. It's early, but Dee's pregnant again." I laughed. "You better catch up soon, Aiden."

He glared. "Ava is nine weeks old. Give me a break."

Reid strolled in. "You mean, give Cami a break."

He folded himself down onto the floor, holding out his arms. "I need a baby. Any baby."

Addi squirmed, holding out her arms, and Bentley handed her to Reid with a frown. He was a natural with kids, but Bentley didn't like to share Addi time.

Reid glanced up from his crooning at Addi. "So did I hear right before I joined the baby circle of truth? We got more little bammers coming?"

I laughed. "Yep."

He raised his hand, and I fist bumped him. He did the same to Bentley. "Congrats! More minds for me to mold. You know, we need to add some computers to the new nursery. Kids love all that, and I can teach them."

"Gimme Addi back," Bentley demanded, reaching for his daughter.

"Nah, she's happy with me."

Bentley plucked Brayden from my arms.

"Hey!"

He ignored me, teasing Brayden with his tie. "You ready for the move?" he asked.

Phase one of Ridge Towers was complete. As Richard predicted, it had sold out long before we broke ground, with a waiting list for phase two. I had purchased the penthouse unit. Four bedrooms, with a roof terrace, and overlooking the water, it was spectacular. Dee was at the condo, packing a few last-minute items. The movers had handled the rest, and we were taking possession tomorrow.

"Yep. All set."

Reid grinned. "I get mine next week. I'm still doing some tweaks on the sound system upgrade."

"Of course you are."

"It's gonna be fantastic."

"Is Becca excited?"

"Yes."

"How's the cottage?" I asked Aiden with a smirk.

He grinned, his eyes crinkling in the corners. "Awesome. We're heading there for the weekend. Cami thinks she wants to stay for a few weeks. Use the peace and view as inspiration."

Van and his crew had rebuilt the place, making it spectacular. It had the porch Aiden wanted, a loft for Cami to work from, and lots of space for their growing family. I knew, one day soon, they would live there full-time, and now I understood why. I was happy for him.

"You all need to come for a visit." Aiden nudged Bentley's foot. "And you need to build."

Bentley smirked. "Soon. Baby number two has shifted my plans a little."

I had to laugh. Babies certainly did that.

"We'll figure it out. And finalize the resort. Now that Ridge Towers is almost complete—" he said with a quirk of his mouth "—and before we start the next one."

We had found another piece of land, and Ridge Estates was in full planning mode. This time it was a gated community for adults. The designs were spectacular, and investors were begging to be part of it.

I took Brayden from Bentley. He snatched Addi, and Reid frowned. He turned to Aiden, who shook his head. "No. You'll have to get your own."

Reid ran a hand through his hair, looking wistful.

I glanced around the "baby circle of truth." My best friends, our children. Life was good—no, it was great. Our company was strong, our personal lives even more so. We had all come a long way. Together.

Reid was an invaluable addition.

I studied him. He had matured and grown into himself. He was broader and thicker. More confident. He kept his hair short, and he dressed in business casual, the torn jeans and T-shirts retired only to the weekends. He was a solid part of our team, and we had rewarded him with a small stake in the company. He deserved it.

I wondered how long until he joined us in our weekly dad and babies meeting with one of his own in tow. I knew it was something he wanted.

He had been through so much and landed on his feet. We had been there with him for a lot of it, but he had pushed to make his dreams come true. I was proud of him.

But it was his story to tell.

And what a story it was.

You've met the men of BAM. Now get to know the rebel.

Reid—Coming fall 2018

Who is Reid Matthews?

A child, abandoned and unloved.

A teen, adrift and disregarded, using his superior tech skills for the wrong intentions.

A young adult, his future overshadowed by his prison record, his life an endless loop of loneliness.

Until he is given a second chance and a new life emerges.

A career he once thought he could only dream of, surrounded by people who show him that family and home aren't simply words.

And a girl who shows him the greatest, most complex code he could ever write.

Love.

A NOTE FROM THE AUTHOR

Depression, anxiety, and other thoughts can make someone feel isolated.

Know that you are not alone. If you are struggling, reach out to a mental health professional.

Someone is ready to listen.

Call:
1–800–273-TALK (8255)

Visit:
www.suicidepreventionlifeline.org
www.afsp.org
https://letstalk.bell.ca/en

A WORD OF THANKS

AS ALWAYS, I have some people to thank. The ones behind the words that encourage and support. The people who make these books possible for so many reasons.

To my readers—thank you for taking a chance on this series. Your love of BAM makes me so happy!

Deb, thank you. Your input is invaluable, your friendship a gift. So many books. Here is to many more!

Lisa, your comments made me laugh and your expertise made it better. Thank you.

Denise, your support is so appreciated. I am honored to call you friend.

Caroline, thank you—your keen eyes and enthusiasm mean so much.

Beth, Shelly, Janett, Darlene, Carrie, Suzanne, Trina, Mae, Jeanne, Eli—I love you. That is all.

Flavia, thank you for your support and belief in my work. You rock it for me.

Karen, my wonderful PA and friend. Of all the blessings in the book world, you are the greatest. Thank you for everything you do. I cannot even begin to list the ways you encourage, support and help. So much love to you. Hugs.

To all the bloggers, readers, and especially my review team. Thank you for everything you do. Shouting your love of books, posting, sharing—your recommendations keep my TBR list full, and the support you have shown me is so appreciated.

To my fellow authors who have shown me such kindness, thank you. I will follow your example and pay it forward.

To Christine—thank you for making my words look pretty!

Melissa—your covers make my books shine. Your teasers and banners are epic. Thank you!

My reader group, Melanie's Minions—love you all.

Finally—my Matthew. Thank you for your patience when you lose me for days. For the times I forget dinner and the pizza guy grins at you again. For listening to me mumble about my characters as if they were standing right there(because they are) and understanding. Thank you for loving and supporting me. You are my greatest gift.

BOOKS BY MELANIE MORELAND

Into the Storm
Beneath the Scars
Over the Fence
It Started with a Kiss
My Image of You

The Contract
The Baby Clause (Contract #2)

Bentley (Vested Interest #1)
Aiden (Vested Interest #2)
Maddox (Vested Interest #3)

ABOUT THE AUTHOR

NEW YORK TIMES/USA Today bestselling author Melanie Moreland, lives a happy and content life in a quiet area of Ontario with her beloved husband of twenty-nine-plus years and their rescue cat, Amber. Nothing means more to her than her friends and family, and she cherishes every moment spent with them.

While seriously addicted to coffee, and highly challenged with all things computer-related and technical, she relishes baking, cooking, and trying new recipes for people to sample. She loves to throw dinner parties, and enjoys travelling, here and abroad, but finds coming home is always the best part of any trip.

Melanie loves stories, especially paired with a good wine, and enjoys skydiving (free falling over a fleck of dust) extreme snowboarding (falling down stairs) and piloting her own helicopter (tripping over her own feet). She's learned happily ever afters, even bumpy ones, are all in how you tell the story.

Melanie is represented by Flavia Viotti at Bookcase Literary Agency. For any questions regarding subsidiary or translation rights please contact her at *flavia@bookcaseagency.com*

www.melaniemoreland.com

Made in United States
North Haven, CT
31 March 2022

17746531R00153